Undersong

Kathleen Winter

ALFRED A. KNOPF CANADA

PUBLISHED BY ALFRED A. KNOPF CANADA

Copyright © 2021 Kathleen Winter

www.penguinrandomhouse.ca

Knopf Canada and colophon are registered trademarks.

Library and Archives Canada Cataloguing in Publication

Title: Undersong / Kathleen Winter.
Names: Winter, Kathleen, author.
Identifiers: Canadiana (print) 2021014355X | Canadiana (ebook) 20210143681 |
ISBN 9780735278226 (hardcover) | ISBN 9780735278233 (EPUB)
Classification: LCC PS8595.I618 U53 2021 | DDC C813/.54—dc23

Jacket and text design by Jennifer Griffiths

Jacket images: (flower) Glow Images / Getty Images; (painting) *Newburyport
Meadows*, The Metropolitan Museum of Art, New York, Purchase, Mrs.
Samuel P. Reed Gift, Morris K. Jesup Fund, Maria DeWitt Jesup Fund, John
Osgood and Elizabeth Amis Cameron Blanchard Memorial Fund and Gifts
of Robert E. Tod and William Gedney Bunce, by exchange, 1985.

Interior image credits: All images courtesy of The Internet Archive
Book Images: (helicopter seeds) page 868 of "The natural history of plants,
their forms, growth, reproduction, and distribution;" (1902), NCSU Libraries;
(bee) page 376 of "The ABC and XYZ of bee culture; a cyclopedia of
everything pertaining to the care of the honey-bee; bees, hives, honey,
implements, honey-plants, etc . . ." (1910), Smithsonian Libraries; (flower)
page 531 of "Cyclopedia of American horticulture, comprising suggestions for
cultivation of horticultural plants, descriptions of the species of fruits,
vegetables, flowers, and ornamental plants sold in the United States and
Canada, together with geographical and biographical sketches" (1900), Boston
College Libraries; (owl) page 41 of "The British bird book" (1921), Cornell
University Library; (bat) page 119 of "A comprehensive dictionary of the Bible"
(1871), The Library of Congress; (dandelion) page 53 of "Dreer's garden book :
1904" (1904), U.S. Department of Agriculture, National Agricultural Library

Printed in Canada

2 4 6 8 9 7 5 3 1

For Dorothy Wordsworth

Sun bursts out before setting—unearthly & brilliant—
calls to mind the change to another world. Every leaf a
golden lamp—every twig bedropped with a diamond.
—The splendour departs as rapidly.

DOROTHY WORDSWORTH, *The Late Journals*

BEE SONG

O hand us her secret pages
Each word a golden mote
Preserve her Incantation,
guard the eternal note!

We ferry her simple terms
within each velvet pouch
consigned to our ephemeral halls
marauders cannot touch

Hand us the words she wrote
for we know all they mean:
Trust us in our timeless flight
'round our conspiring Queen

who will preserve the trove
until mad patent dies
caught in its own manacles,
drowned in its own lies

Her word will never die
as long as we exist:
heaven's daughters are not shy
to delve the sacred list

Vivifying power
of our work and hers—
more potent than male emperors,
more patient than the years

1

Where the bee sucks, there suck I

ooooo

James Dixon's face moves in tiny expressive ways, one moment smooth as a new loaf and the next ruffled like windblown Rydal Water. He was far from bald in 1816, when he first came to Rydal to work for Rotha Wordsworth. Then he had a headful of wavy hair and he smelled like sweet baccy, a scent all the garden creatures loved, including myself, Sycamore, oldest tree of our garden. That summer was a very cold one because of a faraway event that humans here did not know about, though anyone with wings or pollen knew: Volcano! Locals knew it as the year without a summer, and were it not for James Dixon's arrival, many of us living things here in the Wordsworth garden might not have survived. James noticed details you ought to, if you're to be of use to a garden. Small things. Beautiful things. He worked hard and did very little harm.

But now James Dixon is in his fifties, and he sports one of those wool caps that keep the chill off the bald bit. Poor bald head! How poignant the forward rush of human time. James was with the Wordsworths for so long—nearly forty years—that he became intimate with their patterns.

Patterns are the most useful thing in the world. They help us recall what is about to happen.

That is why, on this so-called twenty-fifth of January in 1855, as James sits under my branches later than his usual hour, we know something has changed. The bees know. The slumbering seeds are aware. And I plainly see. His cap is atilt, his step rusty, and he has a funny, burnt scent. We feel his distress before he says a word. It whooshes through my branches like wind, rattling my few dead leaves. One or two bees scouting for signs of spring sense he is not right, and they bolt for my centre where the hive congregates, keeping itself warm. Snowdrops probe green nubs above the hard soil. It will be a week before they hoist their pale ghost flags.

James sits on what he loves to call my knee. His trousers are well-worn, like the creases in his face and hands. He does not possess new clothing or give off a shiny air. Bees love it when old softness emerges and continues on into new time. We all do. Soon the bee scouts venture back out of their entrance and settle on his lap.

Do ye mind, he says at last, if I just sit quiet for a minute before I take on our last chore of all?

He has a round basket at his side and on top of it lies a red book bright as a rosehip, and he also carries his old tinderbox with a few matches he made from splinters of my deadwood, dipped in the bees' wax.

Little Miss Belle noses out of Rydal Mount's side door and sits a distance away on the grass. Normally that dog is never far from Rotha's side. As soon as he sees Belle, James calls out Rotha's name.

Rotha is what Dixon calls Dorothy Wordsworth privately to himself, and to us in the garden—myself and all beings green, living and quick. Rotha is the name of the river that leaps through our haunts, and it is what poor Sam Coleridge called Dorothy when they were young and Sam loved her as deeply as we do now. There will be another Rotha in the family, but there'll never be another like the one we love best, the Dorothy who has slipped off this morning, five years after her brother William.

Who would have thought she'd outlast him? But on the day William died, his sister rose from her bed as if born again! As soon as he died, up she leapt! Making funeral arrangements, flinging windows open, dashing outdoors to fill her lungs with April air. Quick as in her youth, though everyone had feared news of his death might kill her. No. William's death quickened Rotha and made her more present to us than ever. The life of the sister.

James weeps and a few more bees venture out despite the cold. They do that when someone they trust is sorrowful. They hold time, humming around the hive quietly as the person gives way to feeling. They accompany the person, but do not try to console. There is nothing worse than consoling the bereaved too soon.

The January wind rustles my last leaves and the bees keep up their faint hum. And this man who has little left in the human world weeps for us, talks to us. He speaks to us all the time. We are his audience and he is ours. He and Rotha both. But now?

My mam, says James, always told me this: When someone you care about dies, you can tell their story to the bees and they'll keep it, like. Even if everyone else forgets. Bees'll hold onto it for you, then once you're dead yourself they'll scatter it abroad with the pollen so the world never really forgets. That person stays alive and the world hasn't lost them, and you haven't lost them either. What about it? Do ye reckon Mam's right? He reaches his hand forth and five bees alight on it.

Only in our world does James possess anything now. So we denizens of the garden do what we always do for those who acknowledge us the way he and Rotha have done. We eloquesce in the realm of light, wind and water—and with our earthen bodies we listen.

one

ooooo

LOOK AT THAT, WILL YE! James Dixon points at a diamond of glittering frost on a low twig on one of the sycamore's low twigs, and delight flashes through his tears. Rotha's world aglitter! And me, I fell in! Inside the shimmering. Right in I fell, that very first time I ever saw her . . . she lying in the road with her brother. I was only five!

And I says to my mam, Are they all right?

Never mind them two, Mam says. Cracked as two piss-pots, the pair of 'em.

But what are they doing? I asked her.

Hoping the road'll rattle! Then they know the postman's coming. Letters is all those two cares about.

But how will the road rattle, Mam?

Very feeble it'll shake, son, from 'es wheels in the distance . . .

Really?

Get up, son! You're as daft as they are. Honestly, I just washed them trousers. Slaving away!

I felt it, Mam! It rattled a bit like you said.

And sure enough the two arose, he like a black crow and she tiny all in white as if the crow had married a moth, and off they flew toward Dove Cottage . . .

Aye, off she flitted like a moth. Or like a quick, flighty bird racing over the hill. But then stopping while her brother ran ahead. She different from him, stoppin' and startin' and stoppin' and startin' just like a little wild creature. A linnet hopping along or a little rabbit, starting and stopping. Twitching almost, but—she had no idea we saw her. And those eyes! Coal-black but the coal burned with a flame full of its own blackness. Me and Mam hid behind a boulder. Rotha still had her real teeth then and we saw her laughing to the sky and Mam said, She's right off her head. And him, her brother, look—he's gone and run off and left his lovely cloak lying on the ground. Forgets everything, him, he's that daft. But her, she's more than daft, she's mad.

But someone mad is not what I saw. I saw somebody that was a snippet of the whole day. A piece of everything. A bit of birdwing, of leaf, of cloud. Everything shimmering around her. The whole world made of gems!

Such a windy day. She was like something the wind had blown through the day. She would bend in the funniest way! She was, all at once, like a stick and a wing. Like bone and wing somehow laced together and set free on the fell.

After that I glimpsed the shimmer all by myself in droplets on the feathery carrot leaves in me mam's ordinary yard.

I saw it in the quivery bird that stopped right in front of me in the woods.

But later I went to places where I never saw it, nobody

could. Places where no one could find any shimmer in the world. And I feared the shimmer had been only an enchantment, it had never been real, or it was only for children. Aye, I saw bad places. Things that are here already and worse things to come. Things I see very plain whenever I shut my eyes! Or whenever I've been to see my own born-family, Mam or my sister Penny. Nightmares they have had to live. And I haven't helped Mam or Penny, have I? No.

And in all the years since I saw Rotha Wordsworth that very first time when I was five, I never met the glimmer in anyone except her. Even her brother the crow borrowed it from her. William. I wonder if I stole my own bit of glimmer when I nabbed his cloak! When we got up close to it, Mam and me, its lining shone, satin Rotha had mended by hand. Anything glitters that Rotha looks upon with her silver needle or her pen or even only her black and fantastic eyes. And now, where has she gone? Can ye tell me that?

Look how Rydal Lake gleams with frost. And down there, that line of froth—the silver frill—lapping onshore. In Rotha's world everything was all eyes and ears. Things pay attention and you have to answer them. Unless you become dead to the glimmer. And things that deaden you, well, there's no end to those, is there . . . Please don't let me go dead.

THE SECOND TIME I EVER saw Rotha . . . this was a long time ago, mind, long before I came here to work for her. This was when you could still call her a young woman and I was twelve. Seven years after that first time I saw her running for the mail. This time we weren't on the fells, we were in Lady Wood. I was crouched in the ferns hunting mushrooms for me and Mam's tea when I heard the two of them talking, Rotha and her brother.

She sat on a stone covered in moss and her brother loomed over her and he wasn't happy. I heard her whimper. She was crying fit to break her heart, in fact, and he couldn't stand it. He wasn't having it. Some men get that way when a woman is sad. Even if they once had a bit of sympathy they can no longer muster it and they become impatient. They want to get on with their lives, away from a crying woman. I had heard that kind of conversation before and I knew better than to reveal myself because it was private and now William sounded irritated like.

Stop it, he said. It's only nervous blubbering. You are even worse than when our John died.

At this she cried harder, for John was their brother who had died at sea and she had loved him.

John's death was much worse for me, William said. For me, it was business. For you it's only the loss of your own joys and feelings. He sounded very angry.

I lay very still and by and by he left her stooped there and after a few minutes I slithered on my belly a few paces and rose up from behind a slant in the ground as if I'd just come upon the scene. And I made as if to veer off without having seen her but she stopped me. She had wiped her face and she had that quivery transparent whiteness of a flower that has begun shaking raindrops off itself. She seemed interested in the treasure I had gathered up in my shirt.

Are those mushrooms?

This was the first time I ever heard her voice. It's not like any other voice. Ye know that. Her voice is like a gurgling bit of river. Was like. Is. Was. What do ye think? I mean it was so much like a bit of river that for all we know it is still so. When she passed might her voice have slipped back where it came from, into the river? Rotha's voice into the River Rotha. Aye, I'll wager that might be happening now as I talk to ye.

Mushrooms, aye, I says to her then. A few little ones.

What kind—can you let me look?

I haven't got very many. Me mam's very particular about not bringing home maggoty ones.

She had in her own lap a few plants whose roots sprawled in all directions and she untangled a blue flower to show me. I'm transplanting gentians to our new house, she says, but the day is too warm for it. They're wilting even before I can get them out of this wood.

I says, Miss, what you want is to lay a small quilt of moss round them, here.

And I laid down my mushrooms and scooped some moss up and coaxed the blooms from her. I wondered that she did not know you are never supposed to move that kind of flower. I slipped the coldish cushion, green and refreshing like, under the plants in her hand.

Cover them with this mossy flap I says, folding it over them. Her hand was fine and small and she had on a brooch that looked like a drop of blood. Any blue flower, I says to her, is very difficult to move. It wants with all its heart to stay where it is.

I wanted with all my heart, says she in return, to stay just down that lane here in Dove Cottage, but we have been obliged to move.

She had a like to sob so I says, Try and leave that bundle in the moss and don't plant them until night, and they might have a chance.

We were two souls in a shady wood and I got a bit frightened and I don't know why but I said, I have to go home to my dinner now, me mam'll be waiting—although there was no dinner on our table of that you can be sure—and off I ran.

And I never saw her again after that 'til I was seventeen because me and my mam tried moving to Hawkshead but then the bad things happened with Mam like, with me and Penny having to go and live in the workhouse. And Rotha and her brother and his wife Mary moved around a lot an' all. Aye, Rotha kept living with her beloved William even after he married Mary. Their whole lives. And they moved all over the place and so did I.

It was my uncle Jim who knew the odd little Wordsworth fam'ly and their whereabouts more than I did because he had them as customers. Him and his best pal Tommy Thistlethwaite sold them hares and coal and fresh crab. A few times when I left the workhouse to try and stay with Uncle Jim, I tagged along selling his wares. The Wordsworths lived at the old rectory then, but I never saw inside. That rectory was a forlorn place. William and Mary had a baby who died there, Baby Catherine. And their little lad an' all, young

Thomas. Both died and Uncle Jim said the house was damp, it rested in a bog and filled with smoke if they lit a fire, so anyone living there got bad lungs and that's what the bairns died of. He saw all that but I never got another glimpse of Rotha or her brother until I was older.

But I never forgot Rotha in Lady Wood. I did not forget her hands or her eyes that were dark as coal but bright as flame.

Are ye lot feeling sorry for my tears?

Look, don't feel sad on my account. I am heartbroken but ye know as well as I do that before the day is out I'll be all right. I'll be singing my song again on my own. I've got hare broth simmering in my hut as we speak and I'm looking forward to dropping an onion and sage in it and drinking it with the big cooking spoon. Ye know me and my aloneness and my hut and my song.

Flax, chicory oats 'n' corn
Grains for all ye know and thine
Flour, sugar and barley sown
Ring around the old Oak shine . . .

two

ooooo

IT'S FUNNY, YOU KNOW, the way I came to the little fam'ly was really through a bit of subterfuge and smuggling.

That year I turned seventeen, the year I came to the Wordsworths', I barely knew what to do with myself for I was thinking about very hard things I had seen and done at Waterloo only the summer before. And I started doing an awful lot of walking on the coffin trail to try and work it all out. Backwards and forwards all winter through the start of that very cold spring.

That trail as ye know goes right behind Rydal Mount. William was often out raking stones in them days and sometimes Rotha was with him cutting back shrubs or checking to see how herbs had overwintered for their kitchen, sage and chives, and I glimpsed the two from afar, white and black glimmering through the trees and sometimes the hubbub of their voices. I still felt very shy of her. I hardly knew if I was afraid to startle her or if she herself startled something in me.

But this one time her brother was all alone.

He was bent over. I nearly didn't see him but then he

unfolded like a raven waking up and he says to me he says, Hello James—it's young James Dixon, is it not?

Yes, I says. It's me.

He says I've seen you with your uncle—then we exchanged words, y'know about a few gardening things, and he had a perplexed look. And I said are you searching for something?

And he said well, I desperately want to try a plant I have read about, and I can't find it anywhere. You wouldn't happen to know—and then he asked if I knew about something called an Egyptian onion.

And he says I want to try it like mad because it reproduces by an onion growing on a stem, a top stem and then its own weight bends it over—and it's a cluster by then, a little cluster of onions—and it roots by gravity.

Oh, I says?

Yes, he says, getting excited. It lowers by gravity to the soil again and then that little cluster of onions, the ones you haven't harvested, for you can harvest some of them—that's how you harvest them is partially, and you let the other part of the cluster bend down and root itself magically again, so you've got—it's like an Egyptian dance with the connected arms bending and reaching and bending and reaching and it goes on into perpetuity! he says. You've hardly got to ever think about them again once you've planted them. And I wish I could find some. But do you know, I cannot find any. I've read about them but I cannot find one to propagate.

And I says well, I don't know, but if anybody has an Egyptian onion it's the experimental garden behind the rectory of Durham Cathedral. Because I'd been there to that garden on my way home from all that had happened at Waterloo and by then I didn't care a bit about churches or their custodians or what anybody would think of me, and I'd already pilfered a few things out of that garden and stuck 'em in my cap and planted them myself.

So William said, Aye, he says, I wouldn't mind . . . d'you think you could take me there and I might have a look?

And I says to him—it was dawning on me he wanted to pilfer a few for himself—and I says all right, we'll go. Next time you're going to Newcastle let me know and I'll come and I'll show you where they'd be. Because everyone knew the Wordsworths had cousins in Newcastle. But I says it's got to be soon like, before Easter, or in the autumn. You can't pilfer the plant in summer when it's in its full glory.

And he says aye that makes sense. And he says, The only thing is, we won't say a word to my sister Dorothy, because—well she might not approve of our uprooting a plant from a place where it rightfully belongs.

And that was the first inkling I had that William kept things from his sister.

Can you really be her brother, I wondered, yet not know her habit of uprooting a plant ever so tenderly and easing it into a new place to belong?

I was thinking of her blue gentians and wondering where they were by then. I glanced around the yard for any sign she had transplanted them from house to house whenever the little fam'ly had moved. Those gentians cannot stand any kind of glare. So I knew they were not out in the open and in any case they wouldn't bloom until well after Easter. I was looking for their old spikes that show over the frost in a particular shape.

William had a furtive look on his face as he stuttered about the onions. It dawned on me that he felt guilty over his plan of stealing them from Durham Cathedral. Aye, that was the truth of it. The way he'd said *their rightful place*. It wasn't the plants' own discomfort he minded so much as stealing from the important folks at the cathedral rectory. He looked around us now as if half afraid someone might be listening. He cupped a hand to one ear and seemed a bit dazed.

I sensed then something that would become even plainer with time: on his own without his sister near, the brother was hard of hearing when it came to the natural world. He heard human voices, but found flower or wind or trees inaudible, even bird messages or your own voices here, buzzing now round your sycamore. While for Rotha it was the other way around. She heard a faint speech of the flowers or of yourselves far more plainly than any speech from people.

And it was the very same with their two sets of eyes. William had bad eyes but Rotha saw for miles.

Anyway, in the end it turned out I went to Durham by myself the very next week, and I pulled a few early scallions for William of the variety he had mentioned, and he planted them and . . . did Rotha ever enjoy eating them! She craved them. She'd lay them on bread and butter with salt and eat them whole. So that was the very start of things I contributed around this place. After that I did more and more for William in the garden.

William fancied himself a garden designer when he was not being a poet. What's more, he admitted to me right at the start that his poetry situation had deteriorated. He was getting a little bit famous for his poems and people came to visit because of them, and he didn't mind that. He liked the attention. But he let on to me that he was privately feeling as if the poems were leaving him.

Maybe it's because I'm getting a few grey hairs, he said. I'm not sure of the reason, but my writing is getting away from me. The precision of it. It still comes to Dorothy and always did and I hope always will, because if anything comes to me in the way of inspiration it comes to my sister first of all. She is and has always been the first one to whom inspiration comes.

He had laid out a few instruments on and around a chopping block where we sat by the moss shed and he told me what was expected of me. On the block sat a strange little mahogany box whose function I did not at first understand. Against the block leaned two mallets and several hatchets and a couple of wire brushes as well as spades and hoes inherited from the previous tenant, the handles needing to be tightened or in some cases removed and whittled and then refitted. He was attempting that very thing now, fitting the handle into a spade laid on his knees, but without much progress as I could make out.

There's nothing worse, says he, than trying to dig with a wobbly spade.

As far, he says, as outside work goes, I need someone I can rely on to help me with the steps and the terraces we have begun, so there'll necessarily be a fair bit of stonework and lifting and levelling of stairs, then the planting and weeding and clearing dead-fallen twigs. But those last are things an old fellow like me can still do, if slowly. I'm afraid it's the brutal grunt work I'm after from you, but you're young—how old are you?

Nearly twenty, I said. I had added a couple of years on so they would let me fight at Waterloo and I kept them tacked on now.

That is less than half my age, he said, though I feel as if I were twenty yesterday. And I can see how fit you are . . .

He was only forty-six himself at this time and in truth he was a bit bandy-legged but I knew he could still walk for miles and miles, for days on end and uphill as well, all the way over Kirkstone Pass. Everyone knew that. Him and his sister the both of them could walk for what seemed like endless time. So I said, Sir, you'll be able to do anything I can do for a good few years yet, and he laughed at that, he liked it. And while he was laughing I figured it was as good a time as any to let him know the kinds of things I like doing best.

I can do the stonework for you, I says to him, any time you want. And as you already know I'm always looking for ways to increase the health and yield of any garden, whether flowers or vegetables . . . people say I'm a bit enchanted that way but the truth is I have one very old book and I study it. But really . . . I was about to tell him the work I most loved when he interrupted me.

Dixon, he says, it's certain *indoor* tasks I wanted to mention to you while we're by ourselves out here.

He stopped and looked at the grass that had coltsfoot beginning to open, and I waited, but then he looked like he wanted someone to help him out of a confused spot, so I said, By indoor tasks, do you mean helping with the firewood and things like fixing the broken banisters and having a look inside the fireplace as regards all that smoke coming into the house?

Well yes, says he, there is always smoke in every house we've lived in. We can't seem to get clear of it and it has driven us all nearly mad. He still looked uneasy as if there was some other task he meant for me to do. I thought surely he is not talking about paperwork because he has John Carter for all that. I was not overly fond of John Carter but people said he was good with any kind of clerical duties. So I says, trying not to sound incredulous, It isn't serving dinner to your guests that you need help with indoors?

And right away at that he swipes his hand in the air and gives a dark shake of his very longish hair and says, No!

His hair flopped in his eyes and I took it as a sign of the perfect moment to tell him about my particular talent . . .

Or if you don't mind my saying it Sir, that hair of yours, I am pretty good with any task requiring the use of any kind of small blade. These scissors, for instance—I showed him the small pair I keep in my top pocket, stuck in a bit of cork—women all over Rydal ask me to keep their husbands' hair tidy and their eyebrows an' all, and even the hairs coming out of their ears and sometimes their noses. And some women even let me cut their hair.

You think I need a haircut?

Sir, whenever you're ready for one I can do it. I've cut the hair of all hands near me ever since I was nine or ten. I have a knack, like I said, for anything requiring the use of a small blade.

In fact I had learned precise cutting in the oakum cellar at the workhouse, but I did not tell him that.

Scissors, I says to him. Awl. Knife. Any finicky cut or carving or scratch you might need done.

And that's when I took my latest Pace egg out of my jacket and handed it to him.

This one had a swan on it, etched in green, with willow leaves all around, hanging like, as if the swan were just now appearing in a clearing in the fronds. I'd scratched it the night before with my Waterloo knife. I was getting a few dozen ready for Easter. I had painted some green and some black and a few were blue though blue paint is very hard to come by.

This exquisite little goose needs a much closer view, he said.

His eyes were pretty bad even then. He opened the little mahogany box and took out a magnifying glass. While he was examining my swan through the glass I saw that inside the box had popped up two bone circles on slender brass legs, and one of the circles had a lens set in it. Up rose the rings as he opened the lid. What on earth was the thing?

Oh, he said, this is a swan! But this is the loveliest Pace egg I've seen in all my days—how do you do it?

I noticed that one of the brass legs holding the lens inside the mahogany box was loose. There was a tiny hinge on each of the others but a third was missing . . .

Surely, he says, this isn't white ink on top of green paint? Can it be the eggshell shining through?

Like I said, Sir, I am pretty good with anything requiring the use of a very small blade. I've scratched the swan into the green paint. It's a question of being precise and not being in a hurry. And it helps me not worry about anything that might otherwise keep me from sleeping at night. I find it calms me down before bed.

Can you draw a swan like this with a pen?

No, Sir, with a pen I am useless. It has to be a needle or a knife or a tiny metal tool. I notice for instance in your interesting little wooden box, there—if you want me to fix that missing hinge I have a mustard tin full of tiny spare parts, all sorts of bits and pieces I've saved for mending things, and I'm sure one of them . . .

He looked at me anew. I thought, he says, I was going to have to send that box back to London.

What is it? I normally restrain my curiosity when talking to an employer but I couldn't bear not knowing the purpose of the little box only four inches long with such intricate insides.

This goes with it—he waved his magnifying glass—but the lens on legs, see the small disc under it? You put any flower on that and you look through the lens above it and you can see the flower as if you are looking into a cathedral. The spans, the struts, the stained-glass light, its whole architecture appears and you can kneel before it in wonder. Better than a Sunday service!

I was a bit surprised as William often went to church and I had not heard anyone like himself profess that nature was better than religion, although I felt it to be so myself and have kneeled, as ye know, before the gold-lit chambers of many a bonny lily. Not only kneeled but laid down and fallen asleep under the spell . . .

But this equipment, he said, belongs to Dorothy and I'm afraid she hasn't been able to use it for months . . . can you really fix it?

Yes, Sir, I think I can. May I just . . . I went to lean over the thing to get a better look, when out of my shirt pocket tumbled a little shower of objects that clattered on the wood block like tiny dice and I gave a start.

I was embarrassed and I am sure I turned crimson as I tried to scoop them up again with my hand before he could get a good look at them.

There have been many instances since that day when I have been glad of William's poor eyesight, but this time he, in his helpfulness, grabbed one of the little dice as it rolled upon the block, and straight away he felt more than saw exactly what it was.

He looked at me with his mouth agog.

I felt ashamed, but what could I do?

He knew that I had soldiered at Waterloo. So he understood what was in my pocket. When you are on the battlefield and you are prying the mouths of the dead open and extracting teeth it seems normal. All the lads are doing it. I learned before I ever got to Belgium that I should take a sharp pocket knife for that very purpose and that is the pocket knife I own yet. It is the knife I still use to scratch my swans and all the birds and patterns in the Pace eggs. I want to make something beautiful out of my old knife after all the harm it has seen and done.

At home in England you could get a good price for a single Waterloo tooth, but for a whole set, you could live on that for a month, and that is just what I had been doing since I returned. There were several buyers right around here. Cora Freetorch was one. She lived by Paterdale so to get to her I had to face climbing Kirkstone Pass but Cora would buy any teeth I cared to sell her to make full sets of Waterloo teeth for her many customers and she could fix old sets as well. She'd pay for singles or any combination you could supply. People thought she was poor in that hut with no more than a stove and a lambskin on the floor, but Cora Freetorch was never short of a pocketful of gold when I knew her. One reason I was eager for the job at the Wordsworths' in the first place was that I had sold Cora nearly all my supply. The ones in my pocket weren't even part of my inventory but were the teeth I had kept as memorial to a friend of mine who had been killed: Joseph Bell.

Now William Wordsworth rolled one of Joseph's beautiful teeth in his hand. I was ashamed. I was mortified and the sadness came upon me very fast. I didn't know what to say. I cared what Wordsworth must think of me and at the same time all I cared about was getting that white shard of my friend's life back safe in my pocket away from the light and away from anyone, the way I myself sometimes wanted to get away from anyone so I could be quiet and listen to a stream or a waterfall or the wind here in your sycamore.

But the look on William's face.

I thought that was the end of my work for the Wordsworths there and then. He could look very grim, that man. He tilts his head as if he's thinking very hard, then he clamps his teeth shut and sort of sighs through them. It sounds like the north wind. I mean it did. No breath in him now, is there. No breath in any of them. I'm the only one of the little fam'ly left now. Except Mary, but Mary is not mine and I am not Mary's, not the way I was for the others.

But William didn't sack me on the spot. No, not at all.

He held Joe's tooth on a flat hand where it loomed like a relic on the altar in the church where I never go. And he said, James, do you reckon you could use one of your small implements to adjust any of the three sets of my sister's teeth that have been causing her agony every time she fits them into her mouth? Each set needs at least one replacement tooth, and two of them have problems with their hinges.

Dorothy's teeth?

Yes, she is barely forty-five yet her own are nearly gone.

Cora Freetorch is usually the one who does that kind of thing around here, Sir. If you want I can introduce you to her.

Cora has tried over and over again. My sister has sensitivities that Cora cannot surmount. And every time we have made an adjustment someone has to go over Kirkstone Pass and back again and it takes, as you know, all of a day. If you could make a tiny adjustment here and there, well, it would save me a great deal of inconvenience I can tell you. This very tooth, for instance, looks as if it would perfectly fit the gap in my sister's oldest pair.

And he handed me Joe's tooth, and I was very relieved to have it back.

You mentioned inside work? I wanted to take his mind off the unsavoury portion of what we had been discussing. I wanted to forget about putting my friend Joe's teeth into Dorothy Wordsworth's mouth. But William had one more thing to say about it.

It will be important not to mention to Dorothy that these are Waterloo teeth. That they are teeth that have been torn from the heads of deceased soldiers. She can't know this or she'll never acquiesce to our using them. We have to tell her all the teeth are porcelain or at the very worst carved animal bone, and even at that she is liable to balk. She is liable to inquire as to what kind of animal and how it was killed and even what its name was, if it had a name.

I said nothing, taking this in. I didn't want to let on that I felt funny about lying to his sister, or that I felt Miss Wordsworth would somehow know the truth of anything no matter how convincing you were. If you are lying some people know it and she was one of those. And even if they don't know it they as good as know it because something in their blood runs away from the person lying. They know there is love missing or sympathy missing. Something. They can just feel it the way you feel a change in the wind or a current in the water.

Because as I told you, said William, my sister has sensitivities . . . in fact this is exactly what I meant when I said I have work for you inside the household.

Sir?

You've seen my sister, I think?

Er, in the way anyone in the village might have seen her on her walks, Sir. I—when I was a young lad I might have seen her a bit more, as I was often on the fells with my mam . . . I decided not to tell him anything beyond this.

So you know that she is not like other women. She is different.

Is she, Sir?

She is very different. She has to be handled most carefully.

Sir?

I have been the careful one, now, for years and years. I have been so careful that there are bags under my eyes. And frankly, I'm tired and I need help. Is it a terrible thing, to ask, finally, for help?

No, Sir?

Dorothy can be . . . He twiddled his hands round a button and I wanted to warn him it was about to fall off any minute but I kept quiet. I learned a long time ago how shutting up helps you get to the bottom of nearly anything.

She can be exuberant, he said. Too exuberant. Because then she flattens. After the exuberant time when everything is charged and full of a joyful energy, her sun goes out like a blown lamp. Worse than flattens. What is the opposite of exuberant, Dixon?

I don't know, Sir?

I was not about to furnish the poet William Wordsworth with a word, although various words came to mind. I had seen my own sister Penny worse than flattened. But you don't go talking about your own sister to a man like William while he is talking about his. Not if you want to get to the bottom of your job, the job he has in mind for you. There are all kinds of people ready to rant on and on about themselves given the slightest opening. My mam is one of them but I am not. I had seen Mam lose many an opportunity through talking far too much and I knew to stand quiet as a mouse waiting for the job that would instantly benefit myself and that might in time help my sister Penny out of her worse than flattened situation.

At least, in my mind on that day I was daring to allow these hopeful thoughts.

Of course what happened to Penny happened despite all my old hopes, and I now look back on those hopes very differently. But on that day my hopeful thoughts made me hesitate to provide the poet with words that popped freely into my mind, like *grey* or *sallow*. I did not say *maimed* or *wasted*. I did not mention hunger or damp and I said nothing about lungs and I did not mention Penny's shoulder. I wanted to! I wanted to take the chance that William might open his eyes and help Penny Dixon there and then by allowing me to bring her to work at his household, just as he was offering to open the door to me.

No. I forced myself to wait and to listen to the one man in the world who looked to be nearly ready to release the tiny bit of money needed to change my own situation. And not just money. There was hardly hope for my mam, but for myself and for Penny there was something here in this garden and in the Wordsworth household that went beyond what a few coins can buy.

Blasted?

Sir?

Enervated? Whatever the word might be, Dixon, I rather desperately need help with my sister.

Yes, Sir?

And I need it from a person who is not one of our family, and who has the dexterity of someone like yourself. I mean finesse of hand but I also mean dexterity of spirit. I sense this dexterity in your face and now I see it in your beautiful artwork covering the surface of this egg. It is perfect, and it might be only folk art but it has something refined in it, something of the angels, if I believed in angels, which I do not. But if I did . . . do you know what I mean, James Dixon?

Perhaps not quite, Sir. But I do enjoy making the designs on the Pace eggs . . .

Never mind. I see it in you. And you'll see it too, if you spend enough time here with us, in the gardens and in our company. You might be raw now, in fact you look as if you've been out in the wind a few times in bare feet and a woefully insufficient coat.

Aye Sir, I have. But I didn't mind it. You get used to it. You even come to like it better than being too well wrapped-up.

And you seem like a solitary soul, the way I once was . . .

Aye, Sir, I am often by myself, but then again there are creatures and mountains and streams full of fish.

And I respect a man who enjoys his own company. For one thing, he doesn't band up with every galoot in the tavern.

Sir, I never drink.

And you don't seem to have friends—but with us you might feel a modicum of friendship. What do you think?

I could hope so, Sir.

I still did not know what he meant by the indoor work requiring a certain spirit that he saw in me. When someone of William's sort talks to you like that, you feel that they are putting some kind of hope in you, and it lifts you up in a lovely way even if you wish it didn't. They think the best of you even though you are not a rich person or an important man. They see something in you that other people don't see and maybe you yourself don't know is there. I loved it, even though I didn't know what it was William saw and I was frightened he might be wrong. I know what it is now that I own, but I didn't know it then.

Still, I was not a timid youth even though I was shy, and I did want to know exactly what he meant when he said he had other work for me in the house. So far he was talking in riddles. If I was to be of any help I had to know exactly what I was supposed to do. So I said, Sir, can you be a bit clearer about what it is you wanted me to do for your sister?

He went quiet. He often wears black clothes. Wore. He often wore black or dark clothes and that day he had on something that crumpled up as he bent into himself, as if to hold his self dear or tight or apart from troubles that haunted him.

Sir?

I wondered if Wordsworth, no longer young like me, had run out of words. Or words had run out of him. He was a giant bedraggled bird with fresh air gone out of him at that moment. Flightless and wingless and making no sound. Not dead as now but something like pre-dead. I felt he needed me to change the subject.

It has been a colder than usual spring, I said.

Yes, he managed to say. People can talk about the weather no matter what is going on inside them. Our garden, he said, has been struggling.

You'll want help with the sweet peas. They are very tender.

They are indeed in danger.

We'd had lots of rain . . . as ye know. But I knew it had not been the kind of rain our north of England normally has in spring. We were missing that fresh smell that comes when spring is just starting to unlock the green that's trapped in everything, in the soil and everywhere. It hasn't come out fully but shows just little tips. Seams are ripping and the little tips are hardly even showing. It's just that you know the stitches have broken and the green's about to burst out, that's what the rain brings out. The fragrance. And this spring that joy had not come. And it wouldn't come, either. We didn't know yet how there would be no summer at all that year. Although ye lot probably knew. Ye always know that kind of thing in advance. Ye must have been telling each other to hoard whatever drops of honey ye could eke out of that summer that was never a summer.

My sister, William began again. He was trying to find something essential to tell me about Rotha but he ended up telling me an odd joke instead. At first I couldn't make out why he was telling it to me as it seemed unrelated to all that had gone on between us.

Have you ever heard the one, he says, about this doctor? A surgeon?

No, I says.

Well there was this surgeon and he saved a couple of people's lives. Thought he was being very helpful. But after he's saved them, one tries to hang himself and the other one tries to drown himself. And the surgeon can't understand it. Why are they not happy about having their lives saved? So he asks them both. And one after the other they say to him, Doctor, we thought it was all finished, and here's you saving our life! And now we're stuck here and have to make a living and all that goes with it. Doctor, they said, pardon us but now you'll have to foot our bills because by rights we shouldn't even be alive. So he vows after that, this doctor, never again will he save another soul from any accident without making sure first, do they really want to be saved? So one day he goes out with a rowing party, and one of the men falls overboard and starts flailing about. He cannot swim. And our surgeon grabs him by the hair and lifts his head above the water and says, Now then, do you want to be rescued or not? And the poor man gasps, Me poor wife! How would she manage? She's not well, and oh, our seven little bairns . . . And the doctor shouts Ha! Wretched bloke—no wonder you've jumped in! And pops him back under the water to his doom!

William started chortling. He was never a man given to much laughter but at that moment he was quaking. His whole body. He couldn't stop. I wasn't sure, myself, how funny I found the joke. It did not seem funny at all in any way that can make a man like me laugh. I laugh at things. I think I laugh at things. But the best face I could conjure at his joke was simply one that did not look, I hoped, too puzzled.

Sam Coleridge told us that one, William said, once he'd stopped laughing. At a little party. Well we all nearly died laughing at it. We were all busting. Except Dorothy. Once the merriment died down a bit we noticed her brimming with tears. Oh, she says, however could the doctor do such a thing—was he so very inhuman as that? Well. Sam and Bob Southey and the rest of us just about fell off our chairs. But we had to comfort her, and Sam said to her he was sorry. And any time he told the joke after that he told about Dorothy's tears and how they made him love her all the more.

Nobody wanted to let my sister down. When she trusts you, it's like being trusted by the trees.

He said this as if he himself had disappointed or was about to disappoint her most terribly.

She's got no guile, he said, and she is hardly able to laugh at anybody.

We sat in the garden as clouds gathered and it grew very chilly. He recapped what he needed me to do: garden work outside, mostly, and an eye upon his sister's well-being inside. Her mental health, really, he said. Because she never leaves the realm.

The realm, Sir?

That's what you've got to understand, he said. I myself leave the realm. For practical reasons. I step outside the circle. I can look back at it, shining and golden. Rimmed by time but filled with timeless and treasured air. But Dorothy never leaves it. She is always inside it.

Inside what, Sir?

Inside the place where everything in the natural world, each anemone, each oak, each aster, each daisy, each ripple at the water's edge—are you with me, Dixon?

I think so, Sir?

Each rustle of the grasses . . . hangs all about you in the air. Each part listens to one another with the attentiveness of a lover.

He started laughing. It was a different kind of laughter from when he had laughed at the joke. I cannot remember exactly what he said next. Something about the air being charged, every mote of it listening. Did William say the air was listening? Could he have said that? This was a long time ago.

You see, he said, they're all getting ready to sing their song, aren't they.

Who is? I could not fathom what he meant. It would take me all of my years with his sister to understand.

They're all getting ready to sing their song of glory, he said. If this frost ever melts. That's what the poetry is. My poems. Once caught, it all goes on the page: pinned, wings of each specimen—magnificent, annihilated. But my sister! She is awake, attentive in a surround that is also awake. She knows no dead specimen, only charged song. No matter the season.

Charged song?

Did he mean charged as lightning charges the sky? What did he mean?

The clouds opened and a cold sleet fell on us. Shreds of ice lay like coconut in his jacket folds. William folded his sister's mahogany box with the lenses in it and gave me it. I somewhat self-consciously slid it in the pocket containing my friend Joseph's teeth, for I had no other safe place for it. I promised I'd fix it the best I could, and William asked me could I come to the house next Thursday, and that was the real start of my regular work here: part-time at first and then, with the years, more like my whole lifetime.

three

ᴏᴏᴏᴏᴏ

I AM A BIT OF A FAIRY KING when it comes to mending just about anything. From wood and stone to feather and stem, I can usually mend it.

But all the broken things in the little fam'ly!

It was hard to tell what was going on in the house at first. Cold wind thrashed outside and people ousted from their land came begging for bread and coppers all over the vale, but the household seemed harmonious and I felt lucky to be in it. You couldn't really call it a lonely house. The cacophony of that party they had on my first Easter with them! Two roast birds and fresh bread. Their writer friends Charles and Mary Lamb—sister and brother like Rotha and William. Sarah Hutchinson and William and his own Mary in their element, and half a dozen friends. The chatter. The laughter. You'd never dream Mary Lamb had stabbed her mother to death with a carving knife.

Everybody had quietly forgotten about that.

The drinks, the pipes. The firelight on the pots and pans. True, Rotha kept looking out the window for Sam Coleridge who did not come and would never come: he had turned his back on them all by then—but even without Sam there was endless chatter and real affection. And the smells of toasted bread and roasting meat and beef drippings melting on the gravy in silver motes, glittering and welcoming. You'd never say Rotha might feel lonely in the midst of a party like that, but she grew agitated.

William whispered in the corner, Dixon, can you please take my sister upstairs?

So I did. Would you like me to leave you alone? I asked her. She sat at the foot of her bed gazing at a blank place in the wall near the window. Beyond the window your sycamore here was having a hard time trying to bud. Swallows faltered at Rotha's window-ledge trying to build their nest in all that cruel wind. Yet she kept looking, not through her window but at the wall.

Beside her was a fancy hat box on the floor. I already knew what was in it. The box was off one of Mary's hats, a hat Mary often wore to church, so the hat itself was in Mary and William's room. I can't remember the hat. But the box was a green box. It had paisley and knots of rosebuds and some gilt ribbon and it was nearly worn out, but Dorothy liked that kind of thing and in that box she kept her stack of diaries. I knew this because I had gone upstairs one day to unstick the window so she could let air in. She had to have fresh air even though spring had not come. And she had left the lid off the box, so of course I glanced in and saw her diaries. A stack of dark ones, black and blue, but tucked under them this scarlet notebook I've brought out here with me this morning. Something red, you notice it flickering like!

I didn't do more than glance down in the box. But I noticed this red book. I bet ye notice a scarlet blossom, how it stands out from all the others.

Now she pulled the red book from the bottom of the stack and untied it and then unwrapped it—it was the only one she had wrapped up and I had never unwrapped it. But now I saw it had a red cover under its red cloth. The others were just bare books. She stared at the wall as if she saw something through it, and then she wrote in the red book but I couldn't see what she wrote although I wanted to.

I felt as if she had forgotten my presence so I said, Miss—I still called her Miss Wordsworth then—I only started calling her Miss D after we got closer. I said, Did you eat any dinner? Aren't you a little bit hungry?

A bit, she says, but I don't feel like eating meat. What I would love while I'm writing, she says, is one boiled egg with salt on it.

I went back down and brought her an egg and I scalped its top off with my knife and this amused her.

Her diary lay open on the bed while she stared at that spot on the wall again and ate her egg.

I pretended not to be interested in the diary but of course I was, anybody would be, and I saw bits of what she had put down. She had written something but crossed it out, except for the title: *Togetherness Committee*. And Mary's name was there, and *fireside* was there, and flames were mentioned. Half of Sam Coleridge's name stuck out from some particularly strong, black lashings of ink. I had met Coleridge and for the life of me I could not see what all the fuss was about.

He was folded in on himself and uninterested in anything around him. He was a ruined man by the time I saw him. But I knew, I had heard, that when he was young he was one of the loveliest young poets in England and Rotha had loved him. Many's the tongue had wagged over her traipsing through the vales with him alone, lying sidelong on the turf until the stars came out.

In fact, tongues did nothing but wag about Rotha and her brother when I first came to Rydal.

People thought the fam'ly had a bit of money once they moved to Rydal Mount and William became the new tax collector. Oh, they said, William Wordsworth has got buckets of money now, you're in the good books.

When Berthe Briggs came with the eggs she'd get me to mend her tin pail and she'd crow in the lane after, That Dixon, he can do anything, him, shove the arse back in a cat, but he won't let on a word about what's going on behind Rydal Mount's walls! Aye, Berthe and all of Rydal were one and the same in concluding the handyman must know what's going on, let's get him by himself, once he's off duty . . . I had a steady stream of visitors at my hut on Sunday afternoons, prying and thinking of me as the Wordsworth Times, a trusted source ready to provide them with all the news. They all thought I tacked on with the Wordsworths only for the pay.

But the wages are not why I came here to work. I could have made the same money working elsewhere. I could have made more, some places. There is more to it than the money when you are in the company of people who have an exciting way of thinking.

Ye know yourselves, when anybody gets even a little bit famous as the Wordsworths were starting to do, people respect them well enough to their faces. Oh yes, they show great politeness in person. You'd think, after the poet's child was dead—little Catherine—simple as she was, more like a beloved fairy than a child able to grow up to read and write or anything—you'd think when the Wordsworths lost her that people might hold their tongues.

But question number one flying around the vale was, Poor dead Catherine was under a spell wasn't she, her eyes weren't right, was she a changeling? Question number two was, How did I expect anyone to believe that Rotha, a woman roaming the fells alone, had done so without a horde of wild lovers, some of them probably half-human beings in the dusk?

Yet she lets on so as to appear maidenly, they marvelled; surely that's a canny disguise?

And what about the way Dorothy and her poet brother used to carry on before he married Mary?

Talk of the town, all that, and people expected me not only to know everything that had happened before I got there, but to be dying to inform them of the sibling pair's every move.

Now Rotha said to me, Dixon, she says . . . she was tackling the bottom of her boiled egg . . . do you know what I wish you and I were doing?

No, Miss?

Hunting kittenracts.

Swallows banged against the glass—we watched their

fluffy bellies and their forked fishtails and she said, They are trying to swim in an unsympathetic current!

The swallows distressed her.

I wish there was some way we could give them shelter! Did you know, James, that just there—she pointed her spoon at the blank spot in the wall where she had been staring—is a secret window?

I don't see any window, Miss, I ventured.

I felt disappointed for her that I could not see what she saw but I wasn't going to pretend to her that I saw a window where there was none. I felt there was a wee beck starting to flow between us and I did not want to dam it up with fibs. It wanted to become a living stream. I wanted it.

I know you don't, she says. Because it has been concealed. It's a very old window still inside the wall. I feel as if I can see right through it.

This certainly seemed odd to me but I did not explain it away by concluding that she was mistaken or feverish or, as her brother had mentioned, over-exuberant. I sensed even then that I was to learn more from Rotha's strangeness than I could imagine.

I just can't seem to gather myself, she said to me then, when there is a crowd like the one downstairs now. Even people I love, even Mary Lamb, who by herself is a fountain of refreshment to me. But together! They are all talking quite happily to each other and in the wild babble I can't reach a place where I'm listening to somebody and they are listening in return, heart to heart. The way you are now—you're listening, aren't you, James.

I am, I says to her.

But downstairs, she says, it's arm to arm and finger to finger and mouth to mouth and hair to hair and fire to song and wine to bread and meat to soup and ladle to knife—but one heart, mine, wants to run, cowering, shutting the covers over itself, closing the curtain. Making itself as small as possible like a child curled up. Hiding under the stairs! As if something frightening has come to the door . . .

I waited for her to say what frightening thing that was. But she scooped the last of her egg in little white-and-yellow moons on her spoon and continued looking at the white wall where she had said there was an old, hidden window. A window I couldn't see, not even a slight impression in the wall.

There's so much good will and love downstairs just now, she said—all happiness!

I did not mention Mary Lamb's having murdered her own mother quite recently, or the fact that Miss Lamb's brother Charles had brought a straitjacket in a sack in case he needed to slap it on his sister once again. These things went without saying in the Wordsworth house at the time, though it had certainly been said in all the papers.

All heat and cheer, said Rotha. But, James, do you notice none of it is any fainter now that we are here, away from the party?

Miss?

When you went down to get this egg, did anyone notice your presence?

I daren't . . .

They didn't, did they? You were nothing but a shadow.

I can't be sure, Miss. They were all talking amongst themselves . . .

Our absence is—and don't imagine me full of self-pity, James, I'm simply stating a fact—our retreat, our absence—does not take away from their jolly heat, from the heightened temperature of the gathering. She pointed at the real window, the one we could both see: Look, she said. Our swallows have flown away.

I felt a pang when Rotha said *our* swallows. I felt it deeply, and when I think about it all these years later I believe that day of the Easter party was the start of how she and I became a magic team, at least in my own mind. Am I imagining it? Ye lot are lucky, ye have each other—a hive of ye working together, keeping each other warm, always in the glow of one another's natural company, and your old sycamore for shelter, and the whole garden nourishing ye.

But for some of us humans that Easter day was a cold, lonely day like today. Only the twigs of the swallows' half-built nest showed through the rain-blurred glass. It had teemed cold rain that whole spring.

James, Rotha said to me then, can you see those two single droplets of freezing rain suspended on the eave?

Yes, I says.

Just quivering there and reflecting everything, she said, not adding to the warmth of the house nor drawing more than an iota of heat away. I don't mean that the two raindrops are insignificant. I know I am loved, and you must be loved too. Are you loved, James?

Was I?

Rotha had a sixth sense when it came to knowing if you were alone in the world or not. If you had anybody. And I did have somebody—but I did and I didn't. My somebody was not very well. Penny, my little sister. There was something not right with Penny's shoulder, wasn't there? She was hoarse an' all—her voice the last time I went to Manchester croaked from the depth of a dry pit like a noise I once heard come out of a parched baby frog.

Have you got a girl?

No, Miss. I'm far too busy.

Have you any brothers or sisters?

I have a younger sister, Miss. Penny, named for her copper hair.

And do you see her?

I remained silent and Rotha said, Perhaps it is only that people like us do not know how to love a crowd. We cannot find the individual souls in it.

And I felt then that neither Rotha nor I had a clue what was going on in each other's family, and we had not admitted to ourselves why we each felt so alone. That day was when I started wondering how Rotha and I could help each other. Though I knew even then that to wonder this may be wrong, or foolish, or impossible. Because I was only the . . . what is it I heard their visiting preacher Edward something-or-other call me with a teacup in one paw and a goblet of elder wine in the other and currant-bun crumbs all over his gob? The *factotum—What a good mute and earless and eclectic factotum you have—he can re-weave the seat on a beloved old chair or mend any irreplaceable tool!* For all I knew, he was calling me a Peruvian hedgehog. It took me ages to find out the meaning of that word. But it only means handyman.

The rain grew louder and in the din I asked her, Miss—what did you mean by saying you wished to hunt a . . . some kind of a kitten?

William's wife Mary was always on about getting a kitten. Mary longed for a household cat. It was a fierce argument at times, with Mary disgusted by mouse droppings and Rotha defending the swallows and all the other birds that came near. The birds would be massacred if Mary got her way. So I couldn't fathom why Rotha had just now mentioned trying to find the very animal that would destroy our swallows, who were already battling for their lives against the gale outside.

My question made her laugh.

Then she said, You're still the same lad that came upon me while I was crying, aren't you. What a sad time that was, the time in Lady Wood—our baby Catherine had only just died, and Sam Coleridge was so lost to us, you might as well say Sam had died as well, but you wouldn't have known, you were only a boy. It *was* you, though—I know it was you. You're the little lad who caught me crying.

I had no reason to deny this, but at the same time I felt somewhat exposed. I guess I'd thought that with all the growing up I had done in the interim, Rotha had not recognized me.

I'd know your face anywhere, she said. All shy and funny and folded in strange ways, like a darling goblin.

She couldn't have known my mam had often called me a little goblin.

But Rotha was very keen and sharp in her perceptions then, and in my eyes she has never lost that keenness. When everyone around would later lament she was no longer right in her mind I vowed she was the same Rotha as always.

I cannot say why I see her so differently from the general opinion. I only know that she never changed in all our time together, from that cold Easter of 1816 when we were alone together in her room until today. I know she is dead but even so I still feel Rotha has not changed. People don't stop existing when they die, do they? They just go somewhere else. Some place where we cannot reach them.

My mam wasn't an extra wise person. Haha! Far from it. But one thing she said feels very real and true to me now, and it was about the dead. Mam said the reason the dead don't reach out and contact us and let us know where they are and that they are all right is because they are far more than just all right. They are having such a lovely time that if they gave us so much as a hint of how wonderful it is being dead, we would kill ourselves here and now. Don't you worry, my mam says, the dead are only being kind to us.

A kittenract, Rotha said to me that Easter day, isn't a kitten. Guess what it is, James.

I can't, Miss. I don't know.

Think about it.

I'm not a very good guesser.

She crushed her eggshell into pieces like sand and scooped the dangly pile up and handed it to me and said, Do you know what this is for?

I said to her, shaking my head no, Miss, I says—it's starting to look as if I might not know much at all.

Come on, she said, we're going out. Don't worry about the party, we'll sneak out the back door.

The box is still open, I said, with all your notebooks exposed—would you like me to put its lid back on?

No one is going to bother with my diaries, she said. I only put quiet observations in them. The family, Grasmere. The time the Green children lost their parents. The seasons. Times I waited alone for my brother while he was away, written to entertain him. They're all in those books in that box. And my recollections of Scotland. Trips I've taken with William and Sam Coleridge, when we were young and before Sam fell out with us . . .

I did know about the Scottish recollections because there were copies—I won't say flying around, but she had made five or six copies for friends, and there was one copy in her room that she was always working on, trying to make it better and better. It would come in and out of view again as she revised it or put it away.

I don't know where I got the nerve—maybe because the red notebook she had been writing in still lay open on the bed—but I asked her then if I might look at any of her writings. And she said, Why not, they were written for the household. William looks in them all the time, she says.

So right from the start I felt, or I believed at any rate—she would not mind if I knew something of what was in her notebooks.

But she did say to me that day—I've got to confess—Only please don't look in this one, which is for myself alone. And she picked up the red diary off her bed.

It was the only time I had seen her claim a particular object for herself.

So of course that became the diary I longed to see most of all.

I watched her shut it, wrap it, and tie it with a lace off one of William's old boots. It was not a single knot and it wasn't even double, it was a triple knot—but the tool for unfastening it was, and still is, in my pocket. I noticed she hesitated before sliding that book beneath the others. Maybe she suspected she should hide it elsewhere if I was not to look inside. But she stuck it under the rest . . . though that is not where I found it later.

Then we crept out the back door. No one in the party heard or saw us, and she took me along a winding walk William had made past the birches, and what did she show me but the struggling tips of a cluster of leaves belonging to a plant I recognized.

I knew it by the husks of its previous year's flowers scattered around, papery edges tinged gentian blue.

I said to her, You managed to keep them alive all this time?

From their natural home near Dove Cottage, to Allan Bank, then to the cursed Rectory and now here, she said, and you're the kittenlyst!

I remembered William's tone in calling her exuberant, like she had something amiss.

Is a kittenract, I says to her then—I had caught something of her glee out in the wind; the whole outdoors, the wind and everything it touched was her company and I saw she was recovering after fading at the party—is it a cataract that hasn't grown up yet?

And she laughed, and said that now I was a real playmate.

Sam Coleridge made that one up, she said. I noticed the difference between her manner in and out of the house. It was night and day. Sam and I had found a waterfall, she said. Miniature but wild, just rippling and dripping like a thread loosened from a bridal gown. I'll show you!

And she pulled me by my hand up the coffin trail and showed me a falls, a tiny one, beginning to grow ferns around itself though ice shards still lined the rocks, and we sat awhile in the sleet and got wet through while she listened to the water that sounded like bells in a hollow cave: a small voice that combs the bones in your neck and spine with soothing vibrations. It refreshed us and made us laugh.

This was our first kittenract, she said, and forevermore after that we kittenized anything that had *cat* in it. Sam once found a forked stick and pulled a ribbon out of my gown and picked a piece of—you know—that little—tiny yellow pincushion in the middle of the weed that smells like pineapple. He'd flick it at my face and that was his kittenpult. And at the lake, anywhere with a crease in the stones, any tiny indentation—if you could imagine yourself tiny enough to fit inside it, you were in the kittencombs. And if we had any minor misadventure, such as if we forgot to put leavening in the dumplings, or if William stubbed a toe—before his toe got real bad, if he just gave it a knock like, we'd say don't worry, it's only a minor kittenclysm.

I had not known Coleridge was funny and I did not realize until much later that it was his wife, Sara, who made up their secret language, though Sam made out it was his own.

After our day by the waterfall I would not find Rotha humourless even when she grew depressed. I never came to share William's perception of her. I doubted myself in this at first, because I've noticed that people tend to be blind to very obvious things going on around them. I have asked myself, Why should I be any less blind?

Rotha seldom said *I*. She said *we* meaning herself, William and Coleridge, as if the three were one person. It was a funny way she had, and even, later, when Sam and William were both dead, she still said we. I fear I was daft enough to believe I might become part of that *we* once William and Sam were gone.

Practically every day, James, she said to me, we have a kittenclysm. Just yesterday we sent a letter off to the wrong person. And they'll read it and see immediately it wasn't meant for their eyes. But it was only about the curtains so it's a tiny kittenclysm. It was not about anything harmful or troublesome.

She sounded joyful, explaining this game the friends had made amongst themselves. But in the diary she forbade me to examine—is *forbade* too strong a word for the quiet way she asked me not to look? In the red diary I would find a page she had titled *Kittenclysm*, but then crossed that out and scrawled *Cataclysm* instead.

Sometimes no matter how beguiling a kitten is, you cannot deny it will grow up and slaughter the swallows.

four

ooooo

HER BROTHER WAS THE ONE who had hired me, but he hired me to be all and everything for his sister. And it became very evident once I began working regular days at Rydal that two streams were going on as regards my assigned tasks.

For William I did small repairs and brick work and big lifting, using my hands and my reasoning to get the family out of practical fixes and various messes. It amazes me how intelligent people like the Wordsworths cannot think their way out of the simplest everyday problems such as a smoking chimney or a leaky sill.

So when I was not doing the gardening grunt-work for William or listening while he hemmed and hawed about how to form his steps and garden terraces, he assigned me small tasks for the household, some outdoors and others inside: papering and sanding, or patching this and that such as the family umbrellas, pattens and clogs, or their bellows and coal-scuttle. And mending the candle tin or gathering straw for the boots or making the candy for ye bees and bringing it to your hive when it became apparent that we were not going to have good weather at all. In fact I found out by only a slight inspection that ye were starving! That spring of 1816 we had starvation all around us with beggars coming to the door and Rotha enlisted me to help the odd traveller, especially if they had young ones, by handing them a sixpence and sometimes giving them clean straw for their shoes, if they had any shoes.

Strictly for herself she asked me to provide very little but there was one thing—James, she said, do you see much fallen wool on your travels? Locks of fleece on the fences, tufts in the brambles? Wool in the sticks and on the stones, caught, from the lambs and the sheep?

And I says, Aye, Miss, I see it all the time, I know just what you mean.

She says well, I gather it myself when I am out walking, to stuff cushions, but any time you're on your rambles, if you don't mind putting some in this sack and giving it to me, I'd love that.

So that was a thing I did wholeheartedly and happily because you can shove a bit of wool in your sack and it weighs nowt. It compresses. And she was delighted with that. She was over the moon. She made me a small cushion for my own and it's lovely. I've still got it. It's got leaves on it. She stitched leaves all around it twined like a laurel wreath, like something off a Roman coin or an emperor's head. It was like a royal wreath that's been lost, fallen on the ground, weathered and left for a long time and found by a child in the field.

Everything she fashioned by hand was like that, wasn't it? It was weathered and a bit lost. And everything she said to me was weathered and lost an' all.

Rydal Lake has an ever-changing skin, she said to me on a frozen day that first year. A smoky sheen, she said, clouded underneath as if by one layer of smoke, yet mirror-shining. She said things like that. *Mirror-shining . . .* or, *cut like a ransacked facet of garnet attacked by an axe!* And as she said the word *axe* she looked fierce and alarmed.

I comforted her and I said don't be frightened—look, the water's lovely green all the way through, clear to the bottom. Look—coins and fish and glass bottles and glimmer-stones. Look at the glinting fish, trying to catch our eye, wanting us to see them.

I'd say them things to her. Comforting things.

Looking back on it all now I can barely tell if William pushed me closer to his sister because he saw she and I were getting along so well, or if he had planned me as a kind of replacement for himself all along. At any rate I did a lot of little things for her, and our resulting friendship—was it a friendship?—it grew gradual, like.

That first summer we never stopped making fires because all the land was so bitterly cold. Furrows from the year before couldn't be worked because they were frozen to mid-May in the fields. I'd gather sticks after Rotha pruned the trees, and I lit them and in those fires I toasted many a slice of bread-and-dripping for my luncheon and ate it happily while she continued her orchard work humming like a wren, though I had my doubts over any gooseberries or damsons appearing. She'd sit nearby for a break and say how she savoured the smoke and wasn't it a pity William could not smell its fragrance, in fact he couldn't smell anything whatsoever, and she had no one with whom to share the fragrance of wood smoke or of lily of the valley except myself.

Can William really not smell anything? I said.

And she says to me, My brother can only engage with certain forms and colours. Fragrance eludes him and I cannot bear to talk of it with him for fear I might seem to be gloating. I have to wait until he reads of fragrance in my diaries and then he can use it in his poetry as if his own nose had smelled it.

I could hardly credit this. Did her brother really read her sensations and then put them in his poems as if they were his? I thought how painful this must have been for him. Knowing glory was there second-hand, like.

All this she confided to me with our heads bent into the cherry wood smoke and our two noses twitching at the waxen bells' musk which floated that May through the cold. Those lilies of the valley are a hardy marvel. Most flowers are. You think they haven't a chance against the wind but away they bloom. And William couldn't smell them! I knew his eyes were bad but between that and not smelling anything and being hard of hearing, no wonder he needed to comb Rotha's diaries for sensation lost to him.

This cherry smoke is lovely, Rotha said of our outdoor blaze. But when coal smoke fills the house from that wretched chimney in our kitchen it fills me with despair!

I knew their chimney smoked and I had my own idea as to why, but I had been busy with my other tasks and no one had yet pressed me to address that problem.

It only smokes on cloudy days, she said, but it reminds us of all the awful smoke in all our other houses that we dreaded, smoke that made us ill—especially the children . . .

I knew she was thinking of wee Catherine and Thomas, both dead with pneumonia, and I said yes, I know the Rydal chimney smokes. Have you checked inside it for any blackened heart?

And she says, do you mean there is something wrong with our hearth?

I felt offended but I did not let on what I was thinking: I know how to say hearth when I mean hearth, Miss, and heart when I mean heart. My name may not be Wordsworth but I do know how to properly say the words I know.

But I did not say any of this. I said, Miss, I meant only that sometimes there can be a heart blocking a chimney.

What in the world are you talking about?

I'll show you, I says. We'll have a look tonight after the fire's died out. Once the fam'ly is off to bed.

And at half past midnight she crouches on the floor while I reach up with tongs clamped on a stick holding a ball of snarly wire and down tumbles the very heart I suspected of blocking the flue, much petrified and charred.

There you are, I says. More than a hundred rusty pins sticking out of this one.

I see Miss Wordsworth hasn't got a clue what to think. Eyes darting all over the place. Those eyes, they darted everywhere. They were deep and—they were like water. They were like the blackest, fastest-running stream, but with pools and becks that slowed or bent back on themselves but then

gushed forward again. People said her eyes were the wild-
est they'd ever seen. Her friends all said so, but I was the
one who saw where gold flecks were located in that stream,
those eyes. And I loved showing her my tricks, like finding a
heart in the chimney.

It's nowt but a sheep's heart, I says. Someone has lodged
it up there for revenge, judging by all the pins. Some previous tenant or their servant. Someone unlucky in love.

I didn't tell her my mam had done this very manoeuvre
after my father left us or that she credited the act with his
having been killed in his accident at Windy Brow forge.
The sheep's heart stands in for the heart you want to bring
to harm.

All that day and into the next week Rotha and William
and everyone in the house talked about the blackened heart
in wonderment. It was as if they had discovered it themselves. I had given them a thrill. And I realized I had a kind
of a hidden influence.

And gradually there grew that second manner of task I
have mentioned, all concerning Rotha, though purely at
William's bidding at first. It had nothing to do with the hefty
things I did for him, such as hewing stone for the terraces.

This second responsibility was a task that was not stated.
It was never outlined or written in any list or note, nor spoken out loud, though it had to do with the things William
had said about Rotha's mental state and how she needed him.

All through 1816, that year without a summer, I was
hardly aware it was being formed, this main duty of mine
concerning Rotha. If I had noticed it I might have had to put

a stop to it. But then again, maybe I did notice it and perhaps I did not want it to stop.

William had complained to me that for no good reason she grieved and grew distant but I could not agree with him. In my company she was never absent-minded and hardly seemed unhappy at all except over sorrows that would make anyone sad.

Visions impressed themselves on her. I mean real visions: a dove in a puddle or anything she saw, whether the smallest bit of sedge or . . . it's funny . . . a little insect, anything. I mean, I'm looking at a bit of clover now, commonest thing in the world, a bit of red clover. Yet she'd look at that and she'd sense the sweetness of every creamy point plunging into the heart where the nectar is. As if she was one of ye. That bloom called to her and she'd take it right to heart, that little bit of clover. It could be her companion for a day. Aye. Some people, it might look as if they're going through life the loneliest person in the world, but they might be the ones that have a companion in a tiny unremarkable hiding place.

My replacing William in her days happened in a quiet stream at the beginning.

All that first spring he would plan to go out with Rotha doing one of her favourite things: hunting waterfalls or climbing the fells. She would talk about it all day beforehand— falls edged with frills like milk frothing from the cow or lavish as a wedding veil! Imagine! Falling waters and fallen water crashing together into an opalescent pool! She said things like that. She got very excited and baked small pies to carry in their pockets. How William could let her bake those pies I don't know. She was all thrill. But then morning came and he would say to me, furtively, Dixon—please, you go with Dorothy instead of my going for I've been called away.

He could be called away anywhere like this at any time, and by the time Rotha flew downstairs and started wrapping her pies—it was heartbreaking—she'd glance around for William like a bird looking for its mate and she'd finally ask me, James have you seen him? And I'd say, As a matter of fact, Miss Dorothy, he's had to go off to Carlisle on an errand to do with his stamp duties and has asked me to accompany you in his stead.

I SUPPOSE THERE MIGHT BE some that would call me worshipful, subservient—a hangdog bloke following after Dorothy, and after William as well, in their gardens, the beautiful terraces that William made to walk in, to compose in, to be with his sister in, although it became plain that he didn't want to be with her as often as she wanted it. Through the years he wanted more and more to be alone. Even his wife Mary had her own activities and could make herself scarce. I fear I was not there for Mary. But Mary was self-sufficient. I was there for William. But more and more, it was for Rotha. Him and her both, that was my balancing act. And whatever William wanted and Rotha wanted is what I tried to arrange and provide. I suppose, heh, there were times when anybody watching me could've said, That bloke's gone soft in the head. Dixon. He's gone along with the madness in that household. Well that's for them to think, and ye can think it all you want if ye like, yourselves.

But I just want to tell ye here and now that I got as much from the Wordsworths as they ever received in the way of service.

Ye have to understand this was the first time in my life that somebody wanted done what I know how to do. What I want to do. The very sort of task that makes me wake up with a song in my heart. Ye must know how satisfying that is.

And as regards my being only a servant, she'd forget. Rotha would forget that I was only the hired hand. I mean, forget is not what she . . . no, she didn't forget, but she . . . She never forgot. But . . . she fully *listened* to anything I had to say. Didn't she?

And she—I mean yes I slept in my hut and I—I never ate inside the house with the family but . . . that cushion Rotha made me is on my cot even now, so lovely. And it's—haha—it's soft, and I like to think that the softness of that cushion matches the gentle way I helped her, gathering the wool. The fleece. But not only gathering the wool. All the ways I helped her over the years. They were little ways, I know. But I like to think they were tender ways. I mean apart from the times when I didn't know what to do.

And I had days off like any servant but . . . And I was a servant, all right. I was their servant. But what I'm trying to say is that I was made to feel . . . I mean, maybe this was a thing that was done by the family very skillfully, eh, but I don't think . . .

They tried—but I don't think it involved effort, I think it was real. I think they really liked . . . I mean . . . I mean I hope they . . . I'm trying to say that . . . there was a string from my heart to theirs, we had heart-to-hearts, it wasn't as if I was some sort of . . . lackey or fella off the street that just came and hoisted stones . . .

I mean, it wasn't like that at all. At least I—I look back now and I hope, I hope I'm remembering it right.

I mean they felt . . . affection for me, I think? I mean I hope they did, because I certainly . . . I've got to stop telling ye all this for a minute for I feel a kind of—dread? A kind of horrible feeling that I might've been wrong—but—I don't think I am wrong . . .

Do ye think I'm wrong?

I got more from them, companionship like, than I ever knew in my own family, the one I was born into: my mam and my uncles, or anyone in all the hellholes I stopped in as a lad.

Ha.

Some people get a chance in their life to touch gold, to live in a kind of heaven while their hands squelch in the muck, weeding. And I've been one of those people. And I think . . . (are those crows cawing in the distance?) . . . I've been . . . I've been a lucky man.

2

In a cowslip's bell I lie

∞∞∞∞∞

Have you been a lucky man, James?

Now you are a decade older than Dorothy was when you came to her, and what have you to show for your dedication? Her story? I, Sycamore, already know the bones of her tale!

How Once Upon a Time there was a lass whose mother died, then her father, and she, Dorothy, lived alone without her brothers, for the children were all separated. Isn't that correct, James? And she lived for a Time with her stern and unloving grandparents, until lo, she was reunited as a young maiden with her beloved brother William, from whom she vowed never to part . . .

I know her history. But the bees have been busy with future events; just this morning they brace for destruction in Benson's Wood and the slaughter of whole tracts of Luckan gowan—their kingcup—to make way for quarry and road. They see a time when the railway will not only arrive, but become obsolete. A time when machines replace their wings, and life as we know it is a quaint antique. The bees sense in every bluebell the myriad ways humans may destroy their haunts. Yet they endure errand upon errand for the world, and though they live many-as-one they feel a supernatural loneliness.

Comfort them, Sweet James. The Royal Botanic Society should call a flower after you, like Sweet William's flower! Tell the bees about your Rotha, who looked inside ten thousand star-chambers—bluebell, potato-flower—and saw each mote as a bee does, each ray or spear or flare, shaking. Tremulous. Never still, but all efflorescence, fluorescence, signal . . .

So that is her red diary on your wicker skep? The wind blows its first pages open! Why don't you read it to us? Why do scout bees nose around your skep? Have you candy in it for them? Why have you brought matches? To melt beeswax and seal my wounds after you prune my dead winter branches? It's half past ten o'clock—time for pruning, raking, preparing the ground for spring. Speak, James, and then act, for today's light is a third gone.

five

ooooo

I RECKON THERE WERE THREE WAYS, says Dixon, that I
ended up reading her diaries.

The first was innocent enough. It was that she grew used
to me. We both cared about the poems William was making
up, him muttering in bits and pieces out on the terraces. But
I cared about her ideas more.

Hers were different.

Have ye noticed how the feet of certain small birds when
they are running over the ground, their feet they go so quick
it's as if the birds are on little wheels?

They tilt up and down a bit, they rock, like, and that is
how Rotha was on her feet, all those first years while her feet
still carried her. *Oh that my feet may always carry me*, she cried
out once. I didn't fathom why, not then.

Her ideas were like scraps of windblown fog or choppy
bits of lakewater but William's had to have beginnings and
middles and endings. He took ideas from her but by the time
he finished with them his were poems and hers were something apart. His were very easy to remember—I got to know
a lot of them by heart—but hers you could never know by

heart, you felt them the same as you'd be affected by a scrap of tune tumbling from a bird you had never heard before or had half-heard while you were dreaming. You certainly hoped you would hear it again. You hoped you might get to know that bird. But then you might go all your life without hearing it again. You might wonder if the tune really happened.

And when I say I knew William's poems by heart, I don't mean I read them, I mean I heard them fall from his lips. He didn't write them down, he said them, he muttered them, he was famous for muttering them everywhere he went, all along the terraces and in the fields and along the lake edge, everywhere. So I mean I heard them and yes they rhyme and—most of them, a lot of them, they rhyme—I mean I'm a—I can read, it's not that I can't, but—I think if you put the words to William's poems down in front of me and I had to read them, I'd get a bit bogged down, you know. But when he said them, well, it's like Shakespeare isn't it—I mean you've got to hear it and then you figure out what's going on.

Well Rotha, she scribbled William's poems down for him after he said them out loud. That's how his got written down. If it wasn't for Rotha I don't know what would have happened to William's poems. Moss would've drunk them all. So he was always chanting them out loud for her to write them down and if he got in a muddle she'd fix him right again. So I got to hear his poems over and over again. And anything I hear I'm pretty good at remembering. But Rotha and her words—well. After she scribbled his for him she wrote hers down an' all. He was hardly going to write hers for her. Nobody was. And hers were nowt like his.

Hers in Mary's hat box, all Rotha's own books—all her own lovely sayings. I mean, what she wrote about every step she took to the tarns, Nab Scar, Loughrigg Fell, all her travels, a lot farther afield than William.

And she started letting me read her books—I could sit for hours if I had hours which I didn't. I wished I had more time. But I had scraps of time between tasks and in those scraps I could sit reading her diaries to my heart's content. They glowed up and you saw everything she had seen, you saw it all shimmering. The diaries lit up my own memory of every place she mentioned and it felt like the magic lantern show my mam's cousin took me to at Manchester when we went there to try and get some money her brother owed us. We never got a farthing but the lantern show was better than gold for me—all that blazing light. Where did it come from? Light blazing from somewhere. That's the feeling I got reading her diaries. Not the red one but the plain little dark-coloured ones.

Last night I went to see the delphiniums. Most were not yet burst but two or three had burst out . . .

. . . & they looked like blue dancing skirts kicked open & two little feet inside, wearing furry little lemon-coloured slippers . . .

& at the graveyard I saw lupins with their pods out after the flower had gone, & I opened these, green glimmering through a skin of silver fur . . . & inside lay the

"peas" just like Rose's kittens, all in a line feeding on their mother pod . . .

. . . & I noticed that the iris leaves bend over in the breeze & their bent top part has light shining full down on it but the base hides in shadow . . .

Bits like that, with the lemon slippers, but other bits were crying like . . .

All the rosetrees are now fullblown, though they do still have buds on them. They show every stage of the rose now. Their foliage is crowded with buds, one-petalled flowers, fullblown flowers, & the pollen-yellow hearts of flowers that have had all their petals blown off. The old-fashioned garden rose-tree has a white rose, a modest one, in bloom right at its edge. For the pink rose tree it looks as if the blooming has been excessive: the tree looks ravaged, used out, as if it were ravaged by the cloying blooming of too many roses. I think it looks as if the tree is sick. Sick of roses . . .

So I read her diaries and Rotha said it was all right and I got pleasure out of it. But the second way I studied her diaries was not for my pleasure but was work William asked me to do.

I mean William was not a bad man. He had every intention of being the world's kindest brother. He had made a promise to be exactly that. A promise to himself and a promise to Rotha. And he kept that promise, sort of. He never left her destitute, did he. Not in the matter of money or a roof over her head.

I can remember Rotha telling me it was all arranged between herself and William that he would inspect her diaries. In fact she wrote them for him when he was away and even for times when he was right there, for as I've told ye, his eyes were that bad and he couldn't smell a thing and this got worse as he got older.

And he told me himself, Dixon he says, it isn't only my eyes and nose. People come to Rydal to glimpse the great poet and here I am unable to feel any of the youthful things I once felt. Those things have gone from me . . . But they have not gone from my sister.

Aye, William was right there.

No, Rotha never lost what her brother lost. She could grow older and older—ancient, it didn't matter, she was the same. Her feet would betray her, aye! Though I am the one who found a way for her to ride the wild way of a sprightly wren. She flew on my little wheels! Aye, I made her the wheels once she was not able to walk. The little wagon. No matter what happened to her legs I would get Rotha outside and in her element. But I'll come to that later. Anyhow she kept writing and never stopped.

But in William's mind her writing was not for herself. It was all for the sake of him and his poems.

What I remember is one day William said, Dixon—you claim you are good with pointy little tools. He hands me a nib and he says, see how you make out with this. Rotha was out traipsing the fells that day and he brought me up to her bedroom and opened the box that had her diaries in it.

He never opened her red diary, only the black ones and the blue ones. He had me read them out to him and copy bits for him into a notebook of his. Her handwriting was very hard for anyone to read even if they did not have William's terrible eyesight. And writing things down with a pen, well he found that irritating.

He considered pen work drudgery. Scratching, he called it. He hated scratching. It got in the way, between the idea and the poem. He wanted someone else do his scratching. Rotha had done it. At times his wife Mary had done it.

Now it was my turn.

I noticed early on he seemed to want to go upstairs only when Rotha was not present. She was out here in the garden or gone to the post office or flying over the fells. She was still fleet as a lark then. Later when she was not as well, William would bring me upstairs to read her books while she slept, which made me feel uneasy.

I asked him, Sir, if you don't mind my asking, why don't we look in the books while Miss Wordsworth is awake? Perhaps she could help us decipher the penmanship and make our work go all the more quickly.

And he said never mind that, Dixon. She'll get caught up in the memories and we won't be able to get her to turn the page. We'll be here all day. And my sister cannot discern between a passage of literary value and a mere sweep of strong emotion. So let's you and me just get on with it by ourselves.

And I said to myself, Well William is the one paying my wages.

He said he only wanted the perfect timeless things she had set down: the natural, floating things, not details between. The words he fished or made me gather and move from her world to his own were like pollen and nectar ye collect.

We harvested his sister's weightless and golden thoughts.

He did not have anything like those in himself.

He would wait as I read, and he held one hand up in the air like a clock hand ready to strike the moment I read something he wanted to clasp. There was a quality in the air whose name I can't remember. There's a word I can't reach. One that sounds like church bells set to clang, but something binds them aslant in the tower.

He'd say to me Dixon, see what my sister had to say on April the nineteenth.

Went for a walk in the mild thin air, I read out. I had to be careful not to go too fast.

Watch that you miss not a word, he'd say. Don't run the words together. Don't miss the ends off! *Watched the black river with a frost-silvered willow hung low over the water, bent with the weight of the silver, one tip touching the river, dispersing some of the small, white froth-ovals floating on top—listened to the sounds of rain, river, lake—water gullying everywhere— saw three little birds . . .*

What sort of birds, William interrupted.

I don't know.

Damn it does she not name the bloody birds?

No, she just says—

Never mind that page then. On to the next! What does it say?

The next page, Sir, is about Mary not liking it when plates are stacked together for washing whilst food is still on them . . .

Never mind any of that. Who cares about food squashed on plates! Get us back out of doors.

Figurines on top of the larches—a witch riding a broom, Napoleon galloping on his horse—many of these figures seem to be riding fast—

All right, that's better! Go on.

—Nothing in the woods is whiter than the snow of blackberry blossoms on the dark green leaves, & the leaves are dry as bones under the few raindrops that sit on them like tiny crystal balls—

Keep going. Write that one down.

—& water sparkles among the reeds, its voice a flute in the undersong of wind, thrush and reed—lights in the grass—& the lake glimmers through the lilac leaves—skeletons of the lilac flowers stand on the treetop, brittly swaying—a strong wind blew the lilac leaves so they became folded hearts—half-hearted, & it tore the skin off the lake revealing glittering silver blood— like ripped metal—the sound of the wind went hollowly around the hills like a soft-headed stick scribing a spiral on cymbals—

Yes, write it down! We'll have all that.

Sir, Rotha is stirring. She looks as if she might awaken.

No, he says, she's had twelve drops.

He meant the laudanum for her headache.

Read on, he says, sounding impatient.

I had tried their laudanum myself one day when they were all out. I was curious. I never drink a drop of alcohol because I have no interest in making a fool of myself like some fellows do, wandering over the roads in a chaotic fashion, saying things they shouldn't say, telling all sorts of their own and other people's secrets. I like to keep my private information to myself. But in the interest of understanding the little fam'ly I thought it wouldn't hurt one day while they were all down at the lake to take a dozen drops of the medicine they each took at various times, to see what it did.

The best way I can describe it is to say it sanded the edges of my worst hurts.

It made me nearly forget the plight of my sister for a start. Imagine forgetting Penny. Who would want to take medicine like that over and over again? That makes you forget someone that dear. But then I couldn't remember Waterloo in my usual way at all. Waterloo did not jab me behind the eyes to remember the dead or things I had done or times I had been terrified out of my mind. And that kind of numbing was something.

Laudanum makes your worst sorrows hide behind soft young trees. After I tried it I knew better than to ever try it again for I saw at once why half of England was dependent on it, for it is stronger in far smaller amounts than gin. Takes the sting out of the worst details—it even stopped troubling me that Rotha had my mate Joe Bell's tooth in her mouth. In fact, the laudanum told me that perhaps now whenever Rotha spoke her voice had a trickle of Joe's in it; her voice remembered his. What an idea!

Even after the laudanum wore off I did not forget the thoughts it gave me.

William shouted, Dixon, keep reading, please!

Wild roses on the path along the shore—some of them still folded like ballgowns. Wind makes a merciless hash of the soft-leafed ash tree . . .

Is that all?

That's it for that page, Sir.

What about the next?

Mary is peeling potatoes—the sound a soft scridge scridge of the knife, the softer bubbling up of water in the pot, the creak of the kitchen chair as Wm shifts while reading the paper—& the knife, scridge scridge—a little like the snidge snidge of the razor-grinder's horse eating grass yesterday—or

Forget about peeling potatoes, he cried. Let's mark down the snow of the blackberry blossoms though. And the half-hearted lilacs—was it folded hearts or half-hearts? What did she write?

It was both, Sir—I copied it down for him.

At first I had no way of predicting which of his sister's words William would want to keep or leave alone. And bit by bit I grew able to tell. He did not want to hear about potatoes or their peel or their blossoms. Whereas for her, a potato flower was as important as any other.

He never brought up the red diary and for a while it disappeared. But one afternoon I spied a corner of it sticking out from her blankets and I said, Sir, do you mind my asking about that red diary belonging to your sister? I nodded towards it casual like.

No, he says. I do not mind at all. He did not sound put out or on the alert.

So I says, Sir, might you like me to have just a peep inside it for you as we have not looked at that one before, as far as I remember?

It is not an important document, he said.

No, Sir?

Not at all, he said. The red volume, unlike the others, contains not a fragment of literary merit.

You cannot use it for your poems, Sir?

The red diary is of no use to anybody at all. It is nothing but a record of my sister's feelings.

six

ooooo

HER FEELINGS!

I think people show different sides of themselves depending on their company, and I might be flattering myself but I feel as if when she was with me, Rotha was clear as the pool under the kittenract where we went many times even after she lost her foot power and I became her trusted steed. She was clear about her feet. She knew something was happening. But before it happened she was not only clear but merry. She made up more and more of her own words. If an apple shrank and wrinkled she called it shrinkled. She called Cockermouth where she and William were born that Cockamoodle place. She was forever playful when it came to words, though she claimed not to have William's talent for poetry. I did not think this true. I thought, on getting acquainted with her notebooks, that she had a wild streak no one could match. Certainly not her brother. She suited me down to the ground as a companion though of course I was only a servant.

But I mean one servant can be entirely different from another servant, can't they?

It's funny how two people looking at the same thing can see something different from each other, isn't it. I've often thought that. You can take a walk with somebody and you can return home and the other one can flummox ye with the things they've noticed and you didn't have a clue, and same the other way around. You can tell them something you would've thought plain as the nose on your face about what ye'd seen, whether it was a migrating duck off its course or a tree that needed pruning or even something as simple as the way some reeds are getting to overtake, you know, other plants that were wanted to proliferate. Anybody not interested in anything like that, they won't even see it. It's completely invisible!

So I suppose it's not really unusual that John Carter, ye know him, the other servant who helps William with his secretarial work and the stamps and everything, but I mean he does a lot around the place as well and as ye know we don't overlap so much as pass one another on our various rounds. He saw things very different from the way I saw them.

Especially concerning Miss Wordsworth, which is what he never ceased to call Rotha even when she begged him to use her first name. She could not get a human response out of him.

Though I have to watch it. My uncle Jim used to say lad, your da might be dead and gone but he'll be in your blood and you'll have to watch out you don't turn out like him because sadly the man had massive trouble putting two an' two together.

I says what do you mean, Uncle Jim? I was only about six at the time.

Well, he says, the conclusions your dad would draw from something were amiss, y'know, meaning they weren't what anyone else'd ordinarily draw given the same evidence. Your da often used to get the wrong end of the staff. I mean he never suffered badly for this, now, he had a way of going easy over the ground and getting by. That's what he did isn't it? Tramped everywhere, who knows where he'd end up. One time he'd been away to Brighton. He come back and he says well there's a lovely beach, not a grain of sand. They've taken all the sand away and dumped lovely smooth pebbles there instead! And I says they've done what? I'd been to Brighton. I'd seen that beach myself.

He says to me Jim, he says, they've replaced every speck of sand with lovely round stones, all along the waterfront, and I says man you're daft, how would they do that? An' he says well, you know, an army of diggers must've come and carted every bit of sand away and replaced it with—I dunno where they got the stones but aren't they lovely, all colours just like birds' eggs. Speckled! And green veins in 'em an' blue spots and red spots like blood!

Lad, your father had a fantastic time exploring those stones and picking them up in 'es hands and enjoying them. I says you're always jumpin' to barmy conclusions. I says man Brighton is a stony beach and is now and forever has been and will forevermore be world without end amen, and it got that way by itself. But o'course nothing I could say would convince your old man of that. So all I mean, son, is be careful you don't start thinking too much like your da.

And I think my uncle Jim did suspect I might turn out

like my father—not able to put two and two together without some sort of mix-up. I mean ye lot don't have to take
what I say as gospel, it's just I am trying to look at, you
know, William and Rotha and myself and dear Mary an' all,
everything I saw over our many years and, ye know, this is
just me trying to . . . look at it all for ye . . . and yes, put the
two and two together. For ye now, telling you all this, now
Rotha's gone.

So about John Carter, the Wordsworths' other servant,
he says to me one morning it was the most curious thing, he
says William is . . . he's having trouble, y'know, with Miss
Wordsworth again.

This was probably a year after I started with them.

And I says John what do you mean? Is she sleep-walking
again?

Because Rotha was, I'll grant, a sleepwalker at times, and
one of the housekeeper's jobs was to keep an ear out and not
let her roam all the way to William's room. Many's the night,
I was told, she'd end up on the edge of William and Mary's
bed fast asleep in the morning and sometimes on the floor.

But John Carter says no. He says Dorothy's on the lament
about never seeing her brother and he's always out and he's
not coming up to her room to see her and he's eating his
mutton at different times from her mealtimes or he's just
not there.

And I said well, John man, I've been working on it. I've
been trying to keep her company.

By rights I couldn't really argue with John Carter. He
had a point. I had gone to Stickle Tarn with Rotha only days

before. At the summit I had thought she might like to dip her feet in the water and I was unwrapping the pies and putting our lemonade in the shade of a rock when I saw her throw herself on the turf. And she cried something out very loud, but whatever she cried the wind carried away.

Pardon, Miss? I says . . .

William, she says in a heartbreaking tone, is a different man when he's alone with me.

Aye, Miss, I says, I reckon we're all different according to who else happens to be around.

But my brother is hardly ever alone with me, in fact he's never alone with me anymore.

Aye, Miss, William is a busy man.

When he was alone with me, we had a world! Everything else, all his business and all the parties and people talking on and on about small things, they are not our world. They are things he tells me he must endure. I always believed him. Tell me, James, what does he say about it to you?

I had not yet managed to repair her botanical magnifying glass. At that moment I wished with all my heart that I had mended it so I could draw her back to the exact observations she loved to make out of doors. *Calyx, stamen, ovary* . . . But I had not found the right parts—the pins I fastened it with kept dropping out.

William doesn't endure his business, does he? He enjoys it! What has he told you, James? You are the one with me now. Sometimes I wonder if my brother has brought you among us so as to prevent his being alone with me ever again . . .

I didn't know what to make of it all. We sat like a pair of stones. Us and the wind. And then very quiet I started up a song. Not my old, private song, but a new one I had made up after coming to work for the Wordsworth family. I only hummed it, as I did not feel like letting her hear the words in case she recognized herself.

But she said, James, that is a lovely tune. Has it any lyrics?

Not really, I said, which was not true, but I am convinced she could always spot an untruth, especially one coming from her brother or from me.

She said it *has* got words hasn't it.

So I says Miss, it is a song I made up about . . . about a dear sister.

I didn't know you had a sister, James. Is she older or younger?

Penny is younger, Miss. I realized Rotha did not recall I had already told her I had a sister.

Sing it for me. If they belong to such a tune as that they will be words I'd like to hear.

Clouds raced over our heads and there was nary a soul to be seen for miles over the Langdales, and Lake Windermere glittered far below us and it seemed safe enough to give in to her request. Sometimes you feel reckless.

Once upon a time a very wild girl
clambered the fells all night:
Her eyes two living lumps of coal
with diamond flames alight

Her feet were clouds all tiny and fleet
that raced o'er sky and vale
And I yet see that same wild girl
In the rain and wind and hail!

And as I sang my song the wind crept in with my voice. I looked at Rotha and she looked at me. The song was about a sister all right, but whose sister?

I was not sure if my song calmed her or further agitated her and it took a meeting with some stitchwort—counting and naming its parts—to bring her to her regular precision of mind where I knew she would be safe.

And while we were yet up near the tarn she said, If only I had money, James. Do you know what I would have done?

It took resolve on my part not to answer, But you do, Miss. You do have money.

For compared with myself and my kind, such as our Penny now destitute in Manchester on account of her injuries not being able to work, Miss Dorothy Wordsworth had plenty of money indeed. Some survival instinct in her had seen to it that her brothers signed over sufficient for her keep. More than sufficient, for she had made them promise extra for books, and for going places she wanted to go such as London, and for giving sixpence to those who came to the door after losing their land. She had plenty for beggars so as to feel helpful in this world. Only those who have extra feel that way. But I said nothing. It was dawning on me that where money is concerned everybody seems to believe they have far too little.

Money! There's either a small bit of your soul or a medium-sized bit or a giant portion that's taken up with money.

My small salary I know how to stretch.

I grow my own onions and potatoes and leeks. I hunt a few rabbits. And like I told ye, I come from a long line of sheep-stealers. But the Wordsworths? Aye . . . William . . . I think money is what changed him. The Wordsworths thought they were going to have money. And then it didn't come. According to John Carter it got lost. They had to wait. And it was years before they saw any of it. It was owed to them by a man that owed their dad. Something like that. And then their brother John got lost at sea and with him all their investments.

Their rent. Their tea. I mean who knows, if I were them maybe I'd have drunk the enormous quantities of tea they drank. How they quaffed it. Maybe they couldn't imagine a day without that consolation. After all the freezing cold wind and rain and sleet and hail, and more wind, and lightning and thunder on their walks—walking and walking. They needed a cup of tea. But Rotha—she stood up for herself when it came to money. John Carter told me. It was when William married Mary Hutchinson and William asked Rotha what she wanted.

He didn't mean, what did she desire?

He meant money. And Carter told me Rotha gave William written instructions, very detailed. A stipend each year. A roof over her head—William's roof. William's and Mary's. That roof, over her head, for her lifetime. Which has happened. I mean we're looking at that roof now. And extra to give tinkers or gypsies or families who have lost their homes. Have I mentioned books? She had to have her books. I mean she read William's but she had to have her own.

Aye, she stipulated all that. And once William promised it to her, she signed off on all her soul's care over the material things in life. Whereas William, that job he had at the stamp office, and his other bits and bobs he had going, well he was the one who had to see to it all. And trying to sell his poems—she helped there. There's no doubt his sister was his biggest salesperson . . .

WELL? DO YOU, JAMES? Rotha asked me again. Do you know what I would have done if I had money?

I had to be careful. The wind from those pikes had a mind to push us both to blurt whatever we felt. I had to watch what I said but Rotha did not. That is another thing money does for a person.

What would you have done, Miss D?

Because money has eluded me but not before love eluded me! And the two, money and love, well, James, surely you yourself know this—without one or the other, nothing can be accomplished. And a woman without money cannot do the thing I should have done.

What should you have done, Miss D?

I should have become like my powerful friend in Borrowdale.

Which friend, Miss D? Though I knew who she meant straight away.

Surely you know my friend—everyone talks of her—they call her wilder than the rivers or mountains. They even say she is mad, but she is not mad at all. My friend is simply free.

Who, Miss?

But I knew she meant her friend Mary Barker. The Barker woman was unusual. She was unmarried and had built a house for herself to live in all alone, miles from another soul. Miss Barker was a wild one all right, traipsing the land all by herself, carrying her paintbox to hidden places and making paintings of thunderheads and crags, paintings she did not need to sell because she was well-off. The Barker woman could surround herself with rock and thunder by day, and with her own paintings of rock and thunder by night.

My friend Miss Barker, Rotha cried, does not have to answer to anyone, and I wish to god I could go and live like her, since my brother is to be only my pretend companion!

I began coaxing her by way of attention to detail.

I pointed out to her this and that bit of plant.

But she said, There is something in both you and me akin to rage, isn't there. Oh! Do you see that anger has the word rage hidden in it?

Pardon, Miss D? I was not up on word games like she was, but I saw some new idea was calming her down.

The word anger has r-a-g-e in it, she says. But anger contains an extra N. Is N for never, James? Do you never show anger?

Miss—I can't say . . .

Or is N for new? Maybe your anger is newer than mine, James, because you're young.

She was wrong about that. My anger went generations back and yes, it did contain rage. But I had mine under control. I knew where my income came from and I knew how to maintain the sweet world I enjoyed so much. My work-hut and my Sundays and my being the lord of everything William thought he created in his gardens. Such is the way with gardeners. We don't serve a human employer. We work for the place that came before the boss and carries on without him.

My friend Mary Barker has escaped, Rotha said.

Aye?

Yes! Miss Barker is free. Whereas I am forever in danger of losing my world in every aspect.

Are you though? I tried not to sound incredulous.

It is not like that when you are a man, she glared at me. Even a manservant such as yourself owns more say in his own freedom than I do. Through money and through reliance on her own mind and her strong will my friend Mary Barker has indeed escaped! But for me, and for anyone without money, being a woman and running free are diverging forces, and agony to contain at once.

Aye, Miss D, I said. The world of money won't help anyone locked outside it. And the world of love is a daft illusion . . . better not cave to it at all, eh?

But as soon as I said that she suffered an episode whose frenzy I needed to quell or I'd never have got her home. She'd have clung to the rocks and remained as lichen under the snows. What a job I had to run after her that day and to bring her home again.

She had a way of vanishing that frightened me. I don't mean that her body vanished.

BUT I DID NOT ADMIT a word of this to the other servant John Carter, not a peep.

And now Carter says, Dixon I know you've been doing the best you can but the fact is, Miss Wordsworth is not settled. She is anything but settled.

And I says, Well is she confiding you this herself? Or is someone else telling you tales?

And he says no, no, no, I see it in the way she is with that dog of hers.

Little Miss Belle, I says—how d'you mean?

John says, Well you know how Miss Wordsworth renders the dog's fur all damp.

I said what do you mean she renders . . . ?

He says have you never seen the times that dog goes around with soaked fur and it hasn't been in the lake it hasn't been in the rain and she's crying over that dog and you know yourself it's only a very small animal. After an hour of her crying over that dog it's sopping wet, man. The woman's not right in the head.

I did not like John Carter's saying this.

For I had paid attention to the same topic, the matter of Rotha's mental state, and had not come to his conclusion at all.

Right at the start of my time with Rotha, when she told me about the secret window in her room, hidden in the wall, I asked William did he have any idea what she might have meant by that. I was trying to get to the bottom of her strangeness and find out how deep it went and if it meant I should believe the things she told me or instead believe the things other people said. Oh, said William, yes, there is a window hidden in Dorothy's bedroom wall. It has been covered up these many years to avoid paying the window tax. The more windows in a house, you see, Dixon, the more tax the owner must pay.

Now John Carter said, it pains William every time he sees that wet dog because he knows it means Dorothy has been crying again.

I said, have you tried slightly licking it?

He says have I tried what?

And I said, The dog: have you tried touching your tongue upon the dog to see if it's a bit salty? Maybe it's not Miss Wordsworth's tears, maybe it's the rain.

He says man, you're as daft as she is.

I went off before I could respond in irritation. I had tomatoes to stake and plenty of other tasks to do that day, and tasks save my mind. I knew John Carter was not alone in his thinking. My own mam had claimed both William and Dorothy Wordsworth were more than a bit daft and so did a lot of others. Most people lumped the pair together. All their muttering and the pacing out in all weathers . . . people said that was why they had to leave their first house, before Dove Cottage. Their lease never got renewed because the villagers looked on them and on Sam Coleridge and thought—no, *knew*—the three of them were mad.

But this was the first time John Carter had said anything to me.

And William paid John to do a lot of intelligent work for him, head-work more than my kind of work. Still it never occurred to me that John Carter might think William had a level head but Dorothy didn't. I mean this was a new idea to me—that William was sane and Rotha wasn't—and I never came to adopt it myself. To me both brother and sister were above and beyond the ordinary.

But I did tuck John Carter's notion away in the back of my mind as something certain people thought.

And I came across it again down through the months and the years . . .

People had much to say about Rotha that they never said about William.

And what I have to conclude—what I want to tell ye now—is that I am of the mind that part of it was simply because he was a fella and she wasn't.

I mean I don't know if that's right or not. Maybe I have got the wrong end of the staff.

But I failed to make any sense of John Carter and the things he said, the things anybody said, regarding Rotha being mad.

I thought to myself, John Carter, you haven't got a clue. So Rotha has been crying. So what?

I mean what's wrong with, if you do find—that she's cried—what's wrong with going and asking her, Have you been crying? What's the matter, pet?

That's what a brother should have done!

Any rate I touched my own tongue ever so lightly to Little Miss Belle's fur, and of course I found it wasn't salty at all—it was only rain that had splashed through the window.

A wee shower of early summer rain.

I mean anybody can recognize rain on a dog. It's not a smell of sadness at all. In fact, what could be happier?

But I did keep in my mind that John *had* seen Rotha crying. She did burst into tears at times but it did not always mean she was sad. Has nobody heard of tears of happiness? What did William call her? Exuberant!

Still, after John Carter said these things, I kept an eye out.

Because it was part of my job to keep an eye out if anybody in that little family had a heavy heart. Laugh if ye want. True, I might not always know how to help, but just being companionable can lighten the atmosphere, even if you never say anything out loud. Even if you're just with the sad person in a quiet way. I think this is where me and John Carter were different.

He thought weather outside had nothing to do with weather inside. But I have always known that with Rotha the two kinds of weather touch each other. Rain splashes through the window and looks and feels like tears. Or thunder crashes louder and louder until you can't tell anymore if it lives in the sky or in your head.

And with Rotha that was something I understood. I helped her withstand the roar of any weather that rose up; thunderclaps or lightning and the like. That was something I knew how to do because I knew the weather was in her.

Right inside her was the weather!

So there was I, doing as her brother had asked me, plodging beside her in my boots.

Crows.

Sere, yellow grasses.

Puddles.

Reflections of bare branches in the puddles.

The lake.

Caw, caw!

Rotha would say, The water's sullen. She'd say James, the hay bends at the waist, its brow touches the mud, desolate. The hay is desolate!

If the gulls cried, she said something was hurting them.

Yes, I answered, the gulls are downright sodden as up they arc but not near as high as they might if their day was sunlit, you're right, Miss D.

The sunbeams have departed the gulls, she said. The sunbeams have abandoned the grass. The sunbeams have left the water.

But she'd never say, the light has left *me*. She didn't need to say it.

I knew that one and the same thing to her were gull and grass and lake and path and her own self.

seven

ooooo

AND I MEAN IN THAT WAY, in the way of being part of nature and loving and revering it, Rotha was a new kind of woman, to me, so very different from the likes of my mam, who was a lot more ordinary and I hate to say it but who I might even have felt a bit . . . I mean, was I? Ashamed of my mam? I mean she wasn't ordinary as such. My mam was very intelligent. Only she ruined her intelligence or time and place ruined it for her.

Ye would think, looking at Mam with her body gone to wasteful ruin, all grey and swollen like, fed on buns and tea and gin and tobacco—*paff-paff, paff-paff,* always the tobacco with my mam, fumes of it, or fumes of gin . . . ye would think she hadn't a sensible brain in her body, but she did. My mam could read very well, and she could certainly put two and two together, especially any time it had to do with money. She sniffed out the aims of people and she had disdain for their scheming. Everybody scheming, she used to say, yet she herself was the head schemer. Aye, if anyone went on and on about the advantages that might be gained by our family once I got in with the Wordsworths, it was my mam. Ye would think I had come across dead gentry on the highway, festooned with medallions and their pockets crammed with gold, and all I had to do in the quiet wind and the wild loneliness was lift the gold off them and be on my merry way.

But let me stick up for my mam here a bit! Don't judge her that fast.

Ye have to look at it as regards things she believed. And she didn't drink as much as lots did. She drank herself out of pain which is what many do, though I don't do it myself. And was it when she drank that my mam dreamed of a different life? Or did she dream of a different life before her drop of gin, and was the gin only to help make the dream move closer . . .

And it did. Once, I . . . her dream came closer and closer whenever I went to see Mam, after I got in with the Wordsworths. Maybe that was my fault. Maybe I praised the situation up too much. At any rate Mam believed I had found her own dream come true. She believed the Wordsworths were like royalty and in fact as far as we were concerned, our family, they might as well have been.

What Mam and Penny thought my new life was like—ha, it wasn't like that at all. But could I convince them? I didn't even try.

Because my mam had a fantasy. She had never been inside the Wordsworths' home like I had. She saw it—it's funny, this—she saw it a bit like the Wordsworths saw it, themselves. A tall house hidden behind trees and gardens, separate from that other world where Mam skivvied for coppers and ate only buns with no raisins, and drank tea that got weaker and weaker as time went on, until it was nowt but a cup of hot water, because she steeped it over and over again until it had no trace of comfort. Not like the Wordsworths' house where tea is plentiful every day and strong enough, aye. Gallons of it!

That was one thing, the tea.

But it wasn't tea, or roast pork shoulder, or even the use of a horse that Mam thought about when she kept on with her Wordsworth dream. Her dream of what I had amounted to by coming to this place.

No.

Mam's fantasy, and Penny's also, since Mam passed on to Penny her notions about my job. Penny had not seen me in my new element. I *wanted* Penny to come! But Penny had only Mam's version. Cream in a bowl, honey from ye lot, with the comb afloat in it to lift out and gnaw like a king. Berries as well—all that on one bowl of porridge!

And quietness.

And flowers.

And books.

Mam said to me son, you've certainly hit the jackpot. Roast pork for you on a Sunday! Aye what would I not give for a nice pork shoulder like that. She said *like that*, as if she had with her own eyes watched me in the Wordsworths' kitchen seated at their table spearing a slice of pork with a silver fork and putting it in my mouth. Slick pork grease on my lips. My mother saw this in her mind's eye. She had a bright imagination, perhaps as strong as the imaginations of the Wordsworths themselves. And in her mind she had seen the roast, and the silverware all polished, and a fine table-cloth. These things had not really happened but Mam saw them clear as day. She and Penny fancied jonquils on the table, a real la-de-da situation with me as a kind of honorary Wordsworth enjoying the spectacular fruits of that life. You couldn't talk them out of it.

And if I am honest with ye, my mam's imaginary Wordsworth family and my own imaginings were not very different at first. This is why I can't bear feeling ashamed of Mam. I was not forced to stay in her world. If my life here is not what Mam thought it was, or even what I hoped it might be, it is still a world far grander than ours. Mine and Mam's and Penny's.

But I found out I had a capacity to appreciate things William said or wrote, and things his sister said and did . . . I soaked up their world and I knew what it was made of. Mam did also. Even Penny. It didn't belong to us but we recognized it. We were wishful. We were waiting. But we would never claim it. What can I call the Wordsworth atmosphere?

Loveliness? Shelter? How is it ye regard your hive? Full of sweetness and shade and protection? Fragile and filled with gold treasure the whole world wants but hardly anyone can have?

When I started here I thought of myself as coming in from outside. Coming into shelter, into paradise. But very soon I saw that William and Rotha were doing the same thing! They were coming in from outside. Coming into shelter, into paradise. And paradise was pretend. Even for them. It was a moving painting or it was that lantern show I told ye I went to see in Manchester with Mam's cousin. It was no more real for William or Rotha than it was for me or my mam or for our Penny.

Was it?

Sometimes I cannot make out the real difference between the Wordsworth family and mine, as far as our ideas go about shelter from bad things in the world—things causing blight the way foul weather or fungus can come to ye and to your glory realm and to your hives and even your very bodies, if you are not careful and if you are not blessed.

How does paradise touch some people like a lantern beam? While other people, like Mam and Penny, fumble in the gloom?

It doesn't take long for copper to tarnish and it did not take long for my shining sister Penny to lose her youth and her health. I wanted to help her, even if that only meant bringing her here to the Wordsworths' made-up paradise. For the Wordsworths have not lived in the real world!

Did Mam start the notion of my getting Penny a job with the Wordsworths? Or did I? Did Mam say she wished Penny worked beside me instead of at the factory in Pendleton? And did I chew on that wish until it was mine?

Because it did become my thought.

All my first year here at Rydal and maybe my second, I could not make out how to bring that thought up with William or his sister. I mentioned Penny whenever I could, reminding them that I had a sister and that she was a very hard worker.

I spoke this as if I was talking to myself but I made sure William overheard. After all, I am my sly mother's son, thought I. But William did not bite the bait. I was doing it all wrong. Or I was not the son of my mother, who'd have spilled the information naturally, completely innocent like. And because I was so woeful at it, it soon became all I could think of. Mention Penny as a good worker and hope someone would take me up on the idea. But my attempts fell on deaf ears until one day Rotha was reading the paper and there was an article in it about Manchester and she flung the paper in the fireplace. I watched the word *Manchester* flame up then shrink to grey with a gold edge and then collapse. It was one of her last fires of spring. I remember because I was measuring the fireplace to fit a new summer board over the hole. I know it wasn't my first spring there because that first year we had no summer. So it was my second or third.

Rotha shuddered and she said, James, I am most glad I do not have to look very often at a street in that town!

And of course I was all ears since Pendleton, where my sister worked, was on the edge of Manchester.

So I said, Manchester, Miss? I made out as if I was very carefully double-checking my measurements for the fireplace. My sister works there, Miss, I said, although I had told Rotha this before.

But in truth at that moment my sister was out of a job. Something had gone badly downhill with her shoulder. My mam had her at the house and was trying painful exercises to get it to rise back up evenly with the other shoulder. Because Penny had been working at the same spot on the floor in the same position from the age of eleven and was now nearly sixteen. She had become a piece of the machine. Her shoulder had ground itself down low like a worn-out machine part and my mam had it strapped up with bandages night and day, but I wasn't confident of the result. Or I was pretty sure what the result would be and did not want to admit it to myself. Here was I, very comfortable, while Penny . . .

An awful place, Rotha said. A sister, you say? I had thought you mentioned a brother.

No, Miss, a sister.

A sister?

Yes, Miss. I kept my surprise to myself, that she did not remember all that I had told her about Penny. As a matter of fact, I said, Penny is off work on a little break at the moment, and I have been wondering . . .

Is she? How nice for her. I myself am very glad that our own tranquil paradise means I hardly ever have to look at a filthy industrial city such as Manchester. I do hope your sister has a chance to come back to the Lakes.

Yes, Miss. I was going to ask you . . . I mean if you and your brother didn't mind . . . if it would be all right for Penny to come and see me for . . . a short visit.

Heavens, James, you don't have to ask me that. It is up to your family, surely, whether your sister comes to visit them, is it not? And we can certainly spare you the few hours you would need to go and see her, yourself.

Rotha had misunderstood me. Or I had not said it properly, the thing I wanted to ask, which was whether it would be possible for Penny to come here, to Rydal Mount, to recover in the fresh air and the peace here, as the Wordsworths themselves repaired their own health whenever the world beyond our little paradise affected them too much . . . but I had not managed to say it. And now if I said it, the thing would come out all wrong. It would be presumptuous. I could not figure out how to ask. I envisioned Penny curled up in my hut where I had a spare blanket and straw to make an extra bed. She would be no trouble at all to the Wordsworths! But I could not for the life of me find a way to paint this picture in Rotha's mind without it sounding preposterous.

Thank you, Miss, was all I could think of to say. Her working hours at the mill have been long, I said, and my sister does need a rest.

Yes, Rotha said. I have just now read that the government has sent inspectors to the Douglas mill and to other mills to assess whether the floors are really as bad as they all say. Inspectors! But, James, anyone could tell them the answer to that. I could tell them, myself!

Miss?

I was not sure what she meant as I could not picture Rotha having gone inside a mill and seen the workers.

Anyone could, she said, who has visited the streets of Manchester and seen the youths maimed like people who have come home from a war.

Miss, I said, that is true, for our Penny's workmate Rhona got caught by a strap on the machine and flung against a wall and broke every bone in both arms and both legs and has to . . .

Stop! Rotha said, and she shot both arms toward me with her hands splayed as if I had thrown my yardstick at her face.

I realized I should never have spoken. What had come over me?

I did not continue about how Penny herself would never stand straight again. I did not say how her shoulder skewed her spine. Nor did I mention Penny was thin as a nail since thread and dust clogged the air and landed in the porridge you ate as you worked, more thread than oats—you ate the thread you milled and breathed pieces of it until your lungs were full but your stomach empty and you were let go as soon as they caught you spitting blood.

I did not say any of that, because the look on Rotha's face meant if I said another word she couldn't take it and Penny might not be the only young Dixon out on the street. I had a glimpse into Rotha's hard-heartedness that minute. It was something I took in. If she heard or saw even a glimpse of something that didn't go with her vision of paradise in that closed-off, shaded world of theirs, Rotha Wordsworth wanted it gone.

What made the mill send Penny home at last wasn't her shoulder or her lungs. They sent my sister packing with a note. Mam told me they kicked her awake in the drying-room at one o'clock in the morning. Penny hid there instead of being driven into the cold in wet clothes after her shift. They all hid. In the wool. Under the baskets. But when the overlooker kicked Penny she jolted up and went through the motions of her work though her machine had stopped for the night. Like I told ye she had turned into a machine herself, or a wrecked or manic part of the machine going on and on after the controls were off. The note called her unfit due to laziness. But is it lazy if you keep working while you are asleep? I don't think lazy is the word and what the word might be I do not know.

But all I said to Rotha was, Sorry, Miss. I understand. It's just that my sister, Penny, has been having a little trouble with her health, and . . .

Are her feet all right? Rotha asked.

Her feet, Miss?

Yes. As long as one's feet are all right, then everything is not lost.

She looked down at her own feet and I realized she was worrying about them, about being able to cover the miles on foot that she wanted to cover. She was not thinking about Penny, but about her own freedom. Wild miles on the hoof. Would the miles always meet her? She suspected something faltering in herself and this was when I caught wind of it. That moment when she asked me about Penny's feet.

AND AFTER THAT I STARTED noticing Rotha talked often about feet.

Mostly the feet of women older than herself. She kept a running commentary. Poor Molly, for instance, the Wordsworths' old servant who had died before my time. Rotha described to me how Molly shoved her poor ankles into her boots deformed like. Her legs didn't come out of the boots straight. Her shins overflowed like puddings from a pan and her legs were ready to topple like a couple of water-logged larches!

And William rubbed his sister's feet. That was one thing he did do. He only asked me to do that whenever he was away from the Lakes.

Once when I did rub her feet I saw they had the start of a bunion and I said Miss, do you wish me to make you a splint to straighten it up? Because I knew how to make one out of willow. The bark fits around a toe and besides that there's medicine in willow that stops any ache.

But she said no, thank you, James, it's not bunions I worry about. Bunions are insignificant. Nor am I the least concerned by blisters or corns. Calluses, however, quite interest me.

They interest you, Miss?

Yes, in fact, I welcome calluses since in the right places they can increase the working lifespan of a person's feet.

Ah, I says, like an extra bit of leather?

Exactly, she says. I have a few calluses and I don't mind them at all. It's not those small inconveniences I worry about, but larger, systemic things that start elsewhere in the body but end up affecting one's feet so that the feet cannot do what they were designed to do. That is what frightens me.

I wanted to ask her what she meant by systemic things that start elsewhere, but I kept quiet. Like I have said, it behooved me to learn when to keep my mouth shut with the Wordsworths, and when to speak, in order to gain and keep their trust and to learn all the things I needed to learn.

So yes I kept quiet about her fears until out of thin air she would begin ruminating on them.

I was giving her feet a rub and she says to me, James, she says, you, now, you're a lad of no more than twenty-two. You'll have nothing the matter at all with your feet, will you? Not a thing. Your feet must be like the feet of Mercury, adorned with wings! And she looked at mine more than a bit jealous like. In fact she looked at them as if she'd like to chop them off me and have them for herself.

As a matter of fact my littlest toenails had both cracked right down the middle but I didn't tell her that. The nails cracked because my boots were tight. They had got soaked and dried out enough times that the leather had shrunk. And in the toenail cracks I stuffed globs of your bee wax to keep dirt out and to try and repair the nails. But they were a sight. Any gardener that doesn't have filthy feet is no gardener at all is he? And filth had ground into my feet. The dirt was ingrained. I knew if Rotha ever saw my bare feet what a fright she'd get, although hers were not as white or spotless as other women's feet. Her feet were brown as a child's that has been playing outside all summer. But they were nothing like mine.

But I says no, Miss D, I have no problem with bunions or blisters or anything like that.

And, she said, I can see for myself your ankles are not swollen.

No, Miss, my ankles are all right.

But she says mind you watch that lopsided sole on the heel of your left boot. It means your gait's uneven. And

James, I warn you, your second twenty-two years will whizz past twice as fast as the first! By then that foot won't know what hit it—look at William's poor toe!

Yes, Miss.

Gradually is how it happens, says she.

That was when I noticed she was forever remarking on the state of everyone's feet and shoes.

And aye, she mentioned wings. Because those feet of hers were like your wings are to ye. Your wings get you pretty far over these fells and lakes, and her feet were wings in her mind. Everyone's feet were wings in her mind. And you have to give it to her, the shape of feet with their toes is a bit like fans or wings with the feathers sticking off. Hands and fingers an' all. Wings and feathers on our bodies. If only we could fly! Ye lot are the lucky ones.

So I noticed she started caring about feet. And once you notice something you can't help seeing it over and over.

It did not matter who came to Rydal. Friend or foe. Lad or lass. Mrs. Dobson down the hill or Mrs. Luff or any of the relatives. First Rotha would greet the person face to face, but then, to herself, she'd note the condition of their feet. I saw her looking at feet and I heard her talk and yes I saw what she wrote. And it was true that William had a very bad toe and it plagued him and stopped him from walking half the distances his sister trod.

Have ye ever noticed how people will admit something out loud but only in a half-told fashion?

At first when I climbed the fells with her after William asked me to stand in for him—it was all I could do to keep up with her, and she twice my age! It's funny about that isn't it. Rotha was twice my age when we started together, but today she would be only thirty years older than I am, not twice my age at all. Far from it. Time brings you closer in so many ways. But at first we would fly uphill and on our way back down she'd say, James, aren't our feet wonderful? How they get us up here so efficiently and without any trouble at all?

She said without any trouble . . . but even then she glanced at her own feet as if they were getting ready to run away without her.

And by and by she worried about them more and more. What did she know? Even before they failed her, she stared at them as if they were already starting to lose their miraculous powers. And I'd say, Miss, is it your feet? And half the time she'd say no, it's not my feet. But the other half she would say perhaps it is my feet. And if William was not around she'd let me give them a rub.

I felt sorry that he was gone although my hands were better suited to the job than his. She was missing William's hands and to cheer her up I admitted to her that I had made up a song about feet, did she want me to sing it?

The song is a song about the wandering life alone on foot, I said.

I sang it to myself when I wished I could go back to when my da's family were travellers, a time I only know by song or by old tales that flicker like a faint campfire. But I did not mention that to her. I don't think she wanted to hear too much of my story. She was very comforted by the fact that I was a quiet and strong person who did not demand anything in the way of attention. She hated it when people gabbed on about themselves, which in my observation nearly everybody does. It's amazing to me, really, how they don't notice that nobody really cares about anybody but themselves.

James, she said, you know I'd like any song you care to sing. And I do think she meant it. Times when we were outside and I made myself believe she forgot I wasn't her brother, she opened a part of her mind that allowed song or fancy or other things I had to give her.

So I sang part of my walking song.

My caravan has a little brown roof.
My caravan has two blue windows.
My caravan has a pair of funny little wheels,
They go slow they go far over the hills, over the fields
I wouldn't trade my little caravan . . .

And I stopped and said Miss, do you get the riddle?

Oh, she says, it makes me want to fling myself on the turf and waggle my bare toes!

Because it's about feet, Miss, that song. It goes, *My caravan has a pair of funny little wheels*, and those are your feet, see?

I want to learn it by heart, she says.

The little brown roof is your hair, I says . . .

She got it right away. Two blue windows for your eyes, and like I told her the pair of funny little wheels well that's your feet, and the little caravan can take you wherever you want to go—it's your earthly form you have as long as you're alive. I have one and Rotha Wordsworth has one, or did have—and my sister Penny. No matter who you are or how much money you have or have not got, you have your little caravan.

It's not a complicated song, but my songs never are, not like the poems of William or Sam Coleridge. I don't think I could ever have sung my songs for the men.

I even hesitated to sing for Rotha for fear she might repeat my song to William.

A song—or anything secret—is valuable until the wrong person gets wind of it and thinks it silly or unimportant.

A great deal of my time with Rotha was like that—precious to me, but if anyone knew the things we talked or sang about or made or played as time went on . . . Like the maps we would make of all her old journeys so she could take them again in miniature when she was old—

People would think we were both off our heads.

But while she still had the use of her feet—before they started obeying her fears or whatever it was that began elsewhere inside her and moved to her feet—I sang My Little Caravan for Rotha. And outside when it was windy and no one heard us I sang it for her that many times, soon she was singing all the verses with me, happy as a lark.

As long as her funny little wheels worked all right.

I mean as long as we sang and as long as we brought the botanical glass and she got in right close to all your flowers, she was happiness itself. Even flowers that were only a spangle in the undergrowth. I could hardly see them but they spangled out for her and in she went like ye go in.

Not like this grey day of her death.

No. Colour raved everywhere.

Yellow of yolks and butter in the sun fresh-churned. Bold blooms she'd bring home and stand on her windowsill. Coltsfoot and speedwell and columbines. She'd ask them, do you mind my taking you home?

And they nodded. They said she could take them and she did. But the spangles, the jewels, the tiny stitches hiding or half-hiding . . . *a violet by a mossy stone, half-hidden from the eye! Fair as a star, when only one is shining in the sky* . . . that was something she whispered.

You don't pick certain ones. Even if they say yes. Rotha showed me that.

I am very good at hanging back, wait and see. And with both Rotha and her brother, what I saw and heard wasn't run-of-the-mill. It was worth thinking about.

There's always things you find when you're looking for something else.

And bit by bit I found out there were two of me. Two James Dixons. I mean maybe there were more than two. Maybe we've all got a dozen me's in us or more.

Loyalty was breaking me into different bits.

One for William; planning his gardens, placing the stones where they fit together without anything binding them, no lime or clay, only what gathers naturally—a bit of soil blown on the wind. A natural placement of plain things, one against the other in the wind and the rain and the sun and sleet. Mosses gathering in the cracks and garnishing the stone with velvet as time passes. Me and him planting shrubs that sprayed in a fountain William called the fountain of refreshment.

Aye, I thought, Penny Dixon and her workmates could bloody well use a fountain of refreshment. That thought came to me strong but I kept on working with William and his fancy fountain that had no water in it. His was a fountain of leaves. It was a fountain for a poet who had no lack of water. Who was not parched in a factory where if you did not fall asleep you might be lucky enough to capture a cup of your own sweat.

You have to laugh at someone who can ignore everything going on right under his nose!

I had to quell my feelings. I had to be careful of scorn if I wanted to keep my sanity and my job.

Part of me felt proud of all the work I did for William. I built up a reputation with him for a seriousness and a kind of seeing I'd had from the time I was born. That sight of mine was a seed, and being with Rotha and her brother made it grow.

But the first me—my old self—knew fine well that we were in a kind of false green world.

And my old self is the one who wanted to rip away the fantasy and know what lay under it. I knew something lay under it. And that is why I began wandering into Rotha's bedroom alone.

Her room was different without herself or William in it.

All quiet, like, all white.

I felt wary of her mysterious window that was covered so no one could see it. It was no longer a visible window, but still . . . I felt it, an eye open inside the wall, watching me steal in.

I should not have looked in the red diary Rotha kept for herself alone but part of me could not resist. An old part of me that was not loyal to William or to her.

I felt the hidden window stare at me from in the wall.

You can't see me, I told it.

And I untied Rotha's red diary and put my nose close to her very difficult scrawl.

For this I can only claim that loyalty has its limits when it comes to the shadows in our souls.

3

There I couch when owls do cry

∞∞∞∞

D ear James! Everything in this garden was warm and alive that year your dear Rotha became aware her feet were mortal. You were her young servant and her own youth had only just blown away over the mountains—was that not the year she went running, running up those mountains with her strange friend, Miss Something-or-other, to catch one last wisp of immortal youth? But it's cold up there! Not a Sycamore kind of place at all. No tree larger than a creeping larch. Not even a single anemone. Even the bees hardly venture there for fear of blowing away.

And those feet of your Rotha! They had started to run a little less wild, hadn't they, on her legs that had once been so lithe. Some fluid or poison trickled down, drop by drop, through her belly and legs, and droplet by droplet into her feet, and she felt it. Oh, she did. And James, reliable James, attuned to your Queen's minutest tremor: what was that poison?

eight

ooooo

THE VERY FIRST PAGE I opened—I only glanced upon it
where her red book fell open—was so ablaze I could hardly
stand it.

> *Rubies—sharp-cut. Faceted rubies yet with parts melted,*
> *Smashed—poured & sprayed, aglitter on her kitchen*
> *floor—& a thrust of silver—undersides aspen show*
> *whilst making their castanet song to the universe. Then a*
> *crack! The kind lightning is made of & thunder only*
> *remembers . . .*

I slammed the book shut and did not know what I had
seen. A thrust of silver? Red glittering on the kitchen
floor . . . I remembered the murder Mary Lamb had com-
mitted against her mother. Rotha never mentioned that. No
one in the Wordsworth family uttered a word on it. That
slaughter was something the whole village knew but nobody
in this house seemed to remember. And yet in her red book
it continued fresh as if Mary Lamb's knife slashed even now.

Did Rotha Wordsworth think the scene horrible or beautiful?

The way she wrote it! Stronger than her brother's poems but no verses and no rhyming and no space down the edge. I knew William did not rhyme all his poems. But his were tall and thin like himself, with space around them. Hers sprawled over the page. What was she about?

When I feel strange, that's when I go out walking.

The lakelands are themselves a trance and on them your mind slips into a trance of its own. So you're floating. You're a trance within a trance. That's when the ache of anything drains. Grasses whisper ache away. The thrushes flitter it away—it just dissolves.

Willows sway.

The water keeps moving.

There's a thing I feel. And Rotha feels it as well.

Felt it.

We did agree on it. That when you pass under the branches of certain trees, over your head there's . . .

In your hair as if a loving hand . . .

A mother's hand. Not a mother like my mam. Some other kind of mother has smoothed your hair in your dreams. Shifted the path of your dreaming. Of your song. I could cry thinking about it. The peace walking under a tree can give you. No matter if you've seen some terrible frightening trouble. And who hasn't?

And yes, she took the laudanum—Rotha. They gave it to her and they made sure she took it. She didn't want to, though.

If it weren't for her trusting her brother and Mr. Carr so much she would have asked me to pour more of it in the geranium than she did, and she asked me that quite often. She said it made the geranium bloom where it made herself wilt.

Any spoon of laudanum you might swallow never mends you as a tree mends you.

I've often thought ends of the willows are hands. What a light strong touch willows have got. I love when they smooth my head.

Ack listen to that crow! Raw and scratchy.

Here's the second bit I read.

The terror that befell Mary Lamb will never befall Mary Wordsworth, will it. For our wife Mary is far too giving in every aspect. Mary Wordsworth will never let a crack appear. Mary Wordsworth loves it when every moment of her waking life is spent in service for others. Mary Lamb, however, was not like that—

Mary Lamb stabbed her mother with a kitchen knife unto death. Mary Lamb splayed her mother upon their kitchen floor & the blood sprayed & dropped & dripped & splattered on the stones. This is not something Mary Wordsworth would do.

Mary Wordsworth harbours not an iota of resentment. Mary Wordsworth is full only of devotion for her husband, Wm, & for me, his sister, Dorothy, isn't she. Nothing could possess her to do what Mary Lamb has done.

I hardly knew what to make of it.

So yes I walked outside as soon I got the chance. Ye fly and ye go in your buttercup chambers and the blue halls of your morning glory and ye know glory not only in your minds but all through your pockets and wings and then you pass that light on in your honey to us all, ye do. Ye have your golden ways figured out. But I don't fly, and I don't make honey. I only walk to clear my own head. I walked all the time the Wordsworths were alive and I will have to keep going now that Rotha has followed her brother into death. Over the years the medicine I give myself has not changed.

So I walked after I discovered things that lay in the strange red book, and Rotha saw me walking. She watched me out the window. A pale face at the glass, like. Talking to me without a sound.

Take me with you.

But I kept on alone. I had to. And when I came back, she says, James, you know I have been dreaming and dreaming of a very long walk of my own.

Yes, Miss, I says. I know.

I knew she had in her mind to fight her strange worry around her feet. Her feet still worked then as far as anyone else could tell. But according to herself there was something to worry about. She wanted to bring back her young scrambles. Uphill all the way. Something even more strenuous than her young escapes.

I says Miss, you're looking for an extra upness.

Up, up, up, she says, I have to see if I'm still able and how high.

Right, Miss.

The last time I exerted all my leg-power was twenty years ago!

Yes, Miss. I remember seeing you when I was a wee lad and thinking you were the wind. You're hardly any slower now, though, Miss—

Oh, I'm afraid I might be, James. And where those twenty years went or who stole them from me I do not know.

No, Miss, the time flies for me an' all.

But I, she says, feel in me the beginnings of a wooden death and if I want to thwart it I have to climb, and I am bound to do it before these legs forget how. James, I have seen you mend your shoes and rub ointment on your feet— what is that stuff?

Lanolin, Miss. Off sheep.

Do you think it good for preparing one's feet for rough terrain?

Yes, Miss, lanolin is the best.

And she says well you know I am dying to see if I can still climb the high hills around Borrowdale . . .

Around Borrowdale, Miss, I warn, is quite high mountains rather than mere hills—

Yes, she says, I know they are high.

Very high, Miss. Nobody goes up there, only the sheep.

Then do you think you might procure me some of their lanolin? And perhaps also reinforce my shoes the way you mend your own? What is that tool? Can I please hold it?

It's my stitching awl, I says. I hand it to her and I says for a laugh, Miss D, of course I will give you my awl.

And she laughs as well. She has a smashing laugh.

Had.

You think she's come to the end of her world with sorrow untold but then up she wriggles like a trout and leaps into the sunshine. And she says James, you have been giving me your all now since you were a boy, and for that I thank you from the bottom of my heart. And she lifts her pincushion which is heart-shaped and flips it upside down and slides a pin out, and it's a hatpin with a pearl animal head. Some animal I do not know. Like a deer but not a deer. And I have it to this day. I have a wool band I wrap around myself when there is a draft, and I secure the end with the pin and I swear it renders the wool twice as warm so as to give off its own heat like embers long after a flame has died.

I suddenly wanted to ask her why her diary had blood and Mary Lamb and Mary Wordsworth all in the same breath on one page. I found something awful about it. While she was laughing and handing me the pearl pin, a desire to know rose up in me. When you get someone's confidence and they are off guard . . .

I knew Miss Lamb was still in London and I wondered was she better these days or not? I knew her brother Charles was responsible for her and that was why she was not locked up. Could a person get better after a thing like that? Lamb is a funny name for a woman who slaughters her mam. And what about Mary Wordsworth? *Not an iota of resentment . . . Full only of devotion . . . Nothing could possess her.* This all ran through my head and I was dying to ask but I knew I should not have looked in Rotha's red diary—and I managed to accept the pearl pin off her and thank her without asking her a thing.

For how does a beloved servant question his mistress without turning into a prying nuisance? He doesn't, is the answer. Instead he does what is asked and then some. He does a sort of work that gets done with no one quite sure who did it. A kind of enchanted tasking. And the tasker waits and watches the little family, and in particular he especially watches his Rotha to make sure she will be all right whatever circumstance may befall, at least while he is present. He decides she should never be frightened. For she might not be his own sister Penny but she is someone's sister. Someone who has made himself scarce and has not realized what his sister is thinking and writing. William thinks she is only writing about her feelings which are not important and if they overflow he has asked the tasker to take care of the problem so as not to let those feelings flood Rydal Mount.

So I accept the pearl pin and she laughs that smashing laugh and moreover, James, she says, you're the only one who hasn't sounded incredulous.

At your planning to go mountain climbing?

Yes. My brother doesn't want me to do it. Our wife Mary says I am mad. But here you are offering me the foot balm which is exactly what I need. And you are doing it with a straight face. James—

Miss?

Do you believe I can do it?

. . . Aye, I says. By now, I says, I think you can do anything you put your mind to as regards walking outdoors.

And I meant that. I did not lie to her about it.

But, she says, you're remembering me from the old days.

Aye, I says. But time is funny.

And you're still only twenty-two if that, and me, I'm nearly forty-seven. My mother was only thirty-one when she died, and my father forty-two. I hardly come from hardy stock!

Forty-seven you may be, I says to her, but from what I've noticed of your legs—she gave me a funny glance; was she surprised or amused?—I mean, Miss D, that they are strong legs, I says.

You're right, they are, she says, and they are sometimes fast, but I am nevertheless becoming old and William does not wish to accompany me. He cannot take the time from his writing and I suspect the Toe prevents him as well.

She had taken to calling her brother's sore toe *the Toe* as if it held a place in the world as the king of toes. When I told Mam this she laughed all right. Aye, says Mam, the brother's toe is coddled very like our king. Because by then King George was laid down in velvet being fed goatmilk buns soaked in brandy and never coming up for air. And it's true William's toe saw the physician nearly as often as did the king, and he had Rotha talking about the Toe as reverently as if it had a life of its own.

And she says, James, it's not only my legs and feet I'm thinking of. Or my bowels. Because her bowels were bad, they were sometimes good but all of a sudden they'd—but it wasn't bowels she feared now. It's things you have to be careful of on highlands, she says, things we forget about here low down in the vales, and you must know the things I mean.

Getting lost up there, I says.

Yes.

How easy it is, I says.

Nearly impossible not to get lost at some point, says she.

Yes, I says, I know what you mean. You'd never think it looking up at a mountain from down here. For it looks to reduce to a high point from where you can plainly see all that is below.

When in fact, she says—

Yes. The thing is, unless you're at the pinnacle—

Which is so easily prevented! Getting to the highest height—

Yes, any hard gale—

Or sudden fog blanket—

Even snow, I says. For by then we were nearly into October.

Especially snow! Or sleet and hail and the north wind—

Or terrible cold—

Or falling off a ledge after fog or snow might have obscured the way—

Or getting nearly to the top, says I, and not being able to reach the summit, and so not being able to see the way down—

That's it, she says—that last one is my greatest fear regarding the mountains. What if any of those circumstances we have mentioned traps me below a summit, where it can be utterly astonishing how big the mountain is, how far it stretches, and though you are very high up, exposed and far from home, you are not yet beyond the blind wastes as far as the mountain is concerned. You could wander on that level until you perish!

Shambling without food or water, says I.

Yes, and having to muster all your presence of mind in order to simply continue.

Aye, I says.

And we both knew she had often done all these things before in the hills around here. She had been lost and cold. And she had come back home. So then I says, Miss D— presence of mind is a thing you own in great measure.

Yes, I know. That, and the strength in my feet and legs, are all I have, or did have.

I saw then that she was asking me if I believed her presence of mind and the strength in her legs were still strong enough to get her up and down our summits. I said, It sounds, Miss, as if such a climb might give you the measure of what you still possess in that department.

Exactly.

Who are you going to go with?

I wanted her to have someone good. I was half-afraid she meant to set off by herself but I didn't let on. Part of me was crying out to say I'll come with you but I managed to refrain from speaking. Wait and see, that's my motto. Wait and see what she wants.

My painter friend in Borrowdale.

That Miss Barker?

Yes.

I kept silent a minute. Solitary, that Barker woman traipsed mountain crag and ledge, lugging her paints. Now there was a one who knew how to mend her own boots. She was said to be bewitched.

I suppose, I says, if anyone can climb mountains it's Miss Barker . . . but if you don't mind my suggesting it, I can put you onto a fellow who tends sheep in those mountains and he'll not get in your way, but he will be sure to know when a storm is coming long before you or even Miss Barker sees it . . .

At the mention of an old shepherd Rotha lit right up and said, Yes, James! Your shepherd friend will be our shepherd friend.

He won't be obtrusive, I promised. Not auld Thomas.

And she allowed me to arrange Tom's presence and I was secretly relieved. Tom might be seventy-odd but he knew those mountains.

And she says I know, James, I've asked you a lot already but if I am going to ascend the mountains of Borrowdale I have heard there are tiny rare lichen and plants of all kinds, and I wondered if—

The wee microscope?

I'd been fiddling around with it in my hut trying to mend the thing once and for all. Its hinges were not only small, they had a square hollow and I had yet to file replacement pintles I'd managed to scrounge from old pairs of glasses I had collected on my travels.

There's only one or two more adjustments to make, I says, then if you want you and me can go for a ramble to one of the tarns and test it out.

Might I come to your hut and watch you mend it?

At this a leap of alarm hit my throat. My hut! I wasn't having that.

I wouldn't advise it, Miss, I says.

You can't give them everything. My hut is my sanctuary. I didn't want Rotha in it. It was my place. Long as I was the family servant I had to be careful I didn't lose my own privacy. That hut is my own private haunt. Ye lot have been inside my hut. Ye know. Ye've perched on my tools. My saws and everything I've hung on pegs. You've seen the line I drew round them with chalk. Not so I'll know if somebody's gone off with them. I'm not a suspicious man. More so I will be certain I've put a thing back where it belongs. Having things be where they belong is key. You know where to find the right tool for any job as soon as you need it, long as you put it back where it belongs.

My hammers, mauls and spanners! My turn-screws and awls and my old carving set, which is the prize. My wire, my sandpaper, my funnels and hooks—and my scrap paper and a few pencils for drawing out the ideas I show various ones in the fam'ly—Mary pretends interest, and her and William's daughter Dora was a fine hand with needle and thread; the lass enjoyed my creations, my fences or the rockery or any of the small improvements I made over time.

Then there's plant pots, trowels, edging tools . . . all the sticks and tags I use for labelling plants. Ye lot know how important it is to classify! My basket of gauzy bits of . . . haha it goes on forever . . . twine and wool and string and other bits I'd lash on a trellis for sweet peas or anything needing a stake. The scent of earth and boards! Wood, rain, my lovely scented twigs and composted dung sweet as barley malt. Ye know I do sweep the floor but I never mind bits and pieces of dried leaf and other vegetation. That scent means the hut is half in the outside world where I belong. My hut's an in-between world betwixt the indoors and the outdoors and it is the heart of all I know how to make and mend.

Alone in it I would mend the microscope that let Rotha enter into your flower chambers, delving inside them like yourselves. I'm the one who looked after that for her. Helped her go into the heart of all wild rooms-out-of-rooms. But I had to work alone. No one can come in and look over my shoulder while I work in my own space. If they come in, then it's their space, isn't it. People like Rotha and her brother. They control the thinking. And when they control the thinking they control you. And I was never having that.

And funnily enough she did not argue. And I believe that is because she knew her place.

nine

ooooo

AND WHAT HAPPENED NEXT WAS a bit like what goes on with ye bees in the hive, because ye gather the honey yourselves, don't ye, but someone else always takes it away. It's hard to keep any of it for your own survival through the winter, yet without it ye'll surely perish. Still we come and haul away your gold treasure, eh? And we replace it with the candy if you're getting short, but the candy is not the honey.

As September broke into October did Rotha's legs get better or worse? And her bowel complaints? One day this and the next that. I remember I kept thinking she'll never in a million years make it up the mountains of Borrowdale with that going on in her limbs and her bowels. It was then, yes, that it got worse. Right before her climb. But it interrupted itself like. Over a matter of weeks it got worse but then it got better and nobody knew what to make of it.

Rise up, rise up! Get out of your bed and walk!

That's from the Bible, isn't it? That's what it was like with Rotha just before her climb, or it got more like that every day. The occasional miracle whereby up she'd leap!

Then the next day unable.

Mary Wordsworth claimed she was doing it for the attention. I heard her say this to John Carter. Or did John Carter say it to Mary? The two of them considered themselves the sensible ones, I know that.

But Rotha. Headache one day, bowel agony untold numbers of days, and then the leg thing, where she'd tell Mary and Mary would tell John Carter and John Carter would tell me—Rotha's legs are freezing cold and heavy as a pair of marble rolling pins and she durst not move them even if she could because of the pain. Any of this would last a day or two at first, in those days before her climb. Then miraculously she would rise up and get out of her bed and walk as if nothing had happened. And so it was in October that year, 1818, seeming free of her complaints for the moment, off Rotha set to Borrowdale to climb with that Miss Barker.

And poor William while she was gone—he couldn't work on his poems if Rotha wasn't there to aid him, so he worked on his accounts and ah, it was a constant calculation goin' over and over, somewhere between the heart—in the breast— somewhere between the heart and the neck. A constant calculatin' machine, an abacus, never stops, *click click click click click* have we got enough or have we got too little? Is there enough? There's not much. There's not much left. There's not much to come! Accounts in, accounts out . . . He and o'course Mary along with him took care of all that. Paying me . . . I mean, John Carter they didn't have to pay because he was paid for by the, it was included with the stamp job. But . . . *click click click. Click click click. Click click click.*

Money!

Gold hides the seed falling from your sycamore in a spiral. It drowns out the gentle lapping of Rydal Water on the stones. It drowns out the very soft crackle of the rabbit's passage over the turf. It drowns out the wind's voice and the cloud's path. It drowns out the undersong of the leaves and the birds. It drowns out, most of all, haha, the poetry that's welling up, that's wanting to well up, that's dammed inside ye. Dammed.

Rotha being gone up that mountain was torture for William. Why d'you think, he says to John Carter the third day she was gone off—and mind, William's feeling very irritated with not being able to fix a sonnet without her—why, he says, do you think young men are poets and old men are mere husks?

As if John Carter could answer a thing like that!

I mean John's all right but he's one of those people, he's lived in little villages but . . . so John is not a city person, but I think his mam was. So from when John was little, there's something, some reason why the fells and the water and the soil are a bit, y'know, beneath him. And John, even though he's never lived in a big important place like, he gives off the impression that he's a bit above it all here. And he's always got a smirk pasted on 'es face that's more like a mask. He's missing a key aspect of what I like in a person. A gravity where you know it's really the person you're talking to, he's not putting it on.

That's my thinking about John like, and that he would say the things he said about Dorothy—that for one thing she considered herself married to her brother. That she believed deep down in her heart and soul that William Wordsworth was her own husband, and if William had married Mary Hutchinson then Dorothy had married Mary an' all. That was John Carter's explanation for why Rotha often called William's wife "our wife Mary." I had to admit I had no answer to that one. But I mean John Carter gives the impression that he's the, you know, he's the man for William. He's all loyal to William.

Well you cannot profess loyalty to William Wordsworth and be disloyal to his sister. That doesn't wash. This man of William's, John Carter, is unaware of crucial things. Or a piece of him is asleep. There's a bit that is not thinking, a thing in John Carter that doesn't understand and he, ye know when they say of somebody, he hasn't got it in 'im. That's how he, you know, John Carter, that's how he is. He hasn't got it in him to understand a person like Rotha. But he's a loyal clerk for William, I suppose. Was.

But the real sympathy and devotion I'm talking about, and I don't mean being a slave, mind, it's more like having sympathy with anything at all. With the wrens, with the place itself—he's floating around, John Carter is, disconnected from it all. He's missing a connection. He's missing a flame inside himself that warms and melts you into the bigger flame of these people and this place. John just hasn't got it in him.

I suppose I should feel sorry for him.

John Carter, when the little fam'ly can't hear him, rants, Somebody has got to keep these people in line! Somebody has got to keep these people from disgracing themselves by looking completely daft—wandering around, muttering to themselves—living in the selfsame garments year in and year out and year in again. And year out again. And year in again. The same coat, patched all over. Somebody has to make a little bit of money and that somebody's got to be William! And he'd better do his job at the stamp office and not sit around making up verses all the time. Somebody's got to have one foot in this world!

That was John Carter's proclamation. It was his own self-proclaimed job to keep somebody in the little family with one foot in this world. But I'm telling ye that was the disease that made William claw Rotha's inner life and grasp it for his own. One-foot-in-this-world disease. He knew he'd caught it when he wrote *The world is too much with us* . . . Aye if anyone siphoned the spirit out of me that William drew from Rotha I might have a pain in my guts an' all, and sore bowels and stiff legs. William devoured her observations but he spat out her feelings. She saved those in the red diary knowing he had no interest. He delved for morsels of his choice with his pointy nose like a fox.

And I was the fox's helper! I felt somewhat uneasy but he did pay for my keep. I could send a bit of money to Mam and Penny! Didn't we both try to take care of our younger sisters, William and me? Big fox and little fox. Bandy-legged William Fox and the young Fox Dixon.

ON THE THIRD DAY ROTHA was climbing in Borrowdale I hung around with William a bit more than usual because the two of us were at loose ends without her. We worked here in the gardens and he mentioned his dingy shirt and said that Fanny, the maid who helped with the washing and ironing, had pleurisy and could not work. I am a man who sees an opportunity immediately and when I heard this I sat on a stump, my eyes shut, for if I must ask anybody for something—I cannot bear seeing a "no" on their face before they utter it.

I says, Sir if Fanny is off more time than you can spare her, I've a . . .

Oh it's all right, he says, Fanny will be back in a fortnight.

That'd be excellent, Sir, I says, only in case she's not, I have my own sister Penny who's a strong lass and nobody claps a flatter shirt or mixes a better pudding. And her sewing, Sir, Penny's hands are nimbler than mine if you can believe it . . .

Silence. Bitter wind against my face. I unscrewed my eyes to see William look up from his prong with a question mark that seemed to doubt me and my whole place there. Exactly as I'd feared.

But of course, I says, you won't need Penny once Fanny comes back and I hope she gets better.

Why wouldn't she get better, Dixon, he says, and he resumes pulling the horseradish, and I lay awake that night and wondered what he thought. When a higher-up person won't answer you after you've shown them a desire they didn't expect out of you, your heart sinks and all kinds of fears flood you. A stream of shame no matter how proud you were.

That night I did not abandon my dream of bringing Penny into the Wordsworths' fine world, but I vowed not to mention her to William again either, for fear it'd put an end to my own job and so end any prospect of Penny rising.

On Rotha's fourth day off in the mountains with that Miss Barker I had a mind to wonder whether she'd ever come back. She delayed first one day and then a couple more until William was beside himself asking after her—has she come home—he had done all the calculating he could do as well as all the poem writing and moreover his clothes desperately needed washing and finally he worried that she might be lost.

I reminded him of Miss Barker's surefootedness and of the fact that old shepherd Tom would never let them down, and I did not need to remind him that Rotha herself was like a goat as long as she was well, as she had leapt into pure wellness only days before her journey. It was as if the notion of going mountain climbing with her friend had poured life right back into her that had been draining away as long as she lay upstairs waiting for William's company. I think the prospect of Borrowdale with Miss Barker had given Rotha a new passion and William—a bit of a dog in the manger— did not wholly like it.

I know it could seem to Rotha as if it might hardly matter to William if she was alive or dead. But I could have told her that without her William lost substance and became like a flake of soot wisping round these gardens, worrying about not writing and about needing more money. After a week of her absence he worked up a restorative vision of himself as an important poet who must go on business to the city. He allowed Mary to clap and whiten two shirts and off he sailed to his publisher who would, he hoped, pay him to revise a guide to the Lakes that had made him quite a bit of money already, and which bore his name as sole author though only Rotha could have written many of the things in it. Things only she could have noticed in the first place.

So William was away when Rotha came home from Borrowdale to a house going on about ordinary house business: its chimneys clinked as autumn cold contracted the stones, and briars scratched the walls. But the house was silent inside and Rotha climbed its creaking stairs and greeted her diary that always heard. She wrote her feelings about Miss Barker and the mountain and kept the diary with her in the bed. When I went up to her room to bring back the chair I'd patched while she was away I found her in a state of real excitement.

Finally, a living soul, she says! Oh James—you will never credit what we did, what we gained, how high we climbed. I can't wait for William to hear it!

It wore on me a bit how she supposed William might listen to please her when he would—for anyone with eyes to see—take her tale down, not in.

Aye well, I says, you will have to make do with my ear, Miss D, as William is yet in London talking to his publisher—

James! I never fathomed when we started off to the head of Borrowdale past the black lead mine, the guardhouse and

spoil-heaps and the wagonway and all the dirt and racket—
and beyond it Seathwaite . . .

Aye, I says, thinking of Penny. How I had once begged
her not to work in that very mine, where you might be
hanged for leaving your shift with a morsel of lead fallen
by mistake into your pinny pocket, and not enough wages
to keep you fed. And now here Penny was far worse off after
that Pendleton stinkhole. Aye, Miss Dorothy Wordsworth
would pass by a place like the black lead mine blithe as a
moth. She would flit beyond . . .

. . . And then the mountain I thought we were going to
climb—Ash Course they call it, but it is really Esk Hawes—
I believe it comes from German—

And I minded not for the first time how Rotha insists on
very proper names for things. Mind, I says to myself, you
don't get offended over that now. Remember your benefits
in keeping clear of scorn. Remember the Miss D that little
boy James met and will always . . .

So I says, Aye, Miss, Ash Course, I've been up there.
There's a swirly beck with a smashing pool and two ash trees
with deep shade under 'em . . .

Yes! We stopped there, and James, we scrambled to the
top with hardly an effort—it was as if my limbs were the
same as they were when I was young. You saw me then—

I did—

And I have not felt invincible like that since the children
died—little Catherine and Thomas—Or perhaps I have not
been my old self since they were born—I mean my young
self. Oh, James, I do not know when it happened . . .

Aye, Miss, you have had a lot of strain and a lot of sorrow and it is no big surprise if—

—But I found out with my friend that I'm not diminished at all! That's the thing. Troubles are not what they seemed to be, once you are in the mountains.

Aren't they, Miss?

No! Once Mary Barker and I rose to the top of Ash Course, what should we see but—you know it don't you!

I reckon on a clear day you'd see—

—Oh, it was a clear day all right! I have never seen things so clearly in all my life.

Then, Miss, you'll have seen all of Borrowdale and Bassenthwaite as well as Keswick and Skiddaw, all the mountains from here to Helvellyn an' all. And the other direction mebbe all the way to Yorkshire.

Yes, and beyond! And Solway Firth and all the way to the mountains of Scotland.

Scotland, Miss!

Scotland was something the mere mention of which sort of made a fizzle in me and I know it did in her an' all.

But James, even that was nothing compared with what we accomplished next. Miss Barker had her eye on another summit—

The other summit would be Scaw Fell, Miss, and by the sound of it you were already more than half-way up it.

That's it! She was breathless. There was a dancing feeling all round her as if she had run and run and run and wasn't a bit tired, which from the sound of things was about the size of it. She reminded me of myself when I get out in the freedom of the hills.

Scaw Fell loomed so near! But it wasn't near—as we walked towards it, it moved away from us like a great ship sailing off, tricking us, and by and by we saw a dip appear before us and we would have had to climb down and down quite far before we could go upwards once more, so we were disillusioned and instead headed for another height on that same mountain, but closer—

The pike?

Scawfell Pike, that's it! And James, there wasn't a breath of wind. We unwrapped our dinner and the paper lay on the rock without a rustle, and there was no sound—we had left the waterfalls far below us and could not hear even a buzzing insect, only a world of silence and deep air going on forever. And I've since learned that we were far higher than even we thought, as Scawfell Pike has been measured and the mountain-measurers say it is higher than the more distant point of which we imagined ourselves to have fallen short. In fact, James, without intending to do it and without even knowing it, Mary Barker and I have climbed the highest mountain in all of England!

She sat back and looked at me with a very pleased expression.

Have you got your knife? she asked me. I have my favourite pen ready and I wish you might sharpen it, James. The ascent has done something to my desire to write. It has sharpened me and now I need my best pen sharp, but William is not here. Even if he was, he cannot sharpen a pen as well as you. I am going to bring my notes downstairs!

And she carried them down—it was the first time I ever saw her bring her writing into the main part of the house. I tried to make myself scarce but she was eager to seek me out and read me little pieces, and they were so full of life I felt blown to bits as if I was out-of-doors in a big gale nowhere near a house at all.

Was there a gale when you were up there? I asked her. For I could nearly feel the wind. No. I did feel it.

Oh yes, she said. Were it not for your old friend the shepherd Tom we might not have made it back home! He saw, once we were at the peak, a mizzle of gauze fizzing off in the distance over Whitehaven. Mind, he says, we get out of that thing's way, and he brought us to shelter under a crag while the mizzle loomed and blackened and boiled and wrapped seven mountains!

And she read me all about the lowland plants, and about looking through her microscope: flowers in surprising pockets beyond their summer comfort—the violet and the rose—and then alpine flowers, but once they reached the top—what was that? I had to ask her to read it twice. I was hearing it but not able to understand.

Bones, Miss? Mighty neglect?

I know what bones are and I know the meaning of neglect but not when they are put together on top of a mountain. I wanted to ask if I might read the words myself but before I could drum up the nerve she handed me the notes and said James, you read it to me.

So I got frightened because I can read in my head but not always out loud, I mean not properly. I might get words wrong. Their sound. Words I knew from reading, like, but I might not have heard them said. And I didn't want to sound them out wrong in front of her. William I didn't mind—he was used to the way I read her diaries out. But I had never read her own writing to herself before. So I says thank you, Miss, but I have a bit of a sore throat.

All right, then, I'll read it again, says she—*We came against bones of the earth once all the plants stopped, once we reached a height where nothing has green blood—only bone is left. Mighty neglect! The maker of worlds had bones left over from all the animals & people & even all the fish & spines of hardy plants & anything bound down by force of weight—the maker had extra bones & cast them down at the top of Scawfell Pike in a tumble of lifeless petrification!*

Petrification, I says—were you—were you frightened, then, Miss?

It was thrilling. And James, but for your having mended our scope I would not have seen the life, only felt it. I felt it all right, it was fearsome, you're right to mention a fright— who would have thought there is life in austere stone cast aground? Rubble left-over yet important! I had a feeling were it not for that piled rock devoid of softness, no real soft-ness could endure here below. It was as if the bony rock held all endurance for us so we need hardly consider it down here below, but it considers us—

Yes, Miss D, I says, I admit I have thought myself at times that the mountains notice us.

I did not confess that sometimes I found myself talking back to them, as I talk to ye, or that whenever I was away from the mountains I felt lonely, that I missed them. My mam always said when my dad left us that she didn't care because she had the mountain out back of our house for company. Me and the mountain, she'd say. Me and the mountain enjoyed a dollop of bramble jelly on toast for our tea, thank you for asking . . .

And then, James, Rotha tells me, I examined the rock surface, which blazed with petrified paint—lichen that clung to the stones. I unfolded our microscope and saw that lichen is more important than any flower! Lichen is the efflorescence and voice of the bones.

Efflorescence, Miss . . . This was one of her mystery words. I wondered if I would see it show up in the red diary. Sometimes she wrote lists that had no meaning, only a long snake of words, and they were not words you normally hear in the run of a day. She stored them, like, the way Mam lays up her best tablecloth and few tea towels, separate from the ordinary lot.

Sizzling and miniature, she says.

Lichen, Miss?

Yes. Orange, white, green, pink, like the flag of a rock nation, the speech of the mountain itself if only a person knows how to translate it. And James, our lovely magnifier revealed to me that the mountain is always attentive and alive. I peeled my shoes off and felt its grave sermon enter me. It mineralized my bones, James, after everything had threatened to drain all the metal out of me.

You mean it made you stronger, Miss?

We have metal in us, James, and I had forgotten how to restore it. It drains out and you have to make it come back. No wonder that before the climb I had so often to lie down!

But then she tells me a very strange story about the mountain, about looking over the sea far over Eskdale and seeing a ship that ended up being a bit of a wild ship. A ship I couldn't quite understand.

That ship, she says, gave me the best lesson of all the visions the mountain provided that day!

Oh she was delighted to tell me about that ship. I couldn't make head or tail out of the ship story but I didn't let on. I couldn't even tell if the ship was a real ship on the ocean in the distance, or some kind of dream. What did she mean? But I did not interrupt her.

It's all making me realize, she said, I need to get my *Recollections* out again and keep working on them.

Scotland, Miss? I knew these writings were about having walked all over Scotland with William and Sam Coleridge when they were still young and they left Mary Wordsworth back in Grasmere—Mary and William's first baby John was a newborn—and off Rotha and William and Sam went through the highlands as if there had been no wedding, no our wife Mary, only Dorothy and her two beloved men, three pilgrims on foot with a horse and a shambles of a cart that made children everywhere laugh it was so ramshackle. Off they had traipsed over the highlands. She never kept a diary that whole journey but she had not stopped thinking about it ever since, or writing her remembrances and wondering if one day she would publish it. It would be her masterpiece. Yet it lay in a heap forever growing and changing and being revised or laid aside. Perilously lay her notes near her bedroom fire, or on the floor, or they were gathered up and put away but then out they inched once again. And William would say no, don't publish that, you'll never be able to stand the glare of going public. *Public!* He said it as if he truly thought getting published would kill her. Still, she revised her Scottish walk over and over again.

And now William was not in the house to argue and she says to me she says yes, my recollections of walking in Scotland—I could perfect the prose and add it to my account of climbing Scawfell Pike, and I am sure I could reap some income from it—I know I have talked of this before, but now I feel invigorated enough to work like a horse until it is done! If Miss Barker can sell her paintings and live in a house of her own then I can surely do the same with my own word-paintings of all the magnificent climbing and walking I have done—it's only a matter of getting the work out there into the world!

She had all the energy of the October wind from the mountains, a wind that knew her as it whirled round the eaves of Rydal Mount, trying to reach her and talk to her.

And then William came home.

ten

ooooo

AND IF YOU ASKED ME to name the time when it all changed around her walking and climbing and yes her writing, I'd put it square on the nose of that moment when her brother clicked the latch on his return from seeing his publisher in London. He was all ablaze. He brought the streetlamps home from London and waved them round the house 'til they outshone all her thin bright air and bits of lightning fallen off Scawfell Pike which turned to silver and scrappy remnants fizzling out in her clothes next to his new moneymaking project which was the pure hard gold!

By now money outweighed the shining hills for him and he even admitted it with a sad face that said, *There is no other choice, unfortunately.*

My publisher, he told Rotha, has agreed to pay me to revise our guide to the Lakes for all the new visitors dying to see the place. They're all searching, he says, for the very glory I put in my poems. Though I know they'll never find it, not even if they traipse from here to Windermere with my poems dangling in one hand and their cheese and onion sandwiches in the other!

My poems are too—something—he says—I forget his word—the poems are too something—but the Guide! The simplest one of them can buy my Guide and turn to page twenty-one or page thirty-seven and quickly find a place, a name, a tarn or stone or tree or fell all mapped and labelled and described clear as day—the location easy enough for a child to find, and all the flowers documented, and the feelings they produce, or should produce in any reader owning so much as half a heart or having one eye open . . .

And soon as William says that—I mean only once he's finished—does he ask Rotha about her climb up the mountain. He listens for a minute as she begins to tell him things she told me but he interrupts her—

Have you written it yet?

Aye, she says, and he puts his hand out to take it like and she hands him the sheaf and off he goes with her writing upstairs to his private . . . *cryptic*! That's the word. I get mixed up with cryptic and crypt. His poems were too cryptic is what he said. Did he mean like something you'd find in the crypt? Dead like? I dunno. Any rate that's what he said about his poems, they just wouldn't bring enough money to pay the bills. But the Guide now, with Rotha's account of all the things she's seen and done all her days scrambling over the fells and now up the very highest peak in all of England, that was something he could use and sell. For the benefit of everyone in the household.

And while he was working on fitting her tale of Scawfell into the new Guide he'd get me to keep him in fresh nibs and he'd mutter a bit to me now and then, and one thing he says sticks in my mind. It had to do with a violet in the lowland bit below where his sister reached the heights. And I realized he was reciting again. He did that often, recited his own poems, and John Carter thought it was ridiculous but I liked it.

A violet by a mossy stone . . . Half hidden from the eye! . . .

Aye, that was one Rotha recited an' all, for that one was about herself if ye ask me, although it's supposed to be about someone named Lucy who lives hidden away. No one hears or sees Lucy except William himself. She lives all hidden away and no one but him understands how important she is. No one but him cares. And it isn't really about Lucy of course, Lucy's a made-up name. William told me nearly all writers use real people and then just give them a new name so as not to make it seem like they are only writing about themselves and their own families.

Any rate he was copying stuff about a violet down in the Guide and he was reciting that poem and then all of a sudden he says to me, you do know, Dixon, precisely what a constitutes a violet's form?

I think I could scratch a decent likeness of one, Sir, I says, if that's what you mean. For I had done a few violets on the Pace eggs. But he knew that.

So I wondered why he was asking me this and then he goes on and he says remember it has a low petal, that hangs down below the rest?

And I says aye, I remember that. This was nearly November now, but I had seen enough violets in enough springtimes so as to well recall exactly what one looks like.

And he says that low petal, that's my sister, Dorothy. It's really the highest!

Sir, how can low be high?

William got on with riddles like this once in a while. He seemed to like it and I didn't really mind. I forgot most of them but I remember this one now because I was surprised by it.

Because, he says, you know how it's the odd one—a violet bears two pairs of petals, and then that odd one, a fifth, hangs down—

Aye, Sir, I says.

Well, he says, that low one is really the uppermost! Only by virtue of the violet's stalk bending near its summit does it look to us as if that highest petal is really the lowest. I fancy, he says, the two petal pairs being two married couples: myself and my wife Mary, and then Sam Coleridge and his wife. Or De Quincey and his wife Margaret, or any one of us and our wives forming the couplets surrounding that lone petal at one time or another. All alone is the lowest petal, all our lives—that one being Dorothy all by herself bearing the rest of us up.

And that is my sister, he proclaimed. She climbs Scawfell Pike, the utmost summit in England, without even knowing she is in the highest place. To Dorothy it's all just another day's adventure.

He sounded crestfallen about it. I decided not to argue that Rotha climbed Scawfell Pike with her friend Mary Barker and not alone at all. She hadn't been alone. But William seemed to think she had been.

And his pen scratched and scratched 'til I had to recut it a few more times and he filled in the old Guide with many new lines from his sister's life, but nothing at all from the life he himself was living.

Scratch scratch scratch no matter his headache, getting ready to post her living days to London and hammer them into gold he could spend.

As if he could hear me thinking, he says it's all right, you know, Dixon, that I am inserting my sister's observations into my own book. One famous writer in the family is nearly one too many and we have all suffered enough from the glare that falls upon myself as it is. You see heads bobbing outside the garden now, as we speak? Here to see the poet. Imagine our dear Dorothy if she had to endure the exposure of literary fame. Have you noticed especially lately how easily she is brought out of equilibrium into some passionate spiral of thought? And then her bowels start their torment until the strength leaves her legs and she becomes unable to see anyone and cannot even get out of bed.

This did not yet happen often and it had not happened at all since her scaling the high peak. I wondered if William felt at all to blame. I know I felt slightly sheepish as he spoke about the visitors, for I had that very afternoon sold another three of his signatures to tourists outside the gate. I cut them off copies of letters he had dictated but not sent. Myself and John Carter had a little side enterprise going. John was afraid to go and hawk the goods but he did not mind saving the signatures for me in exchange for a percentage on the quiet. But me, I have hawking and selling in my blood, and as far as I am concerned if something was destined for the fire to begin with then it is not stealing to rescue it from there. For instance, whenever I cut William's hair for him what do you think I did with the sweepings?

So when William mentioned the hardships of fame I knew only too well that there were quite a few benefits in it for him and for me. Who sails through life not having done a single thing they feel guilty about? Show me the person who claims that honour and I'll show you a real swindler.

When he read me the final version—his tale of Scawfell Pike that made it seem as if he was the one who reached that summit all by himself—you would think since he used her script that it would sound like hers, but there was something missing. His version was all tied up and had a bow on it like, and he left wild bits out. Any bits that made no sense to him or were a bit unfinished he didn't bother with. And he asked me, What do you think, Dixon? And of course I said I thought it sounded pretty good but that he shouldn't rely on me, he should send it out to people who were used to criticizing. His writer friends. Robert Southey or De Quincey.

But you are a servant and a gardener, he says to me, and if it works for you then I think it might work for the ordinary public.

And I says well, Sir, it sounds all right to me. It sounds like you got all the details about the heights and the plants and particular views from various parts like Esk Vale and Black Combe and Wasdale and Great Gable—

I did not mention things he had left out, for I couldn't quite recall if they were parts Rotha had written, or things she'd only said to me. I did not want to offend William by pointing out gaps but I was curious about one thing so I says to him, Sir, did you happen to forget the part about a ship?

What's that? he says. What ship?

And I knew I had made a mistake.

He wouldn't let it rest, now I'd let it slip.

So I told him best as I could remember, how when they were looking over Eskdale as far as the sea, Rotha saw a ship and she told the other two, Miss Barker and auld Tom the shepherd. Only Tom says then, Is it a ship? And Miss Barker assures him that yes, she sees it too and she has seen enough ships to be certain when something is a ship or not!

And of course auld Tom doesn't argue with her. The likes of shepherds or servants never argue. We might not get hoyed off the mountain but we don't want to risk our living. Only in two minutes auld Tom says real quiet like, he says look at your ship now, it's a horse! He couldn't help it.

And Rotha was over the moon laughing at herself—a gallant horse it was, she says, galloping over the sea. And Rotha tells Mary Barker: Mary, she says, you might know all about ships but our old Wise Man of the Mountains knows even more about clouds!

And Rotha says to me, Never again, Dixon, will I be satisfied with how certainly I know any single fact. For anything could indeed be completely different to what I might suppose. If you see me huff and puff all certain about anything, James, she says, remind me of our ship that turned into a horse! Away with all conclusiveness!

. . . But William doesn't write down a word of this story. He dismisses it.

Me mam used to say each one of us has a secret stone. She said it's between our neck and shoulders at the back, inside. Some people make no headway with it. But other people notice it has a little door. And then that door can open. And inside is what looks at first like a jewel. It's behind a little grate, very protected, deep in the stone inside us all. But if you look closely, if you pay attention to it, the jewel is wrapped in a membrane—it's like wasp's nest paper, it's that thin, and it breaks. It breaks open and you see what you'd thought was a jewel glimmering inside is really an all-seeing eye.

Aye, that's what Mam told me. But again—all-seeing, second sight, extra sight—to me it's, that's not what it feels like. To me it feels like, not have you got a magical, special eye, haha, not—are you going around with it wrapped or open—but are ye sighted or blind?

And either that very day or soon after it a strange fella comes to the door. Someone I had never seen yet he had a familiar look, like someone out of a fairy tale.

William spied his head bobbing beyond the hedges with very wild hair and great orbs of eyes about to pop out of his head like exploding lanterns, a man broad like a keg around but not very tall—That's the poet William Blake, says our William. Quick, tell him I am away and can't be found here for the next fortnight at least, for he's a raving lunatic and I don't want him in my house.

My William doesn't know it but one look at the face of this Blake fellow and I know I can't lie to him for those eyes'll burn through any fib like fire through that wasp's nest paper I was talking about, in fact they have already burned through any cloak I tried to wrap round my thoughts before I say a word to him.

He bursts in the door, this Blake, before I can keep him out. But he surprises me in not caring to visit William at all. It isn't William he wants to see, but the woman who saw the ship that wasn't a ship.

He has heard about it somehow.

How?

I think it was a cloud, I says to him, wanting to be helpful. From up high on a mountain it only appeared to them like a ship at first.

He looks at me pityingly.

I see my William has fled the yard and run down the bank. He has done this before when he does not have it in him to host a difficult visitor and just the thought of this William Blake had given him a blinding headache. I wondered at it, but before I could answer for it Rotha appeared at the top of the stairs looking down at Blake with an expression I had never seen on her before.

The only way I can describe the scene is that when the two glanced one upstairs and one down at the other, a beam lit from Rotha Wordsworth to William Blake like the flash you get if a lamp flame meets a cat's eye. I remembered the eye in us all that my mam described, and I knew Rotha and the Blake fellow both had that all-seeing eye sprung wide open, and our William, William Wordsworth, fled from it. But these two burned and I saw the flash before they turned back into an ordinary pair of writers such as the ones I was used to seeing at Rydal all the time.

I could not hear what they said to each other that day, though believe me I cocked my ears. What they said was muffled and I don't remember much else about their encounter, or truth be told even if it happened on the exact day when William copied down all about his sister's climb or on another day around that time, which is the time like I said when everything changed in the gleam of an eye. I feel as if it was the selfsame day. I know Rotha had her pale green gown on. And I know that the same evening or the one after or no later than two or three days after at the most, I crept in Rotha's bedroom and spied the red diary at her hand, she asleep on the bed with her pen rolled away and ink staining her bedding, and I should not have looked but I did glance at what she wrote about the talk she had with William Blake.

Blake says, she wrote, *that the ship was not merely a cloud but a Vision—*

I remember Rotha and that Blake fellow all fired up in some kind of cahoots none of the rest of the household knew about or understood. I remember her telling me of that cloud, or was it a cloud? On Scawfell Pike. The ship that turned into a horse. And my not understanding.

I remember our William, William Wordsworth, thought Blake should not have been alone with Rotha. It is all bad enough with her own imaginings, he said when he returned after having fled, but—Dixon—*you* failed to shield my sister and now she will not come out of her room.

It was one of very few times when William was angry with me and he couldn't stay angry for long—we both knew it—for hadn't he himself run away and left his sister behind the minute he saw Blake's head bobbing over the goose-berries? Fled, though he somehow believed his sister to be in trouble.

Aye, he said after he found her upstairs unwilling to come down for prayers or even to eat a bit of pudding, that man would be better locked up at Whitmore or Warburton's than free to roam around our paradise here, troubling our peace to match his own madness.

I knew he couldn't mean this, for Whitmore was a bad place to which no one should be sent for we all knew their friend Mary Lamb had been there and what she had seen, if she was telling the truth, and she always, it was said, told the truth no matter that she had murdered her own mother and no matter what else she did. In fact they all said, William and Rotha and everybody, that whenever she was not locked up Mary Lamb was the most sane person any of them ever knew. And according to Miss Lamb they force-fed you at Whitmore 'til the spoon tore the last teeth from your gums and they beat you with brooms, and that was only the start. So for him to say Blake should be in Whitmore I knew our William was far from happy.

And what about Rotha?

A cloud but not a cloud, she wrote, *and Blake bade me wait and watch. Wait and watch and when you find yourself on a ship as foretold by this cloud, know it is the ship of your transformation!*

What did Blake mean by that?

I sat on her bed and read what he'd said and I did not understand what it meant, not then.

—& he said Dorothy, the ship will take you from one life to another—the ship will first falter & run aground—beware that you do not rely on anyone to save you, least of all family. Very least of all the one on whom you most rely for your heart's ease, for that ship is already long wrecked—but lo, from this new shipwreck is born a horse you have rightly called gallant of neck & head, & aboard that horse—if you leap in time—soars your freedom!

That is all Rotha wrote of William Blake's words the day he visited after she climbed Scawfell Pike.

At that time I had no notion what any of it meant. It was not until more than a year later, after we had all been away and she came back from Europe with her brother and their wife Mary, it all came clear.

Aye, the wink of an eye.

Did ye ever notice—ye must've—how you can dwell in one place and things are going pretty well and everything seems to be one way, with sweet accord and a fair amount of knowing what's what—everything has its own place and there is a kind of peace over things, or if not peace then at least there is a comfort or a routine. The house at Rydal was full of a kind of comfort or even I might call it love. Compared with the rest of England I mean, where there was no comfort and things were not full of love.

All I have told ye so far was before 1820 and like I said over the next few seasons I had to go away off and on and so did the little family. We briefly went our own ways. And it seems, have ye lot noticed this? That the minute ye turn your back for even a moment, well it's like what happens in a garden if you leave it. I'll wager this happens to ye with your flowers and fields. Everything goes all topsy-turvy!

Ye head for the clover fields one year and then ye turn your sweet little backs for what seems like no time at all. Maybe ye try a cowslip field for a day or an elder grove or a place where all your honey comes from yet another sort of bloom ye've been meaning to try for some time and suddenly you get the chance!

That's what happened to me, like, and from the way things turned out I am telling ye it must've happened to Rotha at the same time. We both turned our faces away from each other for that instant, and when we came back . . . I find it a bit upsetting how nothing stays the same though I know ye lot know how to keep yourselves safe through the biggest sorts of changes in weather or in society or whatever might befall ye. At least so far. But ye have me beat on that score. The difference in Rotha when the little family returned! You might as well have called a magician into Rydal to hoy a cloth over us all then whisk that cloth away only for us to find we could recognize nothing from before.

4

On the bat's back I do fly

ooooo

J ames, when you leave the presence of our garden, whether you go indoors to Rydal Mount or travel as Rotha and her brother and Mary did to behold cities, or strive to raise your sister Penny from the dead . . . once you leave off touching the land with your own feet and hands and senses . . . once you leave our influence . . .

Have you beseeched your pillow as to what you, or Penny, or Rotha, or I, Sycamore, can do against brutality, except withstand it?

What does it mean to withstand?

Brutality's weapon is the lie that it is stronger than our withstanding. As if withstanding has no power. No. In our presence brutality is pathetic, dwindling. Withstanding is our glory. Our conversation is eternal dignity. We are the realm of life.

Remember that, James, when you imagine yourself bereft.

eleven

ooooo

IT WAS CHRISTMAS EVE OF 1820 that they were to return. Christmas Eve! I was working over in Ambleside the week before when Grace Threlkeld got a note over to me saying the Wordsworths wanted their house prepared for that day and everything ready for the following day, Christmas Day. And they'd like to have myself there to help with the preparations and to be there on the day itself and the days following as well as the months if I felt like staying on. My hut was even waiting for me and I was glad. For the hut was mine and mine only and I slept better in it than at Ambleside or anywhere. So I gave up my Ambleside lodgings and went back to my true home.

Leaving Rydal for that while had made me uneasy, as if my standing with the little family might go wobbly. I didn't want it wobbly. I wanted to be in with them like a wren in its nest. And now I'd be back for Christmas Eve and Christmas Day and Saint Stephen's Day an' all, the very day of the little wren!

The wren, the wren,
The king of all birds—

Saint Stephen's Day
He got lost in the furze—

The wren is a kingly bird yet a humble little bird. That's somehow the way I like to think of what the little family has done for me. They made me a kingly bird in my own spot. Maybe not in an important kingdom but . . . I felt like a little wren with, you know, I'd fluff my feathers and I'd fly here and there and I felt as happy as if I'd been wearing a little crown.

And that's how I felt on the Christmas Eve when I was getting the place ready for their return. Cutting the holly branches for the mantel and a few bits of moss an' all, for I knew how Rotha loved moss. The green of it! I knew just what to do and what to gather and when to show up with it in my arms. That little wren in the song got lost in the furze but I was never lost as long as the Wordsworths gave me a home.

I had not known to expect their return so I had quite a few jobs I was doing here and there around Ambleside. So for me it was a Christmas surprise. But I always found a way to put off anybody who wanted me if the Wordsworths needed me an' all. Mrs. Hills and Mrs. Aglionby and all the rest of them who I have helped over the years—they have all been very kind to me and for that I can tell ye I have always considered myself a favourite of Fortune. But my gratitude has been always and forever foremost towards the little family at Rydal Mount.

And if I'm telling the whole truth, I had another reason to look sharp soon as the note came telling me of the Wordsworths' Christmas Eve arrival—I had invited my sister

Penny for Christmas dinner at my Ambleside lodgings and she was on her way from Manchester. I had sent her the money and she was coming. Ye'd be surprised how much money I've managed to save up. I've even got quite a few railway shares, but don't tell that to any of the family! For they despise any talk of a railway. Although who minds that now, with Mary the only one left? Aye, Mary likely wouldn't be averse to having a few railway shares herself. Any rate, Penny was coming to share my ham and bread with me for a small Christmas at my lodgings, but soon as I heard the Wordsworths were coming home, I felt then that this was my one and perfect chance to bring our Penny over to Rydal Mount and get her foot in the door.

I thought the family would be glad to be home and good cheer would prevail and no one would think twice about Penny's presence.

I told Penny to wait until noon on Christmas Day then come to my hut which I would have warmed up for us, and we would have our ham and bread together and she could wait for me while I did my afternoon's work. And I'd keep an eye out for the right moment to tell the Wordsworths that Penny had come to see me for Christmas, and that by the way she happened to be free should they need a hand with the multitude of tasks involved in settling back into Rydal after their journey . . .

All of that I would figure out how to say in the moment, when that moment came. I was relying on Christmas happiness to carry the day as Christmas Day was as ye know Rotha's birthday as well as the Christ child's. It had always been a time of opening summer's cowslip wine, and card games and mince pies and a great roast and a slab of jellied tongue.

So help me I should have known by that time in my life— I mean yes I was still young but I had been through enough to know that the best-sounding predictions in the world are often the most foolish, and no one can tell what might fall asunder just when you think you have a keen eye for a situation.

So me and the maid Fanny and even John Carter were all looking forward to the family's return on Christmas Eve. We had the house bright with holly branches and the larder ready. But when they arrived—William and Mary looked all right if a bit tired—but Rotha looked to me as if she had all her force kicked out of her. Her force was ousted by some violent sort of kicking! The same as if ye lot were—imagine— flying over your fields with all your summer powers, honey and everything all full-charged, revellin' in your own flying, going Whee! Over the fields ye carouse—

But then ye get the air swept out from under ye by some vicious storm.

Aye, as violent as that.

Some sort of storm had happened, and Rotha stumbled out of the carriage and hardly acknowledged me though I felt my heart leap for her, sad as her state appeared. She was still my wild-eyed Rotha and her curls still bounced. But I saw straight away and I confirmed this over the next days that Rotha'd had her will—to walk, to stay upright, to move, to live the life she was made for—blasted out from under her by a force of, aye some gale force of . . . disappointment.

Some unexpected letdown.

Punctured breath—aye, something took her breath away.

And it's one thing for ye with your wings, but for us without wings ye might need to be told our breath feeds the movement in our legs. Aye, it was all one wasn't it, with Rotha? Her leg-power was all one with her breath. And her breath's what she'd had kicked or pushed out by the time they came back . . .

And I knew there had to be more to it than what William told me, which was that the journey had been long and Rotha was very tired. And when he said it his face was made of very well-placed stones while Rotha's face looked like anything but, or like stones that were dissolving to powder and forming some completely new kind of face as she struggled upstairs away from us.

Will your sister be all right? I says.

And William says aye, you know how Dorothy cannot stand hustle and bustle, and it was true. But when he said it his face closed in over that story very final and clever.

I mean, people are a bit self-clevering, aren't they. You cannot get away from it. They . . . we . . . all want to be thought well of. We don't want to put forth our failings and foolishness. But ye know, from start to finish, from the first minute I ever laid eyes on William's sister, I knew she wasn't self-clevering in any way. She was simply laid out like a field full of daisies. Not simple, mind. Ye know how deep, but even that's not the part I mean. Self-clevering . . . making yourself into a pleasing or nicely complicated intelligent person for other people to look upon and admire. There was none of that with her, but plenty with William.

Admiration?

Haha, I can't imagine in Rotha the bit of people's brains that wants admiration, and nearly everbody's got it. I suppose even pigs and lambs have got it. They want to be looked on with favour. And William did. But she was lacking that bit. You could say she was missing it . . . but that wouldn't be right. Missing is when something leaves a space. She had an absence of something that made for a glory of something else. Maybe glory's a strong word. But I know ye have seen a long view over the fells from up at the top—seen the way things are laid out, just themselves.

Oh the bits of sun fallen like melted coins on the green. Ha, the tarn like pewter. And the old rough stones, nothing to be admired haha, yet you can't help feeling something dissolve that hard, persistent stone in your own heart.

And on Christmas morning she came downstairs early, looking for me to help her with the part I help her with every Christmas morning after we have put the finishing touches on the greenery. And that is the pastry figure of the Christ child, which goes in the pastry manger full of sweet mince.

I hope the mince is all right, she says, as I am using left-over from last Christmas.

You'll have topped the brandy up though, says I?

Aye, she says, in April and June before we went away, and she hands me a bit on the end of a spoon and I pronounce it fine indeed. It has a fatty edge and a fruity depth and is not too sweet and the brandy wasn't cheap, nor were the nutmeg and mace.

Sometimes, I says, mince gets better the longer it ages.

Aye, she says, mixing very cold water into the fat and flour for the pastry, but her hand is trembling.

Are you all right, says I?

I wasn't a good traveller, she says.

No?

The others got up very early each day, she says.

But here we are up before all today, I says.

Yes, she says, but I'm home, aren't I. I am all right when I am home. But on our travels the others rose early while I had not the strength. And, James, I did not see what they saw. I lay in the carriage and slept through the loveliest parts of the road all along the Rhine! I overdid it walking in Ghent and my bowels raged, and James, you know how when my bowels give out, it is not long afterwards that I will lose all power in my legs.

Oh, Miss.

Bowels! Leg weakness! Exhaustion in Brussels . . .

I'm sorry, Miss D.

I loved watching her do the part of the pastry where the fat gets cut into the flour so that it is like wet sand with knobs of fat throughout. It goes from silky fine flour to that knobbly damp sand and then in goes a splash more of cold water and magically she swirls the wooden spoon until it gathers the dough in a fine, fat ball ready for my part. I was sorry that while she seemed so sad at the pastry board, here I was finding it satisfactory to watch the pastry form like God forming

Adam and Eve out of fine, dry dust. For that was what us two were about to accomplish, myself and Dorothy, except it was the other way around. Instead of God making man, man was making the form of the Christ child. You make the ordinary mince tarts like, by the dozens, then at the last comes this, where you make the manger in a wee loaf pan and you make the baby Jesus out of the last of the pastry and you lay him in the manger. And I was the head one for carving the little baby if I do say it meself.

Even though neither of us went to church this was a blessed moment and I waited for her to give me the pastry in my hand, for the feel of it—so fat and cold—gave me a thrill like etching the Pace eggs over Easter. Because with the Christ child I was standing near Rotha and we were making the body of the Christmas child together as if we were its earthly mam and dad. But I never said this to her of course. I wonder what she would have thought if I had.

And I thought of what she said about being home. How she was all right as long as she was home.

Home was a funny thing with her. When she was at home, all she wanted to do was dream of travels afar. Glorious travels, either remembered or planned. Over Scotland's highlands and the Alps and now all those places she had just been, places a man like me hardly dreams of unless there is a war. Days after her last topping up of brandy in the mincemeat she had left England and gone to Brussels and Cologne, and up the Rhine to Switzerland, then Lucerne and the Italian lakes and Milan, and back to Switzerland and then France, for they stayed in Paris a whole month. I was giddy thinking about it.

But she had not been happy.

Were you thinking of home all the while, Miss?

Home, yes, she says. All through the Italian lakes I could think only of our own dear Lakes here. And the spires and glorious towers of Liège I saw only by moonlight, for I lay faint through entire days. The same happened in Cologne. I had to resist the temptation to walk because if I did walk even a little bit too far I would pay for it dearly soon afterward.

But what about London, Miss?

I knew she loved London and I knew she had spent November there and no matter how much she loved the Lakes she saw beauty in London. She saw it when she visited Mary and Charles Lamb. She'd go in a courtyard or back lane and she'd look at the way old stones had worn on the corner of a building and she'd marvel at the loveliness of a puddle, only a rain-puddle. She'd come back and she'd say—I mean I think sometimes she should've been a painter—she'd say James, there was a pigeon in the puddle and I watched it have a drink. Its bright brown eye looked straight at me, and its neck was iridescent turquoise, indigo and amethyst.

And I'd say, Miss, if you don't mind me saying, a pigeon to me looks completely grey.

Yes, she'd answer, but the drab, grey bits only serve to make it shimmer the more.

She'd go on like that and all she'd been to was some sooty lane behind Mary Lamb's house, and you'd think she'd been to that place Sam Coleridge made up that begins with an X or a Z, I forget the name. Domes and that. But I think like Sam she was in that place even when she wasn't there. I mean she could go in any ordinary place and she would see it exalted, like.

And she finishes up the pastry so it's springy like the flesh of a real newborn babe and she lays it on the floured board and she says, London was all right, James. In fact I would like to go back and spend more time with Mary Lamb. But before we got to London I knew I was a failure as a travel- ler. I felt so very far from the way I felt on my travels twenty years ago—or even five years!

I looked at her sideways, puzzled. When somebody has made an impression on you while ye were both young, and later you see them and they have grown a lot more haggard, you mightn't notice them getting old at first. You still have an outdated version of them in your head. It hovers over their new-old self and you don't see at first that big changes have taken place, that the person is closer to death, or some jolt has caved them in like a shore that has been eaten away.

And I knew from my mam that when a woman turns fifty she becomes different. I could see that Rotha had not for some time looked young on the face of it, but I had to make a real effort to see this because to me I did not see the surface of a person and never had. But I could tell something in Rotha had been shaken.

I clamped the urge to remind her how little more than a year and a half earlier she had climbed Scawfell Pike with no hint of weak legs and if anything she had more power than a woman half her age! But I could feel the letdown in her at her European failure, and even as she lamented, I had the feeling there was some shock she was leaving unsaid. What was it?

What had happened to Rotha when they were in Europe, her and William and their wife Mary?

She gave me the pastry and I started feeling the lump with my hands and stretching it ever so gentle here and there to make the parts change to living limbs, or limbs and a body and a wee face belonging to a living child, and not just any child but the Christ child. Baking the pastry Christ was one of the old-fashioned things she loved to do and she took my finished babe in her hands with great care and she says to me, James, you know I once had a little boy child of my own?

And I says hesitant like, Miss, you mean your young nephew Tom? For I knew Tom had been the son of William and Mary and had died when he was little, soon after Catherine, and I did not want to start a mournful conversation.

But she says no, not the son of our wife Mary. Our own son—William's and mine! Little Basil.

Now I didn't have a clue what to say as this seemed very unlikely. But so had other things, like the window concealed in her bedroom wall. So I kept quiet and kneaded the pastry Christ child best as I could without interrupting or looking worried.

And she says yes—William and I had a child together just as Mary and Charles Lamb have theirs even now.

So I says, I couldn't help it like, Miss I says, you mean Mary and Charles Lamb, brother and sister, have a little one between 'em?

And she says yes—a brother and sister can be very excellent parents together, as William and I were for our little Basil.

That's when I wondered for the first time if John Carter and half the village were right all along—she must be raving and how had I not seen it before?

And she takes the baby Jesus made of pastry and slides him in the cooker and I must say he's fine-looking when he goes in and I hope he'll weather the heat all right and not shatter or sink and lose his perfection, and here she hands me a second lump of pastry and says, James, can you please make me another child?

I wonder what she's about. I hope she's not wanting me to make the baby Thomas who died. Or is she trying to have me make young Basil who I don't believe is real? I don't know what to think but then she says, And James, make it a girl.

A girl, Miss?

Yes—a Christmas birthday sister for the Christ child.

At last I twig that she means make herself as a babe, for this is the day she was born. And she says please, James, do make the girl. So I fashion the baby lass and she pops that one in the cooker right beside the Christ child. The two of them together come out looking absolutely perfect.

And she says there. There's little mortal Dorothy and her Divine brother, both born on this day, keeping each other company in the manger. She can be his little doll.

And the way she says doll I remember how only William ever calls her that, and hardly ever, only when he thinks nobody else can hear. Other Dorothys get called Doll all the time, but not her. She's nowt like a doll though she is small. If you could trap a lion inside a doll maybe. Anyway she lays baby Jesus in his manger on the mincemeat, and in she lays the baby Dorothy right beside him for all the world as if he has a doll, and she says, I forgot to make them a pastry blanket!

But the house was waking up—it was getting on for ten in the morning and they were all still tired from their journey but they vowed they would have a good Christmas all the same, with the roast and the mince pies and a few games of cards, but there was one window not done up yet—the kitchen window—and I went out to gather a few branches to deck it out same as the others. And from what I can gather while I was out William came downstairs lured by the fragrant mince tarts that had come out of the oven and he was not exactly jolly but he felt happy enough about the tarts and he poked his nose over the loaf-pan manger with the baby Jesus in it and he says, What's this? And he picks up the pastry Dorothy. And he says, You made a spare? And he cracks the legs off it and pops them in his mouth before she can stop him. And I think, mind ye cannot be certain but all the same, something about that . . . a doll made in the likeness of a person, then someone by mistake, not knowing like, breaks part of it . . . Well my mam had candles like that, she fashioned her neighbours out of stubs while the wax was still warm. And anything good she wished for a certain neighbour, she wished it over their wax figurine. And if anyone crossed her, well their wax figure would meet a pin or two and that was how many a fate was met, according to my mam. Of course ye don't know if the good or the bad was a direct cause like.

But I was out cutting the holly boughs and I got carried away in the woods. I found a sweet-smelling spot to sit, very quiet, and a few snowflakes floated down, and a bird or two sang their carols for me and maybe I dozed off but surely not as long as all that! For I woke and saw by the sky that it was already past noon. And I frowned because I'd told my sister Penny to come to my hut at noon so I could eat with her then introduce her to the family and try and see if she could stay for a little while into the new year. That had been my plan or my hope. And if into the new year by even a few days, why, then, it couldn't be too hard to extend Penny's stay and maybe have her start doing some little job or other. A new start for Penny.

I headed for my hut, praying Penny had waited and could come to the house now properly with me by her side to introduce her.

But there was no sign of my sister.

I went in the house and looked around. Rotha had gone upstairs—I saw the legless baby version of herself on the counter—and William was in his study and Mary off somewhere with the cat Rotha hated because it hunted birds. With that cat beside her Mary was in her own world. So there was no one I could ask had my sister Penny come to the door.

I searched to see if Penny had crouched in some nook waiting for me, her brother, hiding like. Oh, I felt awful. But no. My sister wasn't in the pantry and she was nowhere around the landing or in any of the rooms. So I went upstairs to Rotha's room—Rotha lay on the bed—and I said, very quiet like, Miss, you don't happen to have seen anyone come to the door around noon?

Who do you mean? she says. Were we expecting someone?

Miss, only I told my sister to wait until noon and I would be able to see her today . . .

I thought you told us you had a brother, James.

No. Miss. A sister. My sister Penny.

I knew I had told her about Penny more than once and why she kept hearing brother though I said sister every time, I'll never understand.

You have a sister?

Yes.

She hasn't got ginger hair?

Penny, yes, Miss, she does. My mam called her Penny on account of it.

Oh.

Have you seen her?

I only saw a young red-haired beggar at the back door. A ragged-looking lass. Are you saying, James, that this might have been a relative of yours?

Eh, Miss D . . . I think . . .

For I took her for a beggar and I pressed sixpence upon her and asked her to be off and then I shut the door.

I see, Miss. Did she not ask for me?

I don't know what she said, James. I do not remember if words were coming out of her mouth or if her lips simply chattered with the cold. For my own part I was loath to leave the door open and let our heat out into the cold day, so I shut it rather quickly. I do remember that I thought she would've been a bonny lass if she'd only straighten her back, but she had that sunken look of girls who meet hopelessness in their youth and so look strangely old.

I still held a branch of holly and Rotha noticed it, and she asked if I would lay it on her sill to cheer her as she rested before the evening's feasting and merriment. And I fastened it for her on that sill where the same little wren and robin who had carolled me to sleep might come and visit Rotha. Their carols had come at the wrong time for Penny and I did not know how I could forgive the little birds for singing to me so sweetly in the woods, or myself for succumbing to their voices.

Ye know I could've made the bones of what I need moneywise without this job.

Moneywise I always made do. Going outside and not inside, that's how I manage. And between me and Penny I was the one who no one could trap indoors for a minute let alone a day or a year or a life. But Penny, no. Dank. Deafening. Reeking. Damp. Years. No break for the privy. If the lasses weren't wet enough from the splashing machines, they wet themselves! Whereas me, all along ye found me outside didn't ye? Where scent fills the hay and feathers cling tight to the living birds and my own lungs swell pink and glittering and full of rose-sweet air.

Outside!

Aye, I had all my stolen bits of time—they add up here with the Wordsworths—time when nobody is looking over my shoulder! Even William says to me James, he says, I fear this place belongs to you more than it has ever belonged to us. And when did William ever lie down and fall asleep where the limbs meet the trunk on your sycamore? He's too tall for a start. Whereas me, I'm small enough to fit right in them crooks, and a knot that looks hard to anyone who hasn't tried it turns out to be a comfortable pillow for my head.

The dreams I've had in your tree!

But Penny, when did she ever know any sleep but pure exhaustion? I mean if William caught me dreaming on the job he'd count it as my conjuring some answer to a question he'd asked me. Can I grow ginger between the cabbages? He having read an article about it. Ginger grows sideways and needs little soil, according to the latest Royal Botanic expert. Do I bother William with the argument that it is far too cold in England for tropical plants? No! My whole tactic is this: find a way to do what the master would like done, and when it's done congratulate him on his vision.

And I do what he asks but the fantastic side is all the days and weeks and months of time on my own in the gardens or on errands or anywhere out-of-doors in a free man's air. Free to think whatever I want! Every once in a blue moon William spies me on my own having a moment and he says Dixon, here you are in solitary splendour! A jealous look on his face if I'm not imagining it—for what wouldn't he give to get in his punt and row off to Grasmere Island instead of trudging to the stamp office or having tea with all and sundry or going off to wring money out of his publishers— always on the hunt. When I count up my personal moments of solitary splendour they might easily outspan William's, and for that I am glad to be here. But when I think of how I failed Penny I cannot be glad for long.

Penny. She had to face the world. I couldn't help it. Her brother. She was not her own. That is the point of the world now. To make us not our own.

I was not fit. Because I didn't find a way. A way out. A way of escape. A way of freedom. I didn't find it for Penny. My sister. My sister Penny. The crowd here at Rydal did not care to help me free her.

twelve

ooooo

PENNY MUST'VE BEEN SEVENTEEN by the time Rotha
turned her away that Christmas day. I saw a little sister in
her but she saw herself as grown, though like all the lads and
lasses ruined in the mills she had hardly grown an inch
from the time she started. If anything she was shrunken or
stooped so as to seem smaller than she had been. It galled
her to be treated by me as a bairn, and I admit her face was
grey as an old woman's. She said I was barmy to try and lift
her out of her situation. She herself thought it a better situation than I thought it. I've been doing all right, she says, for
I have had an offer from an old man called Nahum Troake to
be his servant and I think I will do it, so stop thinking you're
any better off than I am!

What does Mr. Troake do for a living? I asked her. She
said nothing and I felt bad. I wondered if the Wordsworths'
situation had rubbed off on me and made me seem as if I
thought over-highly of myself. For there was no question
that in the eyes of the world and in my own eyes I had risen
higher than Penny had.

And for all I knew maybe William was noticing likewise about himself and his own sister.

I wished I could have warned William that a brother can look after his younger sister only so much and then she has her own way of wanting to look after herself. And no matter how sick or poorly or wretched she seems to that brother, if she wants to get up on her own feet and see through her own eyes the older brother cannot make her see through his.

Could I have warned William? Or do I know these things only now myself, after the years that have gone by? Some things I don't know and will never know and other things I know but I don't know how or when I learned them!

For instance I know now that after that Christmas Penny did go to the door of the man called Nahum Troake. It's a hovel not a house, and it is in one of the worst parts of Manchester, and she says yes, Sir, I cannot go back to the factory because of my deformity, and I have no help from my brother so I have come to take your offer. And Penny has worked for Nahum Troake since that day, scrubbing his step and cooking his joint and I have been frightened to imagine what else. He is older than her by thirty years and once when I had a chance to ask her, Penny, is Nahum Troake at least a mild-tempered man?, she told me his temper is no better and no worse than that of any other fella making his living as part rat-catcher, part vagabond. But is he mostly kind to you? I said. She gave me no answer and I have often tried to fathom the look on her face but its meaning I will never know.

And here I was back at Rydal with the Wordsworths and it was them I had to mind, not my sister, and it was not easy. It took us all some time to get used to being there after we had all been away.

It's as if a house knows when you've gone, it knows you've abandoned it and it feels angry with you and it takes its own back against you. Ye feel this in the hives, don't ye. Ye have to be homebodies for the home to take you in as a home should. Each space in house or hive has the spirit in it of whoever lives there and the space gets used to our spirits. And if we go away, our spirits in that house die away like wraiths and then blow away, and when we come back we have to start all over again breathing life into that home.

And that is what I tried to do after the little family came back from Europe. We all worked hard but everyone had a frayed edge, irritated like, or singed somehow, too dry, and crying out from thirst in body and mind. Things didn't feel right and I had no one to talk about it with. I mean John Carter was there keeping William's paperwork up to date and the business affairs in order with the stamps and that, but John had no notion of feelings in the house.

To him everything is made of stone or wood or paper or metal and nothing is made of tears or loneliness whereas I think loneliness is a thing like wood or grass, you can feel it as surely as you can feel a stone. And Rotha when she came back was like a stone separate from the others, and she was heavy and clammy and her legs often would not move, or she chose not to move them, according to Mary for one.

Rotha was disappointed in herself after their voyage but that wasn't it, I could tell that wasn't everything.

Mary, unusual for her, took me aside and asked me what I thought about some of Rotha's health bits and bobs—what Mary called *mysteries*. William never wondered like that. He faced Rotha whatever way she happened to be with each— let's say ailment, for want of a better word. He believed his sister. He accepted what she said and the words that she used for what was happening to her. I felt as if he knew all along why the things that were happening to her happened. And I think he did know back then. He still remembered. But for Mary it was different.

It was as if Mary thought Rotha was covering something up, covering the truth up, by using the word weakness, for example. I mean Rotha often had pain, or she often had weakness. Sometimes she had both pain and weakness. But the weakness itself, Mary was very puzzled by that.

She says, Why is it one day Dorothy can't support herself on her two perfectly sensate legs, but no, she has to be . . . we have to carry her? Yet on another day she can walk quite well, or she can at least allow herself to be brought out to the terrace and stay in the sun for the good part of a day and eat a substantial dinner such as a duck leg and not one but three jam tarts. Two days apart!

Now what's going on with Dorothy today, Mary would say. Is it the pain or is it the weakness?

She sounded very matter of fact but there was something else under the matter of factness. Pain Mary could forgive but weakness was another story. If I myself gave up every time I felt weak, she says, why I'd have been bedridden myself, years ago. One has to keep going!

Rotha's weakness was something Mary found very hard to understand and I suspect she found it hard to believe.

Did I think Rotha was putting it on?

Mary would ask me as if I knew.

And I did know, and I do know.

But some states are not easy to explain to a person missing a kind of sight. I'm not saying Mary was less sharp than the rest of the household. She was very sharp. I'm saying that as regards Rotha, specially over a word like *weakness*, Mary had trouble—she had to pin it down. She wanted to pin down something I knew did not want to be pinned.

Rotha's weakness wasn't only in her body. It was not this muscle or that muscle giving out though sometimes it had that appearance.

If I had to put it into words Mary might understand, though I don't think she will, but if I had to try, what would I say?

(Sigh)

After that Christmas I had the luxury to think about this and to watch Rotha more than in the old days. For William was back in the thick of business talking with John Carter half the time and working the other half on articles, not poems but essays and revisions and that. And he says to me with a kind of desperate look on his face, Dixon, he says, it is one thing to go off on travels such as a Continental Tour, but it is another to come home again and have to re-enter the system of operations from which you extracted yourself to embark on those travels. System of operations is how he put it. I remember that. I remember thinking it sounded like the way the bosses had run things in Penny's factory. All the chains and cogs and hooks and hammers in place.

Which was the opposite of how things were going up in Rotha's room. On her good days she had bits of paper flying everywhere, and her pen and notebooks open all over the place as she tried to write down her memories of the latest tour as well as revise her own Scottish *Recollections,* the book she had begun years before and worked on over and over again, hoping to publish it though William had told her no.

But I was watching her.

And I knew she was not right especially on the days when her legs gave out and she could do no more than lie in bed, and on those days I watched her and waited and I wanted to coax out of her what was going on but I knew the best way for that was to listen and wait and keep taking Little Miss Belle in and out to do her business. The dog nearly considered itself mine, for I talked to it more than anyone and Rotha did not find comfort in it as she had done before.

Would Rotha have changed as much if I had not been apart from the little family while they went to Europe? I wondered often but I tried not to go too far down that road.

My mam accused me of making myself out as far more important to the Wordsworths than I really was. She says I had a cheek that way even regarding my own fam'ly. Thought a bit too much of myself, like.

And not long after that Christmas, on a Thursday in January when William and Mary were in Keswick, the dog became frightened to death because we had thunder and lightning that came close enough to shake the whole place, and dogs loathe that with all their hearts. They don't know what to be doing with themselves, and Little Miss Belle hunkered down under the bed quivering with fright, like, and Rotha was not far behind her in the fear department. I was nearly as bad myself as it was a sky-blackening storm and each thunderclap felt like it had a mind to crack your sycamore and send it crashing through our roof. There was a closer crash right in the bedroom and I said don't worry, Miss D, it's only your cup and saucer tipped off your sill, and she says are you sure, James?

And she is sick on the floor right then and she says James everything is swaying, is everything swaying?

And for a minute I don't know if things are swaying or not because the stench of the sick is great and branches are going mad against the window and Rotha is falling around as if the floor is heaving up and down and she cries out, Where is my brother?

The way she cries it out is bloodcurdling in a way that makes me know it's no good at all to tell her where William really is, which is in Keswick on notary affairs, for he told her that was where he was going and any rate it's a good fifteen miles away so I says hang on, Dorothy—at that moment I call her by the name her brother calls her—I'll clean the mess up, I says, and I'll get lavender and we won't open the window but we'll lie you down on the bed until it passes—

And that is what happens, only as I go to lower her on her bed she hauls me down on it with her and holds me tight, sobbing, William!

Miss, I says, wanting to bring her back to herself, and to know I was me, like. James Dixon, not William, but—

I feared you were lost to us all!

And I ken she is somewhere else. She is grabbing on to me but she is sure she is grabbing on to her brother.

Where are we?

Little Miss Belle is whimpering under the bed fit to break your heart but there's nowt I can do about her now except hum my trouble song and hope it calms everybody down.

I start it low at first to make sure it won't scare Rotha though like I told ye I'd calmed her with a song of mine before but that was a different song.

There's no tune to this one, like. It's more of a rumble with a moaning song that has no words unless I am by myself, and then the words it has only I can hear and the trees or whatever animal or bird is about. But now all I do is the rumbling low part, so holding on to me lying there on the bed what she feels is like what you might feel if you were pressed down into the ground and you sensed a herd of horses rumbling in the distance.

And she says please keep singing. Does she know yet it's me she's with?

And I says, it's not really singing, Miss, as much as it is a kind of old chant.

And she says whatever it is, don't stop.

And it remains this way, her holding on to me and me doing my song with no words, until the thunder subsides. Once I think the cracks are fading off I wiggle away a bit to see if I can get out of Rotha's hold, and she does, she lets me go.

I'll open the window an inch, I says, because the air was sucked out of the room and we could hardly breathe. When I opened it a wild cold breath rushed in and I felt very relieved. I could smell the lavender over the top of the sick, and the rainy smell came in and freshened the room and by and by Rotha rolled over and looked at me and knew I was me and not William. If there is one thing about Rotha it's that she comes back to herself with a clear eye no matter where she has been in her mind.

I was on our ship, she says.

Ship, Miss?

And she says yes, the ship we boarded to come home from Boulogne—William and myself and Mary—that storm!

I didn't know there was a storm, Miss.

It was a week of gales! And we had to stand on the beach with our baggage every day waiting for the breakers to sub-side before they would let us on the boat to cross the channel to Dover. And once they let us on the boat, we knew they should not have done so, for the ship was far too small—it was the only one they allowed as fit to sail the conditions—but it was insufficient, tiny really, with only one real sailor—and the waves wild and the winds malevolent—James, I knew then that I was on the ship that had been foretold and prophesied—

Prophesied, Miss?

And she proceeded—but I felt very sheepish because I knew the prophecy from having read it in her red diary—the story of Mr. William Blake and what he had said about the ship-cloud of Scawfell Pike foretelling a real ship that she would find herself on. I knew the prophetic part of the story already—but I let her go on telling me as if I had not read any of it in her private notebook.

And I resolved at that moment, because of the guilt I felt, that I would have to soon find some way to let her know I had been reading it. Some things are all right done in a devious manner, but other things are not, or things develop in a way that makes you change your mind.

So we shouldn't have been on that ship at all, she says. There was an Irish woman and a little Italian man both curled up down the stairs in beds alongside mine—I descended there to shelter from the waves but William and Mary remained up on deck. And before we were out of the port ten minutes we had a frightful heaving on the waves! Our ship lurched and grated—parts of it flew asunder and water came rushing in—the grating noise went on for many seconds as we ran aground. The sound was like a building being razed. I thought the ceiling would crash down and crush us before water inundated and drowned us! The Italian man leapt off his bed and knelt praying on the floor. But the Irish woman was kind— she enfolded me—she was large and I am so small, it was like being enfolded in a mother's velvet arms.

But the violent tearing-apart sounds kept on going and I saw William and Mary in my mind up top being cast into the sea and I saw everyone at home mourning for us as we had mourned when we lost my brother John—it was just the same as the way John was drowned! His ship was not far from shore either, yet all hands were lost, and now we were re-enacting his death!

All this happened in a few instants and with all my heart, she says, I wished I were a large, strong man able to save people, instead of a tiny person who might as well not even exist. So small was I and so large the wreck and the storm and the roar of the timbers being torn apart . . .

James! When you are in a boat running aground it is as if the boat's bones—its beams and all the solid parts of its construction—are of one piece with your own bones—you become the grounded creature and as you lose equilibrium you fall askew. You know you will flounder and break apart on the stones. Water will flood the boat's lungs and your own lungs, erasing your life's every breath from first to last!

No, I says, for she was quaking. You're here. Back safe.

No, James, she says. I'm not.

Yes, I says. You're safe here, home at Rydal Mount.

And she says no, James, home is not safe. You think it is because you don't know what happened next.

I says what was that, Miss?

She says, James, our ship tilted and swayed but I found my feet and rushed up to the deck. And found William with his shirt and coat off, stripped to the waist!

She waited for my reaction but saw I had not understood.

James, he was poised to dive for his safety and swim ashore! I shouted to him and he was right startled, and he muttered, Dorothy, I believed you and Mary were lost down in the cabins. For he had seen Mary flung down the stairs by the storm although I had not seen her. And he says to me, Sister, I thought there was no hope for either of you, so . . .

I asked her, incredulous, William was ready to swim and leave ye?

And she says he was.

And I says, No, Miss, surely not.

But she says oh yes, I know it true and strong as the storm we have just witnessed.

And I don't know what to tell her for my troubles song is not the right song for a sunken heart.

But don't worry, she says. It's as if she feels she suddenly needs to save me from thinking what I am thinking. She turns stiff and brightens like. I can't make out what kind of brightness it is. There is something about it that I don't like.

We were saved, she says—we were in very hard shape but in half an hour we saw the tide was on its way out, and we were close enough to shore so as not to be engulfed—but—

She fell face down on her blankets thoroughly limp and I knew she had just been through the shipwreck again. I wondered if she had been reliving it again and again while we were all downstairs or outside, oblivious.

She spoke not another word about William having been ready to swim and leave her and Mary for dead. But her plight on that day remains a thing I cannot put out of my mind. Yet there was something in her that refused on the face of it to think any the less of William. She tried as hard as anything to believe he was as devoted a husband and brother as ever.

But in my mind the scene on the ship called into question the idea that he had ever been devoted to anyone but himself.

This is a hard thing for a servant to believe about his master and I am not saying I carry a grudge or that I think of it often. Only it is a thorn, a mind-prick, a puncture hole, in what used to be my dream about the little fam'ly.

A dream is a thing that can live even with a few puncture holes if the wind is right and the summer holds and a garden like this garden grows all around.

Yet somewhere in me on the day that storm came to Rydal and Rotha was sick and I helped her recover and she told me about the shipwreck and William's plan to lunge off without her and Mary, I knew from then on that Rotha could not rely on a single soul, and maybe none of us can. And I vowed to do the best I could for her.

thirteen

∞∞∞

AND IT WAS A FUNNY THING—I started to wonder what might have happened if I'd gone on that expedition to Europe with them.

Would I have left her for drowned in the shipwreck to save my own skin?

Mam says when I get on like that, Son she says, you think you're all right, you think you're better'n anyone else, we all think that of ourselves. In the moral way. We all go yes me I'm the one you can count on to do best. But when push comes to shove, you never know what you might do or not do.

But I think I do know that I would never have peeled my own shirt off to dive in that water without Rotha in my arms safe. Or I hope I would not have.

So I was thinking about that, about going on travels with her over and beyond the ones we did increasingly at Rydal, which were travels without the miles. I mean we walked around the terraces as if they were many miles.

For she had me walk with her up and down and around the terraces like she and her brother used to do. Walking the sacred earth, he used to call it. But she just called it traipsing, plain like. That was how they both composed. The poet and his prose-writing sister. They never sat at a desk. Well, he— he hated sitting and he sat if he had to correct things but it gave him a headache like you wouldn't believe. And if he got the headache that was it for the day. Neither one of them could be happy unless they were outside. And of course early on she followed him and wrote down whatever he muttered. But that was long ago when they both walked their feet off. And both let the ground talk to the soles of their feet.

Only now I was the one tagging along and hanging on her every word.

I kept my ears pricked open in case I heard talk of a new visit to some other place farther than our wee gallivants around Rydal. I made up my mind to be in the right place at the right time as soon as ever a proper new journey was mentioned.

It was dawning on me that home to Rotha was the place she thought about if she went away. But once she came home, all she could think about was new journeys abroad. She wasn't at home in either place, home or away. Her real home was somewhere in her dreams no matter where she ended up.

She said the Lakes around Rydal reflected the skies and clouds and same moon that she had seen in Liège or else-where. They were like mirrors or windows into a dream of being a pilgrim in a far land with her old wagon and one horse like the gypsy. And me, I understood that. And I think I understand it better than her brother William ever did.

And that's why I wished I could go somewhere with her.

Yet it's why, once she was at home again from Europe, after the shipwreck when William was ready to dive and leave her, I understood she felt glad to be home. She loved her home. And when she was away in the Italian lakes or the Scottish lakes or anyone else's lakes, none could compare to her own lakes at home. Because her own lakes at home held all the other lakes in them. But at home, well no matter how much she loved it, off she longed to wander again.

And I wondered, I couldn't help it, what about she wanders away with me?

I did wonder that and I kept my ear out for any possibility. And when it came, it wasn't Brussels or Switzerland or Lucerne and it wasn't steeples in the moonlight at Liège, but it was somewhere. So my ears perked right up.

First she says to me, James—would you do something for me, please? And she touches her jaw.

Yes, Miss? For by now I was ready to do anything Rotha asked of me. Do you need me, I asked her, to have another look at your teeth? For she hadn't been wearing them and I was afraid the hinges had once again come undone and I felt bad about it.

They do need mending, she said. And I am afraid there is nothing more either you yourself or poor Cora Freetorch can do this time. For it is not only my false set giving me trouble, but my last three teeth on the top and those remaining on the bottom are going to have to come out, so it is, sadly, a question of paying Mr. Demergue fifty guineas and having him fit me with a whole new set.

Mr. Demergue, is he the tooth man in London?

Yes and it means I will have to stay with Mary and Charles Lamb and their little daughter and not show myself for a fortnight before all is back to normal inside my mouth.

There she was on about Charles and Mary Lamb's little daughter again, the thing she had told me at Christmas, and I didn't know what to say, for it was absurd, a brother and sister having a daughter between them. So I let that pass. Sometimes I get a bit paralyzed in my talking if I run across a thing I can't make sense of. I sort of shove it in my pocket and try to find a way to make sense of it later.

So I says to her, I says, Miss, is Mary Lamb—but I got stuck again there because I did not know how to ask was Mary Lamb all right, was she at home? Was she mad or well or in-between . . . for Miss Lamb was in and out of the madhouse as we all knew. I mean, I says, how is the state of her health?

Mary Lamb, says Rotha, is of the same state as I concerning her poor teeth.

So she'll be sympathetic, I says.

Yes, and she is sympathetic not only on that subject but regarding every subject under the sun. And sympathy or understanding, which Miss Lamb possesses in uncanny measure, mean more to me at this moment in my life than any amount of what is ordinarily called sanity.

She gave me a look. And to tell ye the truth I don't know where I got the nerve to say what I said to her next.

I can understand that, I says. Miss, might you need a . . . a reliable person's help, if you're to stay with Miss Lamb a whole fortnight?

It dawned on her that I was struggling but she did not twig what I was getting at so I says, Miss, I could come along if you think it would be of any help to you. I nearly said *and save William the trouble* but I thought better of it.

Would you really want to come with me, James, for a fortnight in London?

The thought of it got a bit more real then and I became alarmed and she saw what must have been a look of fright on my face. But was only a small fright. It hung in the room along with her own surprise at the way things were shaping. It was like the air in the room altered a bit, for we were glimpsing an arrangement we had not thought of before.

Miss, I says, perhaps it's not a good idea. I have never been to London before.

Are you frightened of it? she says. Surely not. You've been to Manchester, haven't you? To see your family? A brother, I think?

Manchester is not London, Miss. I did not bother to correct her this time about the brother she still thought I had. It occurred to me that in Rotha's world sisters must be invisible.

Here among the Lakes, she says, there are things just as frightening as any city. Look out the window now beyond the sycamore! The sky looks as if some hand has broken vast amounts of black cake all through it.

Aye, Miss, the sky does look like crumbled treacle cake.

And the wind! she says. Look how it gathers over the tree-tops in the village, ransacking the tips to reveal silver undersides that sizzle and thrash!

It's a mad whoosh all right, Miss, I says.

Let's you and I guess, James, how many minutes it will take for the incoming deluge to drench us. What do you think? How long before Rydal Mount is soaked?

I'd say, Miss, half an hour? I did not like to claim I was sure about the timing of weather, for that's a thing uncertain at all times. I felt uncertain about that and the conversation took a turn that I felt even worse about. I mean she started talking in a way that I couldn't understand, and I was worried. I wondered if the impending storm was going to make her sick like the last one did.

Have you noticed, James, how many souls in the village are women who are getting old?

Here in Rydal, Miss?

In Rydal or Grasmere . . . in Ambleside or any town hereabouts. Women labour down the road on their messages—look, there's Mrs. Jackson who retains fewer teeth than I and has replaced none of them, flashing her black gaps and begging for ale—Parched, she cries, I'm parched! . . . And here I am as toothless and haggard as she is—

No, Miss—

As squat, James—as short, and as insignificant, if you look at me as men look at women, from the outside looking at her, or looking upon her . . . but you don't look at me like that, do you?

No, Miss.

And I did not. For it was as true as anything that to me Rotha Wordsworth was still, no matter her age, a dark slip of night shot with starlight, I don't know why. I'll never know why. But I did not let on to her for I was not sure how that might sound in her ears.

And I am afraid, James, she says, that if I were to describe to you my inner state, I would tell you that my fatigue is so thick as to resemble a fog bank coming in off the sea. Muscular I am not. And people value musculature as it exists in a man such as my brother. Muscle fuels his rage and his inspiration. I am not supposed to have rage. Although lo and behold I have it. You have eaten oats, James?

Aye, Miss, I says. For I had eaten plenty.

And she says, I have eaten oats until William claims I look like oats. I look like a bowl round on its bottom—a bowl full of oats—each oat itself a round entity, oats being blips that nourish; greyish seeds having no legs nor horns nor wings. An old woman is an oat and she is the bowl that holds the oat and she is the spoon that digs the oat from the bowl and she is the mouth that sups the oat and she is the tongue in that mouth. Do you understand me, James?

I'm . . . Miss?

And if she isn't an oat she's a currant bun, inert and white with black eyes, many eyes, but eyes unable to transmit what they see because she is only a bun and is passed by, sitting in the larder. And what is the fate, James, of all buns you have known?

They get gobbled, Miss?

Yes or they grow stale and must be fed to the hens. Already I feel the eyes being plucked out of me by Little Jack Horner. You do know him?

Yes, Miss . . . and I couldn't help it, I recited—

Little Jack Horner
Sat in the corner
Eating his Christmas pie—
He put in his thumb
And pulled out a plum—
And said, What a good boy am I!

Gobbled, she says! And who was in our Christmas pie? Who lay on a bed of currants and plums and was born on Christmas Day?

You mean the mince pie you fashioned, Miss? For the Christ child?

For whom?

She looked as if I had not spoken well and I wasn't sure what she wanted me call Jesus. I couldn't really call him by only his first name. Only people down in the fields listening to the Wesley preachers talked about him by name as if he was a friend they knew. Rotha owned a Bible but I seldom saw her look in it and she was never down listening to the preachers.

The Lamb of God, Miss? I says.

Other than the Lamb of God, she says, looking weary.

I didn't want her to sicken of my stupidity. For I desired to go to London with her. I wanted it suddenly and badly. Just Rotha and me, on the road.

And I remember. Oh! Miss, I'm wrong, for you meant yourself. *You* were born on Christmas Day.

Yes, she says. I was. And I intend to jump out of the Christmas pie to see *my* Lamb, the Lamb who is also not the Christ child.

Mary Lamb, Miss?

Yes, she says. Neither she nor I is anything like Jesus or any man. We are both of us, Mary Lamb and I, something quite other than what Jack Horner imagines. Sitting in his corner with his thumb in his mouth.

Miss?

Get me out of here, will you, my dear James? And pack a bag for yourself and we will tell William we're away for a fortnight while I get my teeth renewed, and he'll think that is all I am about and he will be relieved he won't have to do a thing.

I'll see about the mail coach, Miss.

And tell them we want to ride on the outside and we won't give a damn about the weather.

I'll tell them, Miss. In fact, I says, seeing the look on her face, I'll let them know that weather might be the very thing we desire.

BUT WILLIAM GREW WORRIED VERY soon after she told him of the London plan.

He says to me James, I wonder if you've noticed how my sister is lately and if you think she is fit to go to London at all. I mean, he says, you're the one who's been talking with her more than any of us since we came back from our travels abroad. Have you noticed anything about her speech that might be—he stopped, searching for a word.

I supplied words in my mind but decided to keep them there . . . *vexed* . . . *wild* . . . *trapped*.

—Discontinuous? William says.

Sir?

Fragmented, he says. Not properly strung together. Have you noticed anything like that?

I'm not so sure, Sir.

If I thought, James, that Dorothy—if she weren't able to—it's all bad enough with Miss Lamb's own condition, for heaven's sake. What do you think?

I thought of things Rotha had started to say to me, and I thought of things I had read in her red diary. Water that is not wet. Wrinkled water. Dry water! Sizzling leaves. What had she said? All that. She had told me about a tree being a woman diving head-first into the ground, its trunk her legs waving about in the sky . . . or had I read it in the diary? The thing is, I could somehow understand what she was getting at, in everything she said or wrote. It was wild but I didn't mind it and I did not find it any worse than the wild glare her brother fixed on me now.

Was his nose getting longer than it had once been? How pale his face. Gaunt. Rotha wasn't gaunt. She was plumper now. What had she called herself—a bun! Maybe the bun was worth mentioning to William. But I did not mention it. I didn't want to tell on Rotha. It wasn't herself thought she was a bun, as far as I could see. It was other people thinking it. Him. Her brother. Thinking of her as a stale auld . . . what had he said just now? Fragmented? Coming to bits. Falling into crumbs.

Well, Dixon?

No, Sir, I says. I don't find that your sister is talking in a discontinuous way or a fragmented manner or anything like that. She seems herself, I says to him. Only, I says, there is one thing—

What is it?

And I said, because I was still trying to figure out a mystery, Sir, only she mentioned that—I don't know quite how to say it, Sir, not meaning to give offense . . .

For heaven's sake, Dixon . . .

Well, Sir, only she mentioned that Mary and Charles Lamb have a child together, and I did wonder, I mean— their being brother and sister—

Oh! He waved his hand broad and drapey. Never mind young Emma, he says. That's right. Charles and Mary Lamb do have a little girl whom they have adopted. Emma Isola.

Oh I see, I says. That's all right then. So Miss Dorothy was right—but, Sir, she said as well that—well I think she said you and she had a child as well, and I wondered if perhaps she—I mean my mam tells me sometimes women who have had no bairns sort of pine for them when they get a bit older like, and—

You mean you thought Dorothy had made up an entire child out of thin air and called it our own?

He started to laugh then, a bit cruel like, and I felt ashamed and foolish so I curled up like a snail in my shell and he looked at me and took pity on me and said, Dixon, we had a little boy called Basil, and yes we had intended to be his guardians for a long time, and he was with us a while. Little

Basil Montague. Dorothy looked after him and taught him. But in the end, James, you'll understand, we wanted our travels to continue. Germany, in particular. We wanted so much to succeed in our German travels when we were young.

I said, Sir, what happened to Basil?

And he says, In the end, Dixon, we sent him back to his family. You needn't worry about my sister's sanity on that subject, for Basil was like a son to us, and Emma Isola is indeed a daughter to Charles and Mary Lamb. And about London, James, if you're sure you want to go with Dorothy, and if you keep an eye on her and watch for any decline in her spirit—here . . .

He wrote on a piece of paper and wrapped fifteen guineas in the paper and said the address on it was for more money if I needed it for the care of myself and his sister in London. He gave me a stout bag containing her medicine and said not to give her more than twenty drops at a time but make sure she swallowed at least ten if she suffered any agony or became clouded in her thinking or grew dark-willed or morose.

And for god's sake, he says, do not let Mary Lamb drag her down with her into the mad zone. You know what I mean. That woman is like quicksand.

Yes Sir, I says, and I tried to leave the question mark off. Because he had said similar things to me before and I wasn't sure what he meant that I should do.

fourteen

ooooo

ROTHA WAS EXCITED ABOUT seeing her friend Mary Lamb.

She brushed her hat and got her bag ready in no time with a great bottle of tea and extra chops in case it took us more than the usual time to reach the city. And I spied that in her bag with her letter paper she tucked her red diary. I packed my own bag with some enjoyment. I only have a small satchel, mind, but it was a thrill for me to shake the crumbs out and gather the fewest possible things for a journey.

When we got to London everything was made of the same colour as a big grey pigeon, all the stones and lintels and chimneys everywhere had all pigeon colours and pigeons were everywhere, with the odd purple and gold glint and lots of commotion, and the noise! And she got very excited before we even reached Covent Garden where Mary Lamb lived at number twenty Russell Street right across from the Drury Lane theatre with its big pillars and archways making me feel very small and countrified.

Miss, I says, will I find my own lodgings once you get settled away with Miss Lamb?

But she says no, James, and she catches my sleeve. Her hand is tiny but as strong as it always was. She suddenly struck me as a strong creature while here I was feeling lost in the big city of a London far grander than Manchester. Once in the Lambs' house I felt even smaller for there were cavernous rooms and a smell of old books and mysterious scents I had not smelled at Rydal. Different and again old, like smells from a lost time. Ye know how when ye enter a new house you sniff all its scents at once like any wild creature must when it meets a new place. The rooms were shady and full of stuff. I wanted more light and I yearned to follow the lad cleaning our boots to ask him where I'd sleep instead of waiting for Rotha or Mary Lamb to tell me, for those two were so caught up in one another they forgot I was there, hanging about like an extra broom.

When my eyes got used to the shadows I saw the place was a shambles—and why was Mary Lamb not accompanied by her brother? I'd heard she needed Charles beside her at all times. But it turned out he had gone to see their editor about an essay he was trying to write on dreams and witches and fears in the night, then he was off to a prize fight and after that somewhere else. He could be gone for days.

I told myself not to stay surprised at Charles Lamb's absence, for even if people claim one thing—such as you shouldn't leave your sister alone lest she come to harm—you find gaps where their plans get forgotten and they hope it won't matter. Real time is made up of more hours than they thought at first. They imagine they have all the time in the world. But then other hours they thought would be there get snatched away.

The state of the place!

It was as if a great windstorm had thrust its way through the windows and doors and left everything in eddies and heaps. Books, papers, cups, forks, knives and spoons lay tumbled all over the floor and the furniture, and some of the chairs were upside down. The curtains trailed over plants and chairs like someone had trailed a tablecloth behind them over the fields on the way to a storm-wrecked picnic. One of the upside-down chairs had a straitjacket thrown over one of its legs, and I remembered I had heard Charles Lamb often had to bundle his sister in just such a jacket and walk her down the street to the madhouse. Yet there was a feeling of excitement in the room as if we had come upon the middle of something thrilling going on. It was a colourful room and a room without men if you didn't count me, for Charles Lamb had left no trace of himself.

I tried sitting on a cushion that had cat hair all over it but as I sat I got half-frightened I was doing the wrong thing and I jumped back up as Rotha and Mary Lamb started in talking about their teeth. How finally Mr. Demergue could mercifully see them both, for Miss Lamb had decided to get hers done at the same time so she and Rotha would have the carnage seen to once and for all. I couldn't understand the faith they put in Mr. Demergue or in the whole procedure.

I'll have to have quite a few pulled out before he can put any false ones in, says Miss Lamb, but I don't mind that one bit. In fact, I'm dying to have them out as their place in my mouth is a fetid swamp!

It will release me, says Rotha, from my torture of being between young and old. A nothing place.

Aye, says Miss Lamb. I well know that in-betwixt nowhere.

But surely you're already out of that place, says Rotha. For Miss Lamb was ten years older.

That's what you might think, says Mary Lamb. It's what anyone'd think, looking at my silver hair or my fat middle which has got quite fetching over the last while, I am sure. And the two of them laugh about fat. But you don't have to worry about that, says Miss Lamb, being thin as a key all your life!

That is changing, says Rotha. And no matter how like a key I am, I cannot open just any door. In this state that straddles young and old I can have no lover. Nor, unlike my brother, do I have a following of people fascinated by my wisdom.

Aye, says Miss Lamb. A woman between youth and age is treated like a half-stale loaf. Not tender enough to devour, not dry enough to be cast into a pudding. Perhaps there's mould on her and she'll be tossed out! Not fit to feed hens. But I warn you, my having ten years on you is no use. You might imagine a sixty-year-old woman as being held in high regard but you'd be mistaken. I am not listened to and I fear this will never change.

This silenced Rotha.

I could not help interrupting!

I says, Misses, may I say that my mam—a woman between the ages of your two selves—has told me that for a man to listen to her there has to be no one conscious left in the room, not even a housefly.

This got them laughing.

For if there is a housefly, I says, he will heed that fly before he heeds her. And Mam says it doesn't matter how old or young you are.

Your mam has that right, says Mary Lamb.

But, I says, Mam also says a few men lack the caul over their brains and can hear what women say, and you have to watch who you speak to and not waste your breath with the deaf ones.

But James, Rotha says—how does your mother tell the difference between the caul-brained deaf and men who can hear?

Aye, says Miss Lamb—has your mam got eyes in the back of her head?

My mam's second sight is elsewhere, I says.

I didn't know if I should keep talking or was I saying too much. But the two glanced at me, waiting very eager like, so I went ahead—it is like a stone, I says. In Mam's throat. And it has an eye that can see through her skin and into the head of any man speaking. Even a whole room full of men. And she can tell who is cauled and stupid or who has ears that can hear a woman.

Mary Lamb chortled very satisfied at this. But Rotha went quiet and her eyes looked like a pair of holes, and she says, William used to be like that . . . I felt in my throat, whenever I voiced anything—no matter how astonishing— my brother was never disbelieving. He never tried to dismiss me, and now—

Now? says Miss Lamb with a callous catch in her voice.

I was not sure whether I admired Mary Lamb or feared her.

I remembered what William had said about my not letting her draw Rotha into madness. Something lived in her tone as well as in her words. I was afraid it might leap out of Miss Lamb and into Rotha so that by the time Rotha's teeth were fixed and we got back to Rydal, her brother might not recognize her and he would certainly blame me. For my mam says you have to watch who you spend time with because any kind of madness is a spirit that'll jump out of one person and pounce right into the one next to them before they can do a thing about it. It's not that the madness rubs off on you gradual like, it's more like it makes a wily leap to inhabit two people instead of one. I wondered if Rotha was already catching the madness off Miss Lamb. I suddenly felt a tiny bit worried for my own sanity at number twenty Russell Street, to tell ye the truth!

Where is your little girl? says Rotha.

She is no longer really my little girl, says Miss Lamb. She is my brother Charles's little girl when all is said and done. Charles's very special little pet.

Then Miss Lamb shouts out in a bloodcurdling voice the name of the girl who William had assured me was real.

Emma!

The way she screamed it! I might have lived in the workhouse and my mam might have drunk a river of gin and struggled through a sea of troubles but I never heard the like of shrieking from one room to another in the house the way Miss Lamb summoned Emma.

And in comes a person who I can't call a little girl, not really, with an animal in her arms that was neither cat nor dog. I couldn't tell what it was but I caught a whiff off it and nearly choked for it smelled of piss. It couldn't possibly have been the girl herself stinking like that. That much I knew or hoped. How old was she? Eleven or twelve? Not thirteen, surely? She was thin and sullen with hair like a torn nest yet womanly in some perilous way. Her pet animal was long and slinky and I could hardly take my eyes off it. I felt certain it could fly at me and sink its teeth in my throat. It had a body like an eel, muscled and tense. But no one mentioned it. They talked to the girl as if the horrible thing was not squirming in her arms. So I did my best to pretend I was not on the alert.

Something stole over Miss Lamb in the girl's presence—Rotha had promised me that if anyone in the world had more sympathy than Miss Lamb, she had not met them. For Mary Lamb, says Rotha, is the essence of sympathy and understands me like no other. And I remembered what William had said: Mary Lamb had a fault, and the fault was that she was quicksand into which other people's feelings sank. She couldn't help it—she sucked in everyone else's feelings until they were her own and she could never, in the end, contain all the feelings she'd swallowed. Which was why she went mad and had to be carted off until she came to her pure single self again, with one person's feelings inside her instead of all the woes and shadows of her world. And I saw it. Before the girl Emma came in, Miss Lamb was a sheltered body of ground into which all the rain in the world might fall and bring forth untold blossoms. Her eyes held such a promise I nearly felt like telling her my own troubles.

But when Emma Isola entered the room something quick and dark and invisible strangled all that promise.

And the child in her turn looked very much as if she did not want to be there. In fact she kept her back to Miss Lamb and faced Rotha as if facing a warm hearth, with Miss Lamb a freezing blast at her back.

How are you, Pet? says Rotha.

Very well thank you, Miss Dorothy, says the child in a voice waxen as a lily.

How I wish, says Rotha, as if remembering something blown away and lost, I could have brought mine and William's little boy Basil.

I knew that Emma's meeting Basil was impossible given the years that had passed. According to William, he and Rotha had looked after Basil thirty years before! Yet Rotha says to Emma, you and Basil would have made fantastic playmates, then looks around her as if Basil would pop out if she looked sharp, for he was only playing a crafty game of hide-and-seek. I watched her eyes sharpen to needles, glancing all around the room that was so disorganized a small lad could hide in it pretty easily.

I'm dying to go outside, Rotha said and she started for the door. I tensed, being ready to keep an eye on her as William had charged me. I didn't want to let her out of my sight, not in London. I battled the feeling I had no say in the matter. I felt invisible. No one had shown me a cot or any place to put my bag and I had no idea what my place was supposed to be, unlike at Rydal where all was certain.

Wait! says Mary Lamb.

I can't wait, Rotha says. We must be outside!

I know we must, says Miss Lamb, who hoists herself with some difficulty off her chair and stares at Emma Isola and then at me as if I hold a key.

And Emma, with her eyes welling up, says, Aren't I coming?

No, you're going to stay here with Mr. Dixon, says Miss Lamb to my consternation.

When I get concerned like that, over matters beyond my control, a boiling tide wants to poach my heart like an egg. I get paralyzed.

Show Mr. Dixon what a lovely reader you are, Miss Lamb says.

You promised to take me to the Arcade!

We'll bring you an éclair from Gunter's, says Miss Lamb.

I want to come!

I'll fetch your doll from Mrs. Carruthers's with its new clothes on. Mr. Dixon will look after you, won't you, Dixon?

Miss, I—

He'll slice you a tomato from the greenhouse . . .

No!

. . . and he'll listen while you read him a story—

I don't care about my stupid doll or its clothes! You promised I could have a magic glass! Mr. Dixon doesn't want a story read to him. He's only a stupid servant.

Oh, Emma, he's not, not really, says Rotha. He loves having stories read to him, and your mother and I will bring you an éclair and we will not bother about the doll. But Miss Lamb and I are dying to go on a meander by ourselves—

He *is* only a servant! And he's only a man! Look at him. He doesn't even want to look after me. And I am the only girl in London without a magic glass!

Be kind, Emma, Rotha says. Miss Lamb and I need to catch up on everything we have missed in each other's thoughts. Besides, whenever she and I ramble in the city we climb a great many steep lanes and stairs and—

I climb better than both of you!

But Miss Lamb and I speak to each other without saying anything out loud for ages.

I don't care!

You would be worn out at the end of an hour, begging us to stop and have cake, and it is much better for us to explore in pure freedom and bring you the cake back in its own lemon-coloured box with a silver ribbon you can trim for your hair. And this might be our only day, for tomorrow we have to have very painful things done at Mr. Demergue's and we will be convalescing. Don't you care about our one day of freedom?

No and I don't care one bit about my hair! Emma Isola buries her face in the urine-smelly animal and wails fit to crack the windows. I'm terrified that before I know it I'll be left alone with this child. How am I supposed to look after her? Rotha's the one I'm pledged to watch, and if she has her way she'll be rampant down every crooked street and up staircases and down narrow hills, forever on and on in a maze of alleys unfolding 'til the lamps are lit and me unable to account for her whereabouts!

Very well, says Miss Lamb. Put the ferret in its cage and tell Bernice to dress you and we'll take you and Dixon. He can carry our bags and mind you while Dorothy and I catch up on all we have to say to each other. Mind, you leave us alone and walk behind us and don't interrupt or whinge, or you come straight home, Dixon will see to it. And for heaven's sake bring a book to entertain yourself and Dixon instead of your whining to come home any time before dusk. *My legs are tired! I'm thirsty! I'm bored!* None of that. Do you hear? One word and you're bound for home.

I DON'T GET DAZZLED VERY OFTEN but I got dazzled in London. I wish I could tell ye all that was said and done on our day traipsing through all the best parts—Rowland's for face cream and Lock's for a hat band and cherry wine at Rudd's all very fancy I couldn't believe it, imagine me in all those places!

I had to keep an eye on Rotha while at the same time never letting the child Emma out of my sight, for she wanted to pop down every alley and in every sweet-shop asking for this and that confit and never letting up about her magic glass that she wanted. And Rotha and Miss Lamb were heads-together talking the whole time and whatever they said got the two of them more and more excited until Rotha trembled as if lightning ran through her.

And if ye want to know all that happened in London, Rotha wrote her version in the red book and I'm soon going to read it to ye as I promised. I am.

For I've already read it and I can understand it in part, but I cannot explain it to ye in my own words. Rotha's own words are that different from mine, they're a kind of wilderness or foreign country, and you'll have to forgive me if I don't do a very good job reading them to ye out loud, they are too strange. Though I promise I'll try. But I'll tell ye, Rotha's time in London with Mary Lamb started something up in her, it made her different. Or it sped up a change in her that'd been happening. And there was I saddled with the lass, Emma, and struggling to keep up with Rotha, the one I was supposed to mind. Ye can't mind everyone or everything, for people have their own minds.

Certainly Emma Isola did have her own mind and as we were all about to leave the Arcade she says to me, They are leaving without getting me the magic glass they promised! Sure enough there's Rotha's and Miss Lamb's heads together as one, going off into the street and what does the little fiend do but dig her nails in my wrist making my flesh white then purple and she won't let go until I stop those two ahead and ask them about the glass.

All right Dixon, says Miss Lamb, Dorothy and I will nip in and get her the promised kaleidoscope but we are not taking her with us for she will make the matter last all day, turning this one and that one to test the colours.

There was a tea shop at the end of the Arcade with black-and-white tables and Miss Lamb told Emma to sit and read me the book she had brought while they went to get the thing.

Once they were gone off Emma Isola glares at me and grumbles, You don't want a story at all, do you?

I felt as awkward as the back corners of a cow. I had no clue what to say so I says tell me the story of your last name, what is it again? Though I well remembered what her name was, it being so strange.

So she says it's Isola.

I says is it really? I says that's unusual for a name isn't it?

Isola, she says with her serious face, means isolation, and isolation means—

I ken what isolation is, says I in a tone I hoped she wouldn't find gruff though I must say I did not enjoy such a small person telling me what a word means. I says to her, it means lonely, but you're only making that name up because they wouldn't let you go to the magic glass shop with them. That can't be a real name. I says this to her for a kind of taunt, for I figured she enjoyed having an argument. And now here you are lonely with me, I says, for I'm a stranger no doubt about it. But you don't have to worry, I won't make you read me a story or do anything you don't feel like—and you don't have to tell me your real name if you don't want to.

No, she says! Emma Isola is my real name. She likes being in the right and me being in the wrong. She gets comfortable with that arrangement, and she says do you want me to read you *The Tempest* or *The Taming of the Shrew*?

I said aye, read me *The Tempest* if you can, but Shakespeare is a bit hard for one as young as you, is it not? I know it's very hard even for me! I was secretly proud that she did not have to tell me Shakespeare had written the stories. I have a habit of paying attention to everything at Rydal, and that includes the bookshelves. But Little Miss Lonely had to argue with me on that an' all.

No, she says, taking the book out of her pocket, *The Tempest* is one Miss Lamb wrote especially for children.

But look here lass, I says, you're having me on again. That's one of William Shakespeare's plays. I might be only a servant of Miss Wordsworth but you needn't make a mockery out of me. I do know a few things about books, having lived with the little family for so long.

No, she says, I'm not mocking you! Mary Lamb made Shakespeare's book into a new book for children.

And she gets a look on her face I can only describe as honest and straight as a baby crow. And I like it. Strong and dark, like, ye know how young crows look—they are never without their glare that can seem a bit frightful even in the youngest bird. And she thrusts the book at me, See? she says. *Tales from Shakespeare*, it says on the front, *by Charles Lamb*. Only never mind it saying Charles Lamb, she says quick as anything. Mary Lamb wrote *The Tempest*. Only they put his name on the front and not hers. She writes all the time but nobody knows. Everybody thinks her brother writes it all. She licked her thumb and found the page quite professional like, as if she was my little teacher in our classroom, and I had to stifle a laugh for Emma Isola would have hated to be laughed at.

Be quiet! And she starts reading it out clear as a bell:

There was a certain island in the sea, the only inhabitants of which were an old man, whose name was Prospero, and his daughter Miranda, a very beautiful young lady. She came to this island so young, that she had no memory of having seen any other human face than her father's. They lived in a cave—

See, she says? Easy as anything!

In a cave! I says.

Yes, she says, and wait 'til you hear about Prospero's magic books, and Caliban and Ariel and the storm—and she reads me the whole thing and by heaven I do understand every word of it, *full fathom five thy father lies*, and *where the bee sucks, there suck I*, and the pitiful monster Caliban who is a servant like me and whose mam is enchanted but even more so than my mam, a witch, even. And something in Emma Isola's voice makes me feel caught up in it in a wonderful manner. So by the time we're done here's Rotha and Miss Lamb back already with the magic glass. Here was I thinking it'd drag on worse than a day hoeing turnips in the sleet. She was a right lively lass, Emma Isola.

But she did not ooh or ah over her magic glass for long. Took a look in it but was then back to her normal self which was like a bird on the lookout for some new pip or worm or shiny beetle. The one who took up looking in the glass—

completely taken by it—was Rotha. The thing as I could make out had mirrors all down the insides, and coloured pieces of glass inside, and when you look through the tube and swivel the end towards the light, well, Rotha says, it is like looking through her wee botanical glass into a cowslip or bluebell or some other field enchantment, only in the kaleidoscope you aren't seeing the real flower chambers ye lot know about.

No, she says, I've fallen in the world of a thousand blooms unknown to anything but the imagination!

Ye couldn't drag it away from her, and in my mind that was a blessing, for the very next day was to be the day of Mr. Demergue going at her gums and teeth with his knife and pliers, and I knew that day would be a sore day for Rotha and for Mary Lamb and I was worried both would come back hurt—I've noticed many times that when a person goes under a knife or any big remedy that involves sawing bone, yes the body heals. If you're lucky. But what nobody tells you is you come home stooped and battered with part of your spirit cut away, a bit you might never find again. Or if you get it back it can take years and you'll have changed and the lost piece of you cannot catch up.

Rotha had put great hope in Mr. Demergue.

I'd heard my mam talk about getting her roof fixed with something like the same hope. When I get the roof properly done, Mam said, I'll not have to worry no more. The damp'll never get in!

It was as if damp had infected Mam's own being and she hoped a new roof would not only make her house high and dry but would banish mould or mildew or damp from her legs and her whole body and from her spirit. And that is how Rotha and Miss Lamb talked about what it would be like once Mr. Demergue fixed their mouths.

When we arrived back at Russell Street from our day traipsing the streets, Miss Lamb gave Rotha a chamber with white curtains and ferns on the sill, and I was given a cot in a room that was tiny but clean.

I'll recover while reading, says Rotha. I'll look at Emma Isola's kaleidoscope. I'll meditate on leaf and shadow and half-light. I'll write.

Bernice has covered your chair by the window in white, says Miss Lamb, and washed the curtains. You'll be able to lie down and recall yourself, feel all your membranes and the organs they contain. Dixon will open the window to let air in and shift your pillows won't you, James?

I'm good at fixing pillows, I says. For when I turn a pillow it is cool and sits under a person's head in all the right ways.

Rotha shuddered like a child that has had its complaints heard.

You'll convalesce in shade, says Miss Lamb, and see no lurid day nor eat food you have had to prepare yourself. James will look after us—won't you, James—I can tell you are intelligent.

I hope I can be useful, ma'am, I says.

And, Rotha, says Miss Lamb, you will find rejuvenation and pass from the agony of lost youth into an older, exultant place.

ONLY THE NEXT EVENING WHEN the two came back from Demergue's I saw nowt but despair.

The corners of Rotha's mouth had dried blood-flecks—Demergue had not bothered to warm a cloth and bathe her face, which is what I did immediately after I led her to the bed. Miss Lamb had hardly more spark either as Bernice helped her upstairs. I would have liked at that moment to locate Demergue and remove his own teeth for him. The amount he had charged!

For the first couple of days I hardly knew what to do except bring Rotha broth I had Bernice simmer from lamb bones—I asked her to cook it 'til the gelatin was extracted and the broth glittered with marrowfat. For only bone repairs bone, and our jaw is the foundation of our talking. It's the jaw that sets flight to our words, and her words were what Rotha needed to find. I was frightened she'd never utter another word with that butchered mouth.

And the pain!

But she says James, I'm used to pain. I have known pain all my born days.

I let her sup the bone broth from a spoon I held, and I did not ask her anything.

We were quiet.

She looked through Emma Isola's kaleidoscope, or she opened her red diary and wrote. Penned in it the thoughts of her convalescence, this notebook I have here on the basket for ye now.

Aye, the diary was closer to her in London than I had ever seen it. She lay upon it like a hen protecting its one warm egg not yet devoured by the weasel.

5

After summer merrily

ooooo

W hat can be more ordinary than my voice—wind through my branches, sap gurgling in my wood? Trees cover the earth, as common as stones! Inventors and poets scour their own minds for sparks of life, but Rotha perceived vitality in natural bodies. She knew life was a force no inventor can create, and even now her knowledge remains visible yet unseen, just as the word *real* indwells the word *realm*.

But invention! Progress! Machines to counterfeit myself, Sycamore, and other trees. Bee-sized apparitions to mimic bee work, humming and whirring ever faster, louder than Rotha's undersong of wind in wood, of fluttering wing, of hue atremble in corolla.

Common life will become uncommon. The ordinary will slip underground from whence it once flourished. Not dead, you understand, but in waiting.

fifteen

I WISH, JAMES, that I was a fairy, Rotha says to me, then I'd light on a leaf in your wheelbarrow and off we'd go to the fields and flowers and I could commune with our bees whilst you do your weeding and hoeing.

For by this time she was troubled often by her legs being what she called heavy as marble. Immobile. Every three or four days, like.

So I said Miss D, I can arrange a way for you to get around. For by now I was used to arranging many things for her. Anything you care to name, James Dixon could take care of it.

This was later, as ye know. I mean after London and then after the other time she tried going away to dig in. The last time of all. Digging in, she called it. Off to Whitwick to help William's son John set up his parsonage. And she lived with John alone, helped him write his talks, just like when she helped William with his poems at Dove Cottage. She was going to help John with his ideas. But the son's ears were parched as the father's! *Give me the goblet of your skull and I will drink my fill.* I saw her write that. John Wordsworth

228

drank from her mind as his father William had done until she fell very ill and had to come home, agony of the bowels and paralysis of the leg. And once she was sixty the family hardly understood what was going on with her at all. This understanding fell to myself and I did not find it hard. I deciphered things the others could not decipher or were not able to think about.

Dig in! I'm always digging for home, she says, and they couldn't understand it. You are home, said Mary and William. But I knew Rotha had no home.

What happened was I'd clean my barrow and haul Rotha to one spot one day and another the next. Always out of doors. And that's when she started making the maps. We covered miles. It looked to the others as if we were only going around the terraces like, but it was much farther. We were like ye—we flew. We revelled in ye and your ways and we saw things ye see. We always had. Not as clear as ye see, mind. I'm not saying that.

And she says remember, James, just treat the terraces and the distance you drag me around the lake, treat those yards like many miles. Every yard being a few miles. We're expanding space and time. We're making the most.

And I didn't know what she meant at first. Only that the terraces and the land outlying the house seemed to grow bigger in her mind than other people saw them.

Ye know what the terraces were to the Wordsworths when I first came to Rydal. Ye remember how I helped William build 'em, and they'd saunter, him and Rotha, up and down for hours, winding the miles. He wanted the ground carpeted all mossy or lined with stones and the two of them trod from one end to the other, him composing, muttering, thinking out loud, and she writing down anything he said. She tried writing verses but—she despaired of hers amounting to anything. I am not a poet, she said. No. A different kind of word-making was hers. Aye they both traipsed the terraces in the old days.

And they wound their way along, down, up again, down, up, down—thread like a thread being wound on a bobbin. A gold thread making words. And a silver thread. Sun and moon. Night and day they wound. Frost and sun. Gold and silver. Light, moon, sun, frost.

Wind.

Ah, they wound, those two. Long time ago now. Winding round they wound the paths of the terraces. Up one end, up to the extreme last bit with its gooseberry bush and the plant that has leaves smelling like lemons, up to there and then they turned—like a pair of dancers—like the wheels in the cuckoo clock that so enchanted William. Ever whirring and turning. Wound, winding, sound, sighing, singing, thinking, composing, making. Their winding words. The winding thread. The terraces were the bobbins and on 'em they wound their words. William's in the poems everyone loves, Rotha's in her secret cocoon.

But now he was never with her like that. He was hardly outdoors at all.

We started off with my wheelbarrow and me giving her the few giddy rides in it until William says that has to stop, that is unseemly, my sister in a barrow, please. So I says to him I'm sorry, it won't happen again, but would it be all right, Sir, if I built her a proper little cart?

Now look here, he says, we can't have my sister falling out of some contraption onto the ground. Her health! For he was very concerned about her bowels and her legs and her head and all the pain she felt, though whatever caused it was, he told me, a mystery.

I says Sir, you know me, I'll make sure Miss Dorothy is in no danger, will you leave it to me? And by this time William himself was past sixty for he's a year older than his sister, and he goes off and leaves my question hanging with neither a yes nor a no because he has a lot to do and his time is precious, so of course I maximize the situation and decide for everyone that the space between William's yes and his no is my own special place for me and Rotha.

Though her real place is she doesn't know where, for after London and then Whitwick she tries and tries to find it and cannot. No one has a spot for her in their plans. And they do not look at her writing any more. Oh she writes. She writes her Scottish book and makes copies and gives it to people and they claim to treasure it but I hear Mary Wordsworth tell their friends Mrs. Ellsworth and Mrs. Luff not to bother reading the whole thing. It has a bit, for instance, says Mary, about the flowers in a Scottish potato field! Those rustic insignificant flowers on a potato plant!

This is when ye lot perk up, isn't it. This is when ye remind me ye have been in on the story all along. Careful on me face!

Mary would go upstairs to Rotha's room and find her staring at the wall, or staring through more like it, that part of the wall where the old window was concealed. Mary was perplexed, for Mary never gave a thought to that window.

Here, Dorothy, Mary says, a new book for you to read.

And Rotha says—Mary tells me this dumbfounded—she says Mary, I don't care to read. I need no new book, for I am busy with my own feelings. I'm on an edge.

Busy with her own feelings! Mary's astonished. On an edge! An edge of what?

And I fathom it better than Mary can, but all I says to Mary is, Mrs. Wordsworth, never mind, I'll take Miss Dorothy outside once the rain stops.

And Rotha won't need any book.

But I don't say that part.

The thing about being a servant is you can't let on you see something another member of the family is blind to. And we're funny blind things, people. Ye know that. Ye can see everything but we can see very little. For one thing, ye know about time past and time to come and together with the time we are in, it is for ye all one big golden day. It must be nice. I feel it as soon as I sniff ye'r honey, without a drop on my tongue.

Just the scent. It goes on forever. And that's where we'd go when I took Rotha outside in the little cart whenever the rain stopped. Out to your world.

Our faery phaeton she called it—our rude phaeton, its wheels my liberty—and you, James, my trusty steed.

Ye know our little cart. Ye've seen us traipse the land, me at the helm and Rotha alighting among your flowers. Really your flowers lit on her, aye, dangling on her lap and falling round her shoulders like a garland for the queen of the fairies.

For she was to me a queen as your queen is to ye.

Was it spring of 1830 I built it? I know the year numbers mean nowt to ye. It was spring for we were coming out of the usual lingering sleet and dark. I modelled it on a rough but fairy-like cart she saw a tinker ride with his lass and his pots when she was still walking the roads herself forever on the move. I scrounged the wheels and various bits—the biggest job was only a matter of changing a fixed axle to a mobile one and it meant whittling a knob and reaming a nice deep groove so it'd hold over the rough bits of the terraces. But as it is with any common task that takes half an hour, you might go a week before you get a chance to do it, what with one thing and another demanding your attention. William had been all week trying desperately to write a poem about spring to send to his friend Bob Southey for inspection and he wanted to go through Rotha's notebooks to see what she had written about it first.

My sister has a rough way, he says to me, you can get a grip on that roughness like you would grip a well-knotted rope and clamber up it and spy the view she has—it's like the view I had a long, long time ago. When I was a youth, he says. Before I was even fifteen. Aye, I had what she has then. He says this with a kind of rage and his bad eye watered and his face went mottled like it gets when his head is killing him. Robert Southey is waiting for the poem, he says. Robert Southey was still the laureate that spring and William was practising for when his turn came around. Every year the laureate is supposed to come up with something for the King and William had an awful time getting anything ready by a certain date. He found it was torture. I was still helping him find in Rotha's notebooks the things she had written that might suit him, for by then I knew where everything was in her notes. When you have always done something for a man, done it for years, how can you deny him? Even if you feel awkward about it.

But once I had William satisfied do ye think I could nip to my hut to fix Rotha's cart? No! Because all hell is breaking loose over a bloody chicken. Sometimes I felt like I was in a madhouse. No sooner am I clear of William than Mary Wordsworth needs me to help her get something off her chest about the same chicken she's been on about all the day before. Of all the family, Mary is the stable one. But I knew this made her wild inside with things she'd never mention to William. Instead she'd tell me. I have always been different things to different people in the family, and for Mary I have been a bare corner where she could unload burdens the others never suspected she was tired of carrying.

All Dorothy wants, says Mary, is more food! All last week asking for a whole chicken to be roasted only for herself! A whole chicken! For one small woman! No wonder she's getting fat. And she wants a fire in her room and will want it stoked through the middle of July. Mayflowers will pass. Daffodils will have come and gone. Bluebells will be here. Cows making butter unlimited! And all Dorothy wants is fire in the grate. A hundred degrees in her room, nobody can breathe in it. Or she wants fried fish. Or porridge with but-ter in a molten puddle. She wants new knitting needles but never knits! You should see how much she ate last night, James—no wonder she has problems with her bowels. Then somebody has to clean up after her and who is that some-body? Not that I mind one little bit. Never will I be said to have minded! But mind you, she says, Dorothy with that chicken—it is pure greed.

I said to myself—not out loud—I says no, I don't think that's what it is at all.

The chicken was plump and studded wi' herbs all right, a gorgeous crackling skin—The smell of it filled the house and was tantalizing. I'd have devoured it alone in my hut and it wouldn't have taken me long either. It had fat little legs on it and crisped wings, and Mary knows as well as I do how smashing it is to fall on a well-browned wing and gnaw the crackling and the shreds of meat off it and wash it down with tea or cold, clear water.

I says to Mary I says it is true Miss Dorothy did devour it . . . I stifled a chortle to myself over Rotha's enjoyment of it—like a wolf. A real wild animal she was, feasting on that crisp and fragrant bird.

But, says Mary, it's not the way she devoured it that mys-tifies me. It's how she went on about wanting it all week until I couldn't stand talk of it anymore and had to get you, James, to go have Tom Sharp slaughter the thing. And no, it wasn't good enough we should share it—me, William, Dora or any of us—as I know how to stretch a chicken din-ner amongst company.

I know you do, Ma'am.

Add a few parsnips, the last couple of sausages from Ambleside, Mary says. But no, Dorothy wants that chicken. For my own self, she says. What sort of desire is that, and William going right along with it? Everyone going along with her strange desires, day in and day out?

I mean, I'd hardly call that true. I would call that one of Mary Wordsworth's fantasies—we all have our illusions and I might say that one of Mary's is a perpetual notion of Rotha as a gaping scream. A loud demand. A clamour for more—the kind of lament you hear from one of the trapped hares on the mountain at night. The hunter far off asleep. The trap digging into the creature's foot so it can't move yet it won't die. No wonder the lament can never stop but for one thing alone.

Aye, Mary says, all Rotha wants is more food. But me, I say all she wants is human touch.

Aye. Ye look at somebody ye know over the minutes and hours and days and weeks and years and decades and ye look at how much human touch they're given. And eh, Rotha's little dog, Little Miss Belle . . . that dog clung close to her ankles every time she wrote. The dog knew she was writing. The dog knew that was when its mistress needed a warm body touching her skin, and the dog provided that, didn't it. Now the dog never clung. It wasn't a clinging dog. But it pressed itself against her ankles. She told me this. She laughed. She giggled like a girl and she said, I feel the dog's hot body against my skin as I write. It's lovely, oh it's lovely. And I had an eye on that.

Eating a whole chicken, well that's one way of having another hot body press against your skin from the inside, isn't it. And that's your throat. The ankles and the throat— the dog and the food. And then the fire she wanted. Never warm enough. Never often enough, the fire. The warm body of the wood with the sun's borrowed radiance as she called it. In the flames.

Aye, a warm touch. I could not provide that, other than the few times our little cart broke down. And I took her in my arms. Aye, I did. She weighed, even when she was plumper at the end, not very much more than—than a bird! I mean 'course she weighed more than a bird but, felt like, aye it felt to me like carrying a plump little bird that . . . sank into my embrace. Oh how she sank into my arms as I carried her. And she'd drape an arm over my embrace and gather a mug-wort or henbane or a lovely little—sometimes we'd stop and I'd help her pick a rose without getting pricked. Or an iris. Oh she loved to gather blooms when she was in me arms and together we'd carry them home. Ha like a little bride and groom. Aye, I loved that. I loved it . . . I loved helping her to feel . . . cradled . . . Did she write about that? I had no way of knowing unless I looked for myself in her diary. Oh you look for yourself, don't you. You have a glance, looking for your name.

As for that roast chicken, just burstin' with lovely gold juices. The aroma alone set my mouth to watering an' all, I tell ye. You could not fault Rotha for getting enthusiastic about it. Even so, the mouthwatering appetizing part of it wasn't the real nourishment it gave her. No. It wasn't until we were well into our travels in the phaeton that she told me what it meant.

It was all about the little maps. All the places she had travelled with William and Sam Coleridge on foot or in their own outlandish cart that people scoffed at all over Scotland. Draw me a pair of Scottish maps, she says to me, and we'll affix them to the inside of our cart. Each map had a key on it that she labelled Our Legend. I made one for the lowlands and another for the highlands. She'd pencil in the names of all the lochs and mountain horse-paths and trackless heaths, the castles or any inn where they'd stayed the night. No more than caves, some places they'd stayed, moonlight shining on the dripping roof like melted gems.

And here, she says, draw in the Trossachs, the hills around this lake called Ketterine—Coleridge and I were faint with hunger—look, here is where our boatman put us into a tub so leaky his wife had to ladle the water out—William was so nervous that when we got down the bay he stood up near shore and dropped our food bundle in the water! Spoiled the sugar and the coffee and the pepper-cake—but our roast fowls were intact! Sam and I fell upon them faint with hunger. How I've craved a roast chicken like those ever since, but nothing ever compares with our roast fowls in sauce made of the lake! William had run off—he explored the coast without us . . . Here . . . sketch the heather I stumbled through running after him. I found him sitting alone on a hilltop . . . Here she faltered.

Miss, I says, perhaps it's too much . . . these maps, remembering. You know how good you are at remembering. You take yourself right back there again. I never said *right back running after William*. But I was thinking it. Always running after the one she loved, with Sam Coleridge not far behind. The three of them. And now with our maps she did it all again, through memory, like, and I was her horse. I dragged her wherever she wanted to go and we kept the maps up to date with each new journey we made. The rest of the family thought we never went beyond Rydal.

Thunder cracked her open as if she were sky. I saw it from the time she told me about William jumping ship. Thunder affected her as if it might kill her but then it did the opposite.

I've seen many an animal killed by lightning but there are some creatures that come to life after a thunderstorm strikes them. A pony my uncle Jim had revived itself after lightning struck it down and lived to be twice the age of any normal horse. He changed its name after that, from Blackie to Flash. I remember Flash being a lovely pony with one star glinting in her deep eye and I kept wishing lightning would come near her again, for Uncle Jim says to me son, if it happens again she'll sprout wings!

And thunder knew Rotha. It was forty years since she'd loved Coleridge under the winter boughs if you go by a calendar, but thunder and lightning know no time, like ye yourselves. Thunder told her Sam Coleridge was dying. She was out in our phaeton as lightning flared over Nab Scar. She went rigid with its white light and would not take shelter.

I cannot come inside! she says. I must feel it.

And up she stands in the phaeton, rain running down her face and soaking her clothes. William would be very angry.

Mary an' all, if they knew I let that happen. Three days that was, before the death of her beloved Sam. And when the letter came to say Sam had died, she had already felt him go, standing in our wild little cart in the wind and rain, the thunder crashing through our bodies like a nightmare. Only it was day. Her new kind of day where she's busy with all her feelings and the day crashes into her, full wind and rain.

She was the one that noticed the little gateways. All of a sudden on our rides around the terraces there'd be little gateways everywhere. She was the one—is that right? Or was it me that noticed first? Aye, I might have said it to her because I'm used to—with the rabbit snares—finding tiny— not human-sized but rabbit-sized gateways, and after that, other little ones that all the animals make. I noticed—aye— one in the reeds. Them big reeds that grow tall. People don't like them, frightened the reeds will choke small plants. But I like the way they whisper, and sometimes an animal will have gone in before you and made a—trod down a little area.

Yes it was one of them, leading down to the lake. I says, come on, Miss, look at this.

She says aye, it's a little gateway. And in we went. Yes that's it. I found the thing and she called it by the name.

And ye'll remember yourselves—that was when she stopped caring about all that went on *inside* the house. Stopped forever.

Aye, I don't think most people know about the little gateways. Once you go through them . . .

Rotha kept her microscope in a pocket at all times and let me look through it to see what she saw and what ye see when ye go in the chambers of your blooms. Ah, she needed to read no book! Needed to write, yes. Not read.

She wrote plant names in a guidebook she had and started coming to see ye with her reports of where and when they bloomed. Heckberry! Crab blossom! Anemone! Speedwell! Aye they sped well, our four wheels. Only around the terraces mind, but on our map she covered all her old ground. Our map signified not only Grasmere and Rydal but all the ground she'd once trod with William and Sam. Helm Crag, Stone Arthur, Nab Scar, Loughrigg, Elter Water, Ambleside and up Kirkstone Pass—Geraniums! Gowans! Little star plants with no flowers, or flowers that only opened under the stars like white lights in the darkness leading their way home. Her and William and Sam. Rotha still surefooted as a goat.

I took her back to all that in our little cart.

She nearly forgot I was not William.

The gateways everywhere. We searched high and low. Here under the willows or there in the grasses. There'd be a gateway in the sycamores or in the rocks themselves.

She noticed any tiny difference in sound. I saw well enough but she heard an' all. I mean ye can hear it now, the wind in those reeds, listen . . . (wind sound, whispering reeds)

Aye, that was music to her ears. She loved that. Loved it if a natural sound gently overcame all the other sounds of the village . . . of someone hammerin' and workmen bellowing to each other about a step they were digging, or even William's din . . . he could make a racket when he was working on the terraces. She couldn't abide his mallet on the stone. We'd go through the little gateways and the rushes and leaves softened all other sounds and she would become very peaceful.

Then she'd lie against my shoulder like somebody who— aye like a lass who'd—might I say gone to sleep on the breast of its mother? No. I was still a youngish man in my thirties and she old enough to be me own mam, yet . . .

Aye, in the phaeton we travelled, didn't we, through gateways. All through those late years she called down to me from her bedroom, and out we ventured in the wagon. Into a world far deeper than her brother's.

She'd tell me, Look, James, at that ash tree! Each of its leaves is a lantern. And look how each pendulous lantern is lit! Oh, James. And she'd get out of the cart and we'd run to it. Just her and me.

The others indoors. And she had no need of a cart then.

I had a wisp of Mam's magic in me, and I had my ears, with which I have listened to the wind and to ye and to Rotha through my faithful years. So I knew me and Rotha were in the world between worlds that I had always felt to be just out of grasp. Through her, standing there, our phaeton like something out of a fairy tale with the light catching its ordinary wooden wheels yet changing them—I saw her lamps lit throughout the ash tree.

But after a moment—not even a moment—the blaze faded and she said, crumpled like, so I had to catch her and seat her in the cart propped up by an old cushion, she said that's it, James—it has left us.

In clock-time indoors people saw her in agony, in her bed, trapped in a terrible state of mind. But ye know pollen!

Each golden speck seems as dust to the ordinary eye . . . yet any pinpoint of golden time I had with her in the cart went on forever for us just as pollen does for ye.

That's where my little cart took her and I was careful to keep its wheels oiled and the planks sanded for whenever she wanted to come outside.

No matter that once I'd drag her home and park it against the back of my hut, our cart looked for all the world no more elegant than a barrow with a board for a bench.

sixteen

ooooo

AND WHAT ARE WE GOING to do with ourselves now she's gone, me an' ye lot? Ye bees and all the glory that surrounds ye?

And Mary.

Aye, Mary, alone on the stairs after they laid the body out. Ever alone, that one. A space around herself at all times.

Did ye know—ye must've—we all did—what Mary really was?

Aye, William's biggest poem of all, the daffodil one. Saying he wandered lonely as a cloud . . . yet he was with Rotha when they saw all the golden daffodils. I've told ye Rotha saw them first. And Rotha first wrote their glory, William used her eyes for his poem and her eyes were all he needed but for one detail.

The best line of all . . . where the great poet lies on his couch remembering the golden glory . . . William couldn't figure out how to write that part. How you hold onto a vision after it has gone. Rotha had no trouble letting it fly free. She never tried to capture it! But William would grope. Oh it drove him nearly insane.

How do visions work? William asked the fireplace. It did not answer.

But Mary, sewing in the corner, keeping quiet until she could hold it no more, the missing line growing bigger inside her till it burst forth—*They flash upon that inward eye which is the bliss of solitude!*

Aye, we all knew Mary made up the wisest line her husband ever wrote.

For solitude was what our wife Mary knew more than any of us! Yet she was content in hers.

Mary is that rare self-sufficient person.

And this morning on the landing Mary says to me, James, now that Dorothy has died, don't worry about losing your position with us.

Us, she says to me. As if anyone but herself remained.

And I minded how Mary had said those same words to me when William died five years before. John Carter had made no bones telling me there was only enough money to keep either myself or William's horse. And that horse was a favourite with Mary for it had known William well and Mary stood for a long time with her face against that horse's head after William's death. I nearly said, Mary, don't fret, keep William's horse. I can always find a job don't you worry. But I still had Rotha to think of then. So I said nowt and I stayed, and Mary did have to say goodbye to that horse.

But now this morning of Rotha's own death when Mary says to me, James, you have been faithful to us and I will be faithful to you, I says to her, I'm not a bit worried, Mrs.

Wordsworth. For as you know, I am here at your service if you need me, but only then.

And she looks right into me and I understand her as I have always understood Mary. I have always heard her as I have always listened to everyone here at Rydal and she knows that. Oh, she's a lone one, that one.

Sometimes ideas are struggling to be born. An idea thriving in one place is mebbe something everybody there has known about for ages. And somewhere else, not far away, that same idea or mebbe a similar idea is behind a membrane having a very hard time being able to pierce through, struggling for its life. Aye, I think all of life is like that, ideas struggling to be born. Oh the difficulty they have. And the stillborn ideas, and the maimed ideas, beautiful they would've been had they had a chance to beak or claw or scratch their way through that membrane and burst into full life . . . Mary Wordsworth!

I mean Mary was never one for gallivanting but she wanted to see people. She was not a pondering person. Not a person that needed to write poetry unless her husband was having an emergency. If it were left to Mary, Rydal Mount would be the most temperate and peaceful place on this earth.

But I cannot stay with Mary.

And neither will ye, my lovelies. Aye, I'll read ye the red diary now, today, before we leave, ye and me. And we'll do the thing that I promised Rotha I would do, at the last.

For she reckoned I'd been peeping in it—when I got the chance—I had to peep in the red diary to see if she had put down anything we did together or thought together. I was anxious for it, looking for the story of myself—myself counting—in the whole story of the little family. My place in it. I kept leafing through the new bits looking for myself. As if Rotha Wordsworth would write about the likes of James Dixon. But I kept hoping.

One day she mentioned our little gateways!

Little gateways made of light
Naught of darkness told
Ephemeral Continuum
Inscribed with dust of gold—

And on the very day I read that part—I had been trying to find a time to confess to her that I had stumbled upon her book—but didn't she catch me holding it lovingly in my hands reading that verse over and over again!

Do you like my couplets, then, James?

She stood over me having moved soundless on her small feet.

I had warned myself about the soundlessness of those little feet. They could steal up on a fly or a midge or even a thrush. Not one of ye, mind. Ye'd know. She weighs no more than seven stone but she's spent that much time among ye I think she turned into one of ye at times, weighing no more than a bee herself. Going about on small wings like yours from here to there, now plunged in speedwell, now in the crab blossom, now in celandine—

Oh I felt terrible. A crawl of pure shame singed up from my chest to my neck over my face and closed around my scalp like a fish net closing over a fat trout that was my own stupid head with a big innocent grin on it like, as if she could count on me to be both a dunce and a deceiver. Well I never felt so ashamed in all my life. I might as well have never abstained from drink, only become the village drunk. I would rather in that moment have been anything and anybody but James Dixon, faithful deceiver of Dorothy Wordsworth.

Well? she says—do you?

Bravado was not in me and I never said a word of an excuse for I had no such thing prepared. I knew I was found out.

But Rotha doesn't calculate things the way other people do.

It's all right, James, she says. No need for you to play rigid rabbit. What you've read can't be unread. But tell me, James . . .

She was struggling and I do not want to admit I felt some small power surge up in me like a blade.

Sometimes you cannot help feelings that arise in you. My mam said that. You can't help the feelings, the only thing you can do is watch yourself in how you act.

Quiet, I have discovered, is a good weapon against your own worst self. It feels like a useless thing but it is very useful. I keep a little piece of quiet folded up in my back pocket. I know that with it I have wiped away quite a few of my own mistakes before they spilled over the whole of my world and spoiled it.

I didn't make up the little couplets, you know, she says.

Didn't you? I leapt gentle as I could upon this topic—where she came up with her secret words—instead of the topic of why I was anywhere near them.

They came to me of their own will, she says.

I remained quiet.

Sometimes it works, she said, and sometimes it doesn't. Listening. Knowing which message is of freedom and which issues from the prison of my own smallness. That is why this book is secret. Only in this book do I dare write my own sorrows. Might you read some of it out loud to me, James?

Out loud, Miss?

What about this part? She took the book from me and found a section and handed it back, open.

I tried to argue but she says no, go on. I need to know how it sounds in the mouth of another person. For when William hears me speak in the way of the red diary, he warns me that I might yet join poor Mary Lamb. That I am mentally unwell. So read to me, please. I want to hear how it sounds, myself, with fresh ears.

So I says, Miss, don't mind my nose down in the book and my not looking up, for that is how I have to read, slower than you would do it yourself.

But she says never mind slow, James—I know my handwriting is bad. Read this part about the tree roots—

And I read a bit about roots reaching out like hands, but not reaching for her. There was nothing in their hands for her—and she says, Do you know what I mean by that, James? Do you?

And I says I think so, Miss. I've often felt the roots of trees were a bit like hands myself.

And she says go on then.

And I read as smooth as I could, like. She's right, her writing is slanted and squashed and some of her lines are like string pulled nearly straight with only a few kinks for letters.

I do the best I can and after I finish she says to me, Do you see? How a tree plunges its roots—her roots—like arms into the earth and her beautiful head is underground, and her trunk splits in two as her legs reach into the sky. The tree is an upside-down woman. Head buried in moss, James. Legs flung up like limbs of a great, petrified acrobat! Ears under the ground, unhearing. Mouth underground, unspeaking. One with that tree, James, I have heartwood instead of a human heart and there's nothing I can do to make it flesh. And now you've read it.

I have done, Miss, I'm sorry . . .

Stop it. What do you think? Do you think, as my brother does, that I need a few more drops of medicine?

How would ye lot have replied?

Look down the bank will ye—pieces of ice are floating past us on the lake. The water isn't disturbed enough to wrinkle, only ripple in spots—halves of circles colliding soft on a misty mirror—a mirror with polish smeared on it but no one's wiped the polish off yet with a cloth. Everything soft grey except the reeds, and they're that quiet gold. And snowflakes floatin'. And the old gold grasses bowed and swaying and all the leaves brown as dead mice.

Miss, I says, I'm not the one who'd know if you need more medicine.

No, she says, I suppose you're not. But you have known me a long time.

Aye, Miss, I says, I have. And I wondered then how many more rides in the cart we'd have, though I said nothing about that.

We've eaten quite a few blackberries together by now, you and me, she says. And drunk the juice.

Aye, Miss.

I had wiped purple dribbles off both our chins with my hanky.

Have ye ever eaten a purply-black bursting-with-sunshine blackberry sticking through somebody's fence? Have ye ever—o'course ye have! Ye lot feast and slurp on 'em, I've seen ye with my own eyes. Quaffing blackberry wine with the fairies! And so did we, Rotha and me over the summers. We grew hungry and thirsty with wandering and that's what we ate and drank.

Blackberry is made of a sky dull and leaden but cracking with lightning. A berry like that knows the flight of swallows and robins that've fledged then grown up near the bush—the berry only comes out once the robin has grown and learned its song. All that song and all that lightning and all that blackness and all that rich redness of the robin's breast is in that berry and ye know it—and Rotha did an' all. But more than only taste, she'd look in each drupe of that berry, the little mirrors . . . they were little mirrors, this is the thing. And Rotha knew they were gems. She was a gem-seer.

William and Rotha were once twins inside your world.

Ye'd think nobody like me could get in there. Really, I never thought I would.

It was well-brambled. It was hidden. It was secured from anyone that can't understand, but ye understand. Ye were born inside the columbines. Ye were born between the layers of the leeks. Ye were born in the bluest wings of the blackest bird . . . Ye know. Ye know the land where Rotha lived.

And her brother saw it. William. He knew where she lived, but some people see a thing and they can't abandon themselves to it. They're not wild enough. He wasn't wild enough. Aye, she was never tamed. He had the church. He went to church and so did Mary, but she couldn't. Now why couldn't she? The pain. Oh but the pain was not only medical pain. The pain was a thorny barricade that prevented her from entering the tame world. She wanted William to go the whole distance into the wild land but—he had a grain of caution, didn't he. He was the one that had the grain of caution.

But me—what would I be doing with caution?

Here's the diary, look—she stitched it herself like all her notebooks. The thing is, now like, I've got to do the right thing by this red one, haven't I. You can't just leave it lying around. Her other ones—with their shopping lists for this and that—sewing needles, special ingredients for the custard and bits of material to lengthen the curtains in the room downstairs, and on and on. A mustard spoon, all listed, and, heh, lovely bits and pieces of her day. Then they flip to her real song . . . or pieces of her song like bits of bread along the path or notes you hear of a bird's song. In all her tattered books she's scattering crumbs or taking down the notes from birds' throats as they sing. She's not changing the notes into anything. They're the plain wild notes. And in those books there is no Dorothy. There is hardly ever an *I*. But the red diary is not like that . . .

Here ye go. Here it is . . . I will read it to ye because she asked me to read it out loud in the fresh air after she was gone. All her feelings. Disperse them out of doors once and for all, she says to me. And I'm here to not only read it to ye now, but to do the other thing she asked an' all.

Aye, ye lot won't be long here at Rydal and nor will I, not without Rotha.

Mary will not want ye in the sycamore without Rotha and Dixon to keep ye happy, to tell ye things, to tend ye.

I'm going to be gentle and I'm going to take ye with me. I promise ye that. And if a few wisps of smoke come in it's only me doing as Rotha wanted, ye understand. I'll smoke ye but I won't use much. Every one of her pages I'm about to read to ye now, I'll light each one and I'll blow the smoke in your hollow.

Don't mind it! I'll never harm ye.

I'm only burning the red diary as Rotha begged, for its ashes to fly with all her feelings to where only ye'll find them.

I've put a comb of your honey in my skep and ye'll be safe when the smoke comes in your sycamore, just crawl out into the skep and it'll hold ye.

I'll wait here for every one of ye. I'll wait here for your queen as I waited on my own queen all these years. And off we'll go.

Our wife Mary won't pay no mind and there'll be no harm to ye. For Mary won't be much longer following the dead and then, aye, it'll be strange coming back to visit the little churchyard in Grasmere once I'm the only one left of the fam'ly.

Do ye know the first thing I'll buy with my railroad shares? A railing to place 'round the Wordsworth gravestones. So no one will disturb them, only lichen and moss. I'll bring my flask of tea and I will think about them and all the time we had together. And there'll be lots of visitors like that big spider with yellow stripes, look. Rooks and thrushes and the flowers she loved, and the church bells ringing.

And us.

Rest in peace they say and yes, she'll love that. Hated any hustle unless at the fair like. Oh she loved that all right, hawkers and the pie man, horse traders, lasses and lads at play. As long as she had only to nod to gypsies and children. None of the stifling talk regular people get on with. And she'd say after an hour, James, I've had enough! Take me home into the quietude. As if she was saying let's go to the willows where the cold moon shines. Or bulrushes where a duck might hide. Away from all glare or noise.

Aye, quietude. She said that word so many times it was like a brooch on her breast.

It's daft me talking about the fair in January isn't it. The wind's blown me hat right off. Hang on while I nab it— rolling like a wheel! That's 'im. Aye, the fair's nice. Summer's fine. But Rotha always loved frost and a cold moon. Not another soul about. Under frost glittering on the bare branches. She loved a winter tree.

The little family. Have they left each other desolate?

They tried not to. They tried, each one of them, not to abandon each other.

What will I do with the cloak William dropped in the grass the very first time I laid eyes on him and Rotha? He never knew I kept it. It was a dandy cloak then, but it's threadbare now. It's in shreds! I have it yet in my hut, wrapping up some of the tender bulbs all winter to keep them alive. Would ye like me to wrap our basket in it when we go?

When you see somebody for the first time and you're nowt but five and she's a white moth—away on the wind she flies after her brother, who has left his cloak on the grass in his big rush to meet the mail coach . . .

And you pick that coat up even though your mam says Eh, you shouldn't, but of course she doesn't stop you, your mam can't help but be a bit proud of your nabbing the cloak . . .

I had it for a blanket for a long time.

The red satin lining was the be-all and end-all in finery as far as I was concerned, even if it had been mended twenty times by the time William left it on the ground. Rotha was the one who mended it for him. She mended his everything.

And I never forgot that later day in Lady Wood, with the mushrooms and the blue flowers. She was still young and quick then, and yet so sad.

He had three fairies looking after him, didn't he. He had Mary and her sister Sarah and he had Rotha. People talked. How pampered he was. But he was the one who wrote, *The world is too much with us*—that was one poem he managed to write all by himself! *Getting and spending, we lay waste our powers*. That's what powerful people do with their powers isn't it. Lay them waste. *Little we see in Nature that is ours.* That was his tragedy and we all knew it, and I wouldn't want anybody to think that I hold it against him.

His life was a sacrifice.

For Dorothy held the keys to the kingdom.

Oh, Lady, you held the keys.

Hang on, let's see if her pages will catch . . . I'll try one from the end with nothing on it, only a bit of blotted ink with the word *William* shining through—that's 'im—aye! The ash floats all right, just like that white moth she was on the first day I saw her. And now let me read ye the red diary before we leave Rydal. I've told ye a few bits, now here's the rest.

Motes, ash, softness. Dorothy's word transmute into these, her private pages dissolve and disperse in the air—no one to know them now but myself, Sycamore, and Rydal's bees, riding the wind.

Do you burn the pages because her voice is strange, James? Too strange for human ears and eyes? Is that what you fear?

Can that be the moon floating up already, while it is yet daylight? See how it hangs, caught in my top limbs, even before the sun has gone? Time!

Time is both late and soon, my friend James. Dorothy's death-day is growing late, and the sparks that will soon undo her pages burn with a strange, intense gold.

Her strangeness is my home.

Dispersal—as you know, James—is not disappearance. There was nothing dissoluble about our Rotha! *The naked seed pods shiver,* she wrote. *The pine trees rock from their base.* Comfortless was her world. Would you erase this truth? Innocent child, James Dixon, fulfilling the will of the enchanted housemaster.

Would you like me to say now, like the god of St. Oswald's, *Well done, thou good and faithful servant . . .*

Quietly, stoically
standing by
to pick up the pieces
as they fly . . .

For you were with the little household all along, weren't you, James, making things run as smoothly as humanly possible. While the others imagined that they did everything by themselves. Their imaginations were always the important thing.

But the truth I know is a stranger one. As strange as Dorothy's unspoken words.

All right, then, James. Speak Dorothy's words now, and set your fire to her pages. We in the garden will hold her feelings far beyond Rydal's years, into an age you cannot see.

I, Sycamore, feel the people listening even now, in the gold span outside our little day.

6

THE RED DIARY

X

Wm said no & I believed him. I wrote my recollections of
Scotland five times by my own hand . . . & I fixed it up—
oh—finding the memories & placing them in the correct
locations . . . that was a monumental task. I mean I worked
hundreds & hundreds of hours on it.

I never said it was for anybody other than our friends. It
was not myself that contemplated publication. Was it?

But—I was asked . . . & I—I've always been the same as
Wm & Sam—me on my rock & Wm on his & Sam
Coleridge lying on the grass between us with a blade of
hay in his mouth, chewing on it & thinking, & all of us
thinking. All of us thinking with one mind.

All the same.

That was the promise.

It was the promise I was given: when Mary Wordsworth came it would not change—Wm & Sam & I were all one & the same. We were The Concern.

We were the same.

I was not different.

I did not marry a man & become a wife. That was the promise. I would not become anyone's wife. I would keep writing.

. . . & writing, & writing. So when I asked Wm . . . when I said I'd been invited to publish, it took a long time for me to realize—Wm was trying to find something to say, some reason why I shouldn't. I mean, he'd promised, had he not. We were all one & the same mind.

You won't like it, he said.

The limelight. You'll hate it. You, my dear Sister, who likes so much to hide in solitude. You'll wilt, he said, he the one that wrapped himself up in blankets & hid in the bottom of a boat. He the one that sequestered himself away in the terraces. He the one that wore that black cloak with the red lining—& wrapped himself up in it to be invisible in the night. He the one that groaned if Little Miss Belle barked for it meant unexpected visitors. People coming to see him. Gawk at me, he'd say. Watch me & look at me. I always thought, if somebody wants to hide themselves, they will do it. No one needs to be encouraged into quietness. He had me convinced that writing & being a published writer were two different things. The first was all right but the second, he claimed he wanted nothing more in this world than to protect me from it.

That's the funny thing—it stopped my argument. For claiming no need of protection meant wanting. Wanting more. Wanting readers. Wanting what Wm had. There was a very dark, raven-like aspect to my brother that forbade my saying that I wanted what he had.

So it stuck in my gullet.

A knot at first.

A pain. A sickness. A stab. A mute agony that grew.

I couldn't eat.

Oh I could eat.

But I couldn't digest or be nourished.

I held my desire back—& it was never desire for the bodily love of any man, Wm or Sam or Hazlitt or any man, not Quincey, not any man's body, surely they knew that.

I held myself back from my own body—of published work.

I swallowed a big stone there, didn't I.

×××

There is a me-shaped hole in the path—maybe it has a membrane. Maybe it has just been torn into the flesh of the garden & is skinless.

At night the hole is black & by day it is green. I am an empty space. Nevertheless, people call me by name. They offer food as to a me-shaped god made of light & darkness. Little sandwiches, an orange, buns of bread, a saucer of gooseberry jam.

If the hole that has replaced me speaks, it does so by a deep scream of one who is falling. No one can hear, for if they could, they would rush to the hole-edge, peer through, & be themselves in danger of disappearing.

But I have not disappeared—the me-hole is visible, it is present, it is my shape, it is defined, it is both a Missing Person & a definite shape of me. I am a hole. The hole is truly myself. The hole is horrifying. Is everyone a hole & am I the only one who doesn't mind? I don't mind because I am with Wm & Sam, who are, no, Wm & Sam Coleridge are not holes—they are jubilant glow-worms who have eaten into the leaf of the world & made the me-hole.

Before I was a hole, what was I?

Slugs have green blood. So I am not a slug.

But though I had red blood I was not a man, which I did not like & did not appreciate.

No. The opposite of that: I am a shy body with retractable claws all along my belly: I grow fatter & more substantial, & by the end of my growth I occupy a large part of the path & cannot be got around. Everyone must halt. They consult Wm. He does not want me bodily removed or rolled aside. He has made a vow to leave me as general obstruction. You will never hear from his lips a word of complaint. Mary has asked him to build a lightweight bridge over me out of thin sticks & bits of willow. He won't even consider it: he has secretly asked James to keep my little cart wheels & pegs maintained & ready for carriage at all times of the day or night. This does not please Mary. She would like to get a pair of shears & cut me in two halves.

I have never been beautiful.

We are—Wm & I—interested in roundness: the roundness of my shy-body which can be rolled up- or down-hill . . . & the roundness of wheels, small wooden ones, that can be placed under my body so I can be transported.

They have already started acting on this idea of me as a me-shaped hole. A cut-out, a silhouette, a cameo disappearance. Of course, nothing could be farther from the . . . The membrane is not cut but torn. If you look with the micro-vision of bluebottle or even thrush, perhaps even dog or cat—it has nothing to do with domesticity blinding one—I have never cooked a single meal to be eaten sitting indoors. All you need is clear sight—wash the windows for heaven's sake! Splash waterfall-ends into those eyes as do I.

I hurtle through.

All I need is to go outside, look into a green-lit space, go deeper into star-shaped bits of shade.

Into spider-house geometry.

Into gooseberry stripes.

Into measurements of one mountain against the next.

Around the bark of someone standing silent for its hundredth summer.

Into the veins of a leaf map or remnant of melted stone locked red within another stone. Fur inside reeds. Rampant extravagance of perfume in the dog-rose, look closer—be proboscis suspended by wing—be all eyes in a pile like the

beads of a blackberry which turn out to be fly-eye, buzz-
vision, airborne Eye of membrane-held focus: the
membrane made of something thin as thought.

The membrane is flesh's spit, blown into a bubble & cut &
sewn by fingers of that Dorothy you thought had fallen
down a hole, a green hole by day & a dark hole by night—
Oh she did not fall down it! She is quite easy to see in
there—out there—all you need is a massive eye where your
hunger dwells . . . have you ever seen yourself with an eye, a
massive eye, where your belly once sat? Some of us have
replaced mortal hunger with a hunger for vision that renders
us fearless, renders us without human love. For what is
human love for, if not to see, together, the mathematical
secrets within what dwells out-of-doors? I do not mean
numbered mathematics, but umbrel & shoot as they slow-
sizzle in the gas from water & sun & earth & air. Animals
are quivering question-marks, like us: look at a velvet cow,
how sad its peaceful restraint!

No—we plunged our noses into the ground & breathed
ground's drug made of animate geometry. To meet the red-
breast became an enregistration into the courts of the
traveller-king.

Envoy, that's me.

On my Scale of Decrepitude which goes from zero (Beyond Utmost Decrepitude) to 13 (The Golden Streets), every Indoors is a blundering state of being below five, with dust or crumbling bits or general malaise for its energy & none can stop me longing to go wild.

& what of the Grim state of Manhood? First let me mention that the flowers who know Myself are, some of them, blue & tall. Others have been short & pale cream or yellow. Certain ones such as Bee Balm are red & bear fragrant leaves. All without exception have been varied & original in our conversations. People think that flowers cannot, for instance, be acerbic. This is un-insightful. I have had frequent talks with Chicory, for instance, about the Grim state of Manhood in the neighbourhood.

As a matter of fact, there is one living in this house who would, were I to die, do all in their power to demolish every calyx, pistil, petiole, umbel, pod, anther & filament until the place be a mass of uprooted gore—this would hardly destroy the entities themselves, whose life exists in a Body that cannot be murdered.

This imperishable Body is known about by certain people. It is not Floral but extends to bird life as well as to the un-murderable States of animals, fish & minerals, the mineral Body being elemental as opposed to fluid-animate yet force-filled & in fact basic to all other imperishable Body-forms. (Basic in the sense that there is nothing without it.)

Red Potentilla.

Bell-like flowers lend a ready, listening ear—Nothing
could, for instance, be more sympathetic than a Delphinium
bending to listen to a question put to it by myself.

Of course, any question worth asking reverberates in a
bell-ear for some timeless-time, as if it were a mouthful of
mystery-wine lingering 'round the tongue of a vineyard-
labourer who, in wind, sun, rain & time, has perceived more
about wine's secrets than the most revered & sophisticated
Sommelier.

But as with all forms, Delphiniums come with their particular gentle warning: Our colony slowly deteriorates with
age & there is nothing you can do about it.

Alas?

No—triumph!

For what can be more relaxing than the certainty that there
was nothing you could have done? No recrimination here in
Delphiniums' world.

×××

Our wife Mary has thrown another Book on my bed
admonishing me to read but I am too busy with my feelings

to open it & have been busy thus for years. People are so tiresome in their mad rush to avoid all feelings whatsoever, especially the literary souls all around me—the books! The poems. The endless words. Get me out of this room, out of any book, outside. Had I known when young the things I know now, I would not have married my brother Wm.

Oh, it was quite a wedding. He held onto the ring for ages, blessing it & walking with me & with it under the moon, itself an ever-changing ring trying to come into being: now broken, now filled with molten gold, never quite fitting on my finger because it was the moon & far bigger than any ring, farther away, & moving—always sailing around the stars & the clouds—why did I ever believe it could be made into a Husband ring & slipped on my own finger?

Oh Wm did slip it on, all right. The replica. The ring that has forever since our wedding night—or that morning after our wedding night when he tore it off me—or we both tore it off me—where it has nestled around the finger of our wife Mary ever since!

Mary, so perfect, like the perfect ring which is Not a perfect replica of the everchanging ever incomplete ever knowing moon.

I am sorry, everyone will have to wait if they want me to join the epidemic of reason, the queue of propriety, manacles of safety—no more of that for me. They will have to wait outside the bars of my cage-not-cage. Only those who do not feel their feelings will look on my room, my bed, my post-humous life as some pathetic enclosure. We know—the inhabitants of my mind, & myself—me & my multitudi-nous winged companions, leafed companions, song-voiced familiars—we know we have bolted to freedom. It seems not thus, I know. It seems as if others are the sensible ones & I have gone somewhere inaccessible & restricted. Mary, you come to my bed with books! As if books could ever replace all amongst which I now run free.

Poems? Oh, Wm. Poems? With their structure & gait, they are like dark horses & you barely holding the reins, but holding on, vying for control. Everyone vying for control.

All are afraid of darkness, when all I want is for it to sweep down upon me so I can freely visit the splendours I find by following the light collected in my own mind—not imag-ined, no—but real sight—I always had it & that is why I found it impossible to enter a room of people chattering away about the things in that room. Arguing over tea-sets or the Turkish carpet or the curtains or who was coming down over the road in a new hat.

Take all that away!

I should have shouted this when I was—at what age did it become unbearable? For when we were young, Wm, Sam & I—there was no Turkish carpet, only the frost hung like

diamonds in the trees. Gems upon gems. They could see it.
Once upon a time . . . & then something—did it blind
them? What blinded them & did not blind me, so that I had
to—I was the one who had to hold the gem-world fast when
all around me, all the so-called faithful men around me, had
become—Can I say faithless?

Oh I don't care anymore what I say to our wife Mary, to all
proper ladies of the vale—give me Miss Barker. Give me
the young men I loved, who were wild & not tame. My
feelings might be too much with me but I'd rather that a
thousand times than suffer the pallid consequence of
focusing on a book Mary would have me read, or on any of
the things coming out of people's pale & monstrous mouths.
Laudanum! Oh yes it was convenient at first for me to take
that, it shut me up & kept me quite happy, in their minds,
didn't it. The poppy. The brandy. The diffusion of all sharp
things. Well give me the sharp things now. Give me my
sword. Get that nurse out of here or I will knock her on the
head once more—yes I mean it. I do mean it. I do for once
mean it. Oh yes.

×××

What is love? You think I was a spurned lover? You think
Wm's cracked wedding vow was about my not having a
husband in the earthly sense? When will you know by
looking into my eyes that nothing in me whatsoever is or
ever has been or ever will be about earthly sense? How is it

you can't see? It's because the world is too much with you, yes, late & soon, yes late & soon & all time that is not time. Getting & spending you lay waste your powers, yes, you have given your hearts away, a sordid boon, amen. Little we see in Nature that is ours . . . We? No. Speak for yourselves. What happened to you? You crowd of lost traitors, bereft imbeciles—I am speaking to you now from my saddle on the back of a bat.

×××

Excuse me, what was it you wanted?

Have you people not learned how to get along without me yet? A button sewn on? A transcription of your latest thoughts for the papers?

Hello?

Have you not noticed something is different? It has been some time now since I felt able to pretend to care about any of that. As a matter of fact, it has been seventeen years, twenty-one days, two hours, thirty-seven minutes & seventeen seconds since I cared about your own personal situation. The children have long grown up, or at least they have ceased to need me the way you appear to still need me, or the facsimile of me that you have created for your . . . shall we call it your convenience?

I have been a convenient person to have around, loving as
unreservedly as I do, or did. Forbearance has been important
to me & I know you will agree it has helped this household.
Funny that they call it a house-hold & not a house-drop.
Not a house let-go. Not a house fallen downhill, & not a
house released.

Hold me in your house.

Yes, you have done that, thank you.

You did it & I was supposed to find that sufficient. Was.
I was a convenient person to have around, but now how
things have changed.

✕✕✕

Womanliness!

What is womanliness? I thought I knew, or I thought I
might know. Until Mary Lamb went mad from too much of
it—let's see, what happened again? Ah, yes—her grandma
died so Mary & her family could no longer go to the country
& were stuck in a small London flat. Who did Mary Lamb,
in all womanliness, look after? Her mother, paralyzed in her
body, slept in bed with her like an unmoving log of hate. The
mother who had never shown her any love, not even when
she was a babe & her brother John had an accident & an
infected fever which Mary Lamb tended because she loved

him, & her beloved brother Charles, like my own beloved Wm, was away away in the days, away from the little cramped flat. Away on his own important business. Though he said he loved her—& her father in the flat as well, completely demented, & she had to look after him & her grandmother dead so that the house in the country was no longer a place to which she could escape, & she the only source of an income for the household, sewing cloak after cloak amongst the rest of them & their clamour. Who would not have a temporary frenzy?

Was that womanliness? Or might womanliness mean when I went to Germany with Wm & kept our fire going whilst we both translated German to make pennies? The cold unbearable, & neighbours refusing to believe we were brother & sister, not man & woman living together unwed. We had no language, no friends, & no real fire, as I was—I must face it—a terrible fire-keeper, most unwomanly.

Is womanliness in my love of flowers? In my naming of them, my lying in grass on the soft earth who is, herself, womanly? But no—I left off naming, or I named wrong, or I concentrated on nameless curves, pistils, trumpets. I concentrated on a most unwomanly, piercing blue, for my favourite flowers were blue & they had about themselves something merciless.

Or might I have become womanly through having looked after enough children of other women, when those women

were away or ill or indisposed? Certainly like you, Mary
Lamb, in your mothering of young Miss Isola, did I not
mother my little Basil when Wm & I were still a couple?
Taught him to read? Gave him jam & bread with cream?
Did not suckle him with my breasts but lo, how could these
small breasts suckle a whole child? I am such a small person!
Still, some sort of woman, & not a man. Nobody has sug-
gested I am a man.

Womanly, then, how?

You could say I have roasted a few chops so the fat glitters
& drips & makes mouths of men water like crazy mouths
do when they foam with lust.

Or you could say that when Sam Coleridge & I stood under
the hanging birch bough gemmed with frost, I wore a
bridal veil studded with heaven's jewels if there be a heaven,
& Sam did not deny I was womanly, for if he had denied it,
he would be denying the times we were together with feroc-
ity, though frozen not hot—we had a frozen burning. But a
frozen burning is perhaps not the womanly evidence for
which I search.

I have a bosom, a bonnet, a lump of cheese in my pantry
to share, a tart whose edge I crimped with my thumb, &
that crimping extended the flesh of my thumb into the
pastry of the tart before baking, so that the pastry itself
was like a piece of my flesh—Here, this is my body to be

broken for you. This is my flesh for you to share. Eat it in memory of me.

No, apparently that is not womanly either.

& Whatever all the things might be that I have outlined, doesn't there always loom a time when they become defunct? A time of war, a time of men chasing their own fame, a time of famine or plague, a time of catastrophic cold or storms? When the details of womanliness, or all details whatsoever, become a thing of the past, or an extravagance, or—& this one is very womanly I have been told—a frill?

×××

Eye-skin. Endless intrigue—I have descended into the kaleidoscope. There is a hole leading to a staircase leading to an intricacy of streets with pieces of every colour glass you can name—pea-green, turquoise, garnet or gold— pieces of glass & when you come close you do not need William Withering's optical glass but can look through the transparencies with your bare eyes. Naked flesh has nothing on the naked eye-skin.

Naked flesh is fat & bread, lard & bun. But the skin on the eye is so thin as to be made of fish skin from the depths of the ocean. Eyeball membrane separates me from wonder & the separation is unmeasurably thin, thinner than glass or even than new-formed ice in November on the Lake's edge.

Thinner than thought itself is eye-skin, & who has ever peeled it or looked through it except the medical experts, the surgeons & body-thieves? I have my own eyes to look through in the streets of London with Mary Lamb. Together we name for each other the things we see, & what we see is not what our brothers see! The kaleidoscope is a gift for a young girl who already knows what we know but has not named it. Emma Isola, if only Mary Lamb & I'd had mothers as you have in us. We would have trusted far sooner the visions we saw through our own eye-skins.

The gaping give-mouth in our skulls.

Mary Lamb is older than I am & she is completely porous when feeling my situation or anyone's. Her sympathy knows no bounds if she chooses to award it, & if she does you had better say yes. For Mary Lamb's sympathy has saved me.

I do not think she gives it to everyone, or that she could if she desired, because it takes something from her, much like the spark they say Christ felt depart from him once touched by a woman in a crowd. But Mary Lamb gave me more than the Lamb of God ever gave that woman in the book of—what book was it? I do not remember those books. That woman in that book did not then go on & proclaim her joy from the rooftops but here I am, writing down exactly what transpired for me when I had my fortnight with Mary

Lamb—ostensibly to get my teeth renewed—but in fact to renew my whole Self, through the power of Mary Lamb's own experience. Her womanhood. Her descent into what they call madness. Her murderous past, her matricide, & most important—two blessed weeks uninterrupted by the male members of our families.

Her first instructions came before my teeth were pulled & replaced. Why, I asked her, have I become exhausted in this perpetual & enervated manner that means I drag myself around like seven stones of flour in a sack?

The reason, she said, is the very gaping give-mouth in our skulls, whose openness is a perpetual asking of what we can do for everyone in the house, even when they have not asked us. It is the controlling force behind our every move on behalf of the mother, the father, the husband, the brother, & any baby or child in our sphere. What, asks our gaping give-mouth, do you need, & how may I present it to you? & there we go, walking miles into the village or the town, stooping to pick things dropped on the floor or the ground that might be in the way of our family members or of value to them. Moving this package here & that bottle there, this burden here & that burden there, carrying like a donkey every little scrap & morsel whether it is a jar of milk or a broken heart.

We carry it all, says Mary Lamb, & we carry it down the miles & when we sleep, or so-called sleep, there we are, still carrying gingerly so as not to lose or drop all that requires carrying in our beloved families. So that by the time we are fifty as you are now, my dear Dorothy, you are left with your giving gape-mouth hanging on its hinge ready to wail with tiredness, & your shoulders are tired to the bone, & you are tired to the bone, yet what do you do but keep going, for you do not even realize you are tired, only that you hurt in a blinding way.

Blinding, yes, I said to Mary Lamb, for my vision itself is getting blurred at morning & at night with increasing labours & I cannot read as much as I should. I am losing my reading.

Reading, she cried! You wear your eyes out mending the shirts, all the little stitches for everybody, sewing not only their garments but their broken souls, sewing their weary thoughts with your comforting words but never hearing the one sentence that would quell the bleeding lining of your own perception.

& when Mary Lamb said the bleeding lining of your own perception I did not hesitate to know what she meant. For inside me is a layer like wet silk that lines my brain & heart & bowels & if I am honest it has a wet silken twin that lines my womb, & that one—that one!—has never been attended to. I told Mary Lamb this & she said yes, this is why you have to do as I say whilst you are here with me, while you wait to have your jaw renewed with its teeth & its hinges & its sadness that runs deep as oceans.

×××

I don't know—it's as if someone whilst I slept peeled my
skin off so I awaken all of a sudden skinned & raw with no
knowledge of how I became thus. I look at the hills, & they
have nothing to do with me but have turned their backs.
Their shoulders are blue & their faces are turned against
me. No hope of comfort there, best turn to the trees—but
no, the trees also have become uninterested in me.
Something has changed their sympathetic leaves which no
longer contain green blood but are dry & swish like
threshed hay, the green gone out of them & a greyness
greeting me instead. Granted this happens more often in
August than it does in winter or early summer.

Is it the late summer, then, that gives me this merciless
feeling as if I am nothing to any of the beloved hills & fields
that once held me in their regard?

I wake raw & peeled & bleeding. My emotions have all run
to the surface of my limbs & they writhe there in agony
like orphaned worms. The sky glares down at me with a
merciless blaring blue. Where is the beloved & merciful
rain? Where is mist or fog? Why am I caught in the lamp of
the sun's stare, as if the sun wanted to witness me curling up
& burning with arid fever?

But I lie. It can happen at any time of year. In the tenderest
April shower or the newest froth-greened baby birch

half-leafed bowers, I can be this spectral lone wolf, this animal caught in mid-howl with a cold grimace for a face & a blind sleet-storm for tears, & no reason for any of it. No reason but being a crazy lonely soul with its skin peeled away & its muscle, blood & nerves pulsating purple & blue & garnet like a monstrous wound bound by a membrane thin as a berry's skin—oh but a word will puncture it & my blood will obliterate my world.

If only I were that lucky—if only I could end everything with a needle-prick. I would do it—it would appear like a sewing mishap or simple kitchen accident . . . She was one minute dressing the fowl, & the next, the tip of the blade merely pricked her thumb & she burst like a ripe fruit in the centre of the kitchen, & was whole no more, but shattered & scattered & spilled so that every bit of her became formless—there was a pool where our Sister once stood.

This is what happened in Mary Lamb's mind only it was her mother she pricked & the pricking was not small or incidental but massive, a slaughter. So it was not the same. Yet— if I could simply end my life by seeming to cut my finger with the point of the meat knife or the embroidery needle or the darning awl, then nobody could fault me & nobody need know about this torment I feel, this peeled, raw state that comes upon me in which I feel the cruel ache of having to move & stand & walk & be alive among other living beings, who do not seem to feel these torments at all. Except Mary Lamb, whose raw agony is even more excruciating than my

own. In fact, my own, next to hers, becomes insignificant, &
that is what makes being with her a relief.

I wish I knew what causes the peeled state with its unbearable harshness. If it were aloneness then I would simply try
to spend more time in company. If it were feeling over-
whelmed by social demands, why, I could easily plead a
headache or bad bowels—god knows I often do! If it were
simply too much glaring sunlight I could stay in the shade of
a willow or rest behind curtains like the lovely curtain Mary
Lamb hung at my window during my convalescence there.
But I sigh with incomprehension of my own self, for any of
these things might set me off the wrong way one day yet
bother me not at all the next. I do not know what it is that
causes the light or the darkness to overtake me.

When it is at its worst I cannot even grieve or cry—my chest
& throat & eyes become encased in a leaden shield. I go
around like this for days or even weeks, not knowing what
caused it or why it started, though I can always pinpoint the
moment at which my joy departed . . . & then—a moment
later & who can tell when it might happen—joy flies back
into my body exactly like a wild bird that has been away &
flown back of its own sweet accord!

I wish I could beckon it somehow when I feel ready to give
up, when my body becomes immobilized, my legs wooden
& my fingers dead, & my mind unable to remember the
idea of any kind of future, let alone a beautiful one.

At home at Rydal of course I do not tell anyone this. I do not tell Wm, who would medicate me.

& I certainly do not mention it to our wife Mary, who would admonish me—who would say—who has said—For heaven's sake, woman, rise above it! Every woman's throat has a burning coal stuck red-hot in it. If we patiently endure as we should then the coal will eventually behave itself. The coal will tinkle & dwindle to grey & settle into words we can share with the people around us as if they were normal words. As if they had always been normal words & not a wild woman's incendiary wails—is what our wife Mary would say. Not out loud, of course. Never out loud.

Is London a dream?

Or is it real? I never know!

I dreamed not once but many times that I travelled its lanes, the back lanes behind the grand displays are the thing, places that begin in a narrow passageway then beckon with colour & sound just around the corner. A shout, a scrap of garment hung to dry, white that contains all colours or blue reflecting in a white garment from the sky above all the soot—blue filtering down or mauve filtering up from the shadows.

All the lanes, the little ones, the little busy ones, there they start all narrow & they last long & blossom out as if into fireworks, or the bloom at the end of a stem, or the fantastic scene at the end of this, the toy we found for Emma Isola— yes, your mother's friend has not forgotten it. But it is not a toy, inasmuch as every grownup in London has one in his hand & peers into it for dear life, to escape this world & join the indescribable glories of heaven.

I say I dreamed my London walks & I did dream them. I dreamed them in Grasmere & in Germany & I continue to dream them as I grow old in Rydal. For each night once my eyes shut upon the spangled fields where Dixon drags me in our cart, upon what should they open but sister-gems of the city! I doubt I only dreamed London's most beguiling streets. Yet I think—though I'm strangely never sure—that the most tantalizing, the mistiest streets, faint or lurid in equal mea- sure, all jewel-clash like Emma Isola's new toy—the purest streets, the most dreamlike alleys with the best stories or fragments of tales—those I did dream. I walked them with these same feet that strode the Lakes.

I love London, when I am in it, every bit as much as I have loved my country home with all its flower gems, its lake- shimmer, its diamond crowns sparkling in hidden places, its cascades of silver, falling water. The city is all this & more once I am in it. It is only when listening to Wm that I forget & believe it dirty or fearsome or a place in which

I might get lost. Listening to Wm you would think we were a pair of fragile & new-hatched swallows unable to stand a smudge of chimney smoke or eat a Cheapside bun. Maybe Wm is that fragile.

✕✕✕

It's wonderful how I can roam the streets invisible. A man lords it over a woman but once in the streets of London, hark! He is constantly seen as a mark—offered compan-ionship or wagers or the latest swindle-toy or defunct pocket-watch—or offered nothing but the unseen hand filching from his trousers soft as a feathered bird that has no bones. Yet a woman past fifty can walk the streets for an hour & be seen by no one at all. As if by magic, she is unseen like the wind itself, known only by other women her age, for we see each other with special eyes that live all over our bodies.

Yes our bodies are covered in sensitive eyes.

Some of the eyes see in the way normal to ordinary eyes: they see form & hue & can read signs or tell when a thun-derhead looms. But our other eyes can do all sorts of things. They can smell, only it is not a nose-kind-of-smell they know, but a sharp curling of the air from a doorway or back lane—we know if someone is being hurt or maimed or loved in the shadows—& some of our eyes can hear, only it is not an ear kind of hearing—it is more as if our skin has scales like tiny herring scales except these are old woman scales, yes, we have them all over our skin & all we have to do is adjust them like miniature sails in this direction or that, & we can sense any sound through six walls, through an earthen roof over a work cellar, through a bell tower high over St. James's Street. And lies!

We have eyes lining our throats like keyholes, & where are the keys but in the raindrops or songs of street starlings & the keys tell these, our throat-eyes, all sorts of songs-of-the-day, such as how long it will be before anyone notices us noticing them, which is very long—in fact months & sometimes years or even forever.

We can, & this is the part Mary Lamb & I most enjoy in our fleet-footed romps around London, we can stare into the faces of all & sundry & we can, with our combined old-woman bodily eyes, read the fortunes therein, all the woes & waiting, all the hurt & betrayal, all the hope & lust, all the forlorn aloneness, all the greed or very occasionally greed's opposite which is a pouring-out of love so great no one but we can discern its end, for it has no end. This is something we see in the hardest places, where women older & more invisible than ourselves sit by themselves thinking no one can see them at all.

We can stare all we like, with all our eyes, at all these things, & nobody knows.

Our age & sex have drawn over each of our heads, Mary Lamb's & mine, & over the heads of any women like us in age or sensibility, a silken cowl.

×××

The late, great Antoine Lavoisier, shouts Mary Lamb, finding his name in the Gazette after our egg bun, for they were comparing his discoveries with those of a new genius named Faraday. Dorothy, do you remember Lavoisier's most famed finding? *Rien ne se perd, rien ne se crée: tout se transforme.* Ha! I could have told the world that the moment I turned thirty. In Nature nothing is lost, nothing created: everything transforms . . . She shoved the paper in her bag to show her brother when he came back from the prize fight. She still showed Charles everything as I used to show Wm.

When we turn thirty, according to Mary Lamb, we become old in the sight of men. Then in our forties our blood runs like the gore of slaughtered pigs & each step squelches in a red flood & our bodies become suddenly changed—on some ordinary Wednesday our arms become someone else's arms. Our faces become those of our fathers. Our sense of smell alters. As a small person I have always smelled the ground as my nose is nearer it than Wm's nose. But now I sniff deeper in the ground & in the air high above it, for scents have whirled into a vortex whose point is attracted to my nose. Sardines! Earth! Feces! Carnations! Peppery &

coppery or stinking of sweet, rotting fish—all of London inhabits our noses.

Nothing created nor destroyed! Mary Lamb sings all the way down Bennett Street, euphoric.

I am not sure, she cries, that the Gazette realizes our former youthful hunger has but been transformed!

. . . & I knew what she meant. Late-summer air pressing my skin was now unbearable like the insistence of a lover when one is sated. The air itself our lover! The scent of rain our passion. Utterly sensual, the feeling of simply being alive; it can ache just to walk down the street. I am ransacked as the bee unpetals her late rose. By accident the passing bee unhinges the last pink flake . . . & then what? The swelling of the hip. The filling of the hip with paste, not liquid—orange, not pink. The sweet, pasty sugar & a gnarled star atop it all—oh nothing is destroyed, only transforms. This is a fact all women know before being told by Monsieur Antoine Lavoisier. Spring in a woman's body is hardly sensual compared to autumn & winter—when, against ice & snow & monochrome of black & white—against skeletal life in the waste ground along the Thames or the edges of our beloved Lakes—the fruited hip with its gnarled star is the fragrant rose transformed from soul to body in a transubstantiation not of church altar & not of the body of any man whether that man be young or old.

Matter, marvelled Mary Lamb as she hauled the Gazette out of her bag to examine it once more. Why only matter? Did Lavoisier think only matter matters & did he not realize how matter extends into feeling & perception?

I halted beside her while a man with pots dangling from his belt & a hen under each arm had a mind to crash into us on the downhill cobbles.

Mind where you stop, he says—a pair of right cows!

This is where you are wrong, Sir, said Mary Lamb, for I am a lamb & my friend here, she is your quintessential goat.

He spat at us but she deflected the gob with her newspaper & off he tromped with a page of it stuck to the rump of his fattest hen.

Dear Lavoisier, we wrote at the Lotus Café on the bits of paper I was never without in case an idea came into my head in field or steeple of wherever I might walk in this life.

> *We, authors Mary Lamb and Dorothy Wordsworth,*
> *thought you might like to see our list of things which, besides*
> *matter, are neither created nor destroyed. We feel we owe it*
> *to Science to suggest the following additions, though our list*
> *is by no means exhaustive, we realize.*

*Only look at us as one pair of observant women whose
advanced Age allows us to imagine we have noticed a few
things that behave like Matter and that we believe are of
the same category, being of denser or more amorphous
concentrations . . .*

Our advanced age, laughed Mary Lamb, pleased with
herself.

Allows us to imagine! I said, getting into the spirit.

*Here, then, is our list of items which, like Matter, we
Believe "ne se perd, et ne se creé," but only transform:*

Tears
Love
Yearning
Hunger
Rage
Pain
Ecstasy
Thirst
Unknowing
Agony
Jealousy
Mourning
Humiliation
Triumph

Dream
Wind
Cloud
Rainbow
Abandonment
Companionship
Hatred
Terrible Mistakes

Together we compiled a list that was in danger of using up my entire store of spare pocket-paper.

Our list went on.

Our list could have been endless.

Over some entries we laughed & over others we cried.

I had not been prepared for the feelings our list would unleash & I did not realize until trying to sleep that night & thinking it over, that it was not the list that made me feel loss or gain or love or wrongness or any other feeling.

No, it was not the list.

But it was the making of the list, & it was the companionship of Mary Lamb during the making. For she was the one who saw so much that had, for me, remained unspoken for years.

Antoine Lavoisier's name, when you break it apart as I often do break words to see what falls from their cracks, contains the word *la*—feminine form of the—& *vois*—a form of the French word meaning to see.

. . . & I thought, as I broke his name in the lamplight filtering from Russell Street, how Mary Lamb herself was more of a she-who-sees, a seer—mad or not mad, I did not care what men called her—more of a seer than any eminent scientist.

Where will we send our letter? she asked me. To the celestial academy where Lavoisier is eating the fruits of his discoveries? He will be swallowing a heavenly profiterole at the moment, bless him, & perhaps washing it down with cognac . . .

In the end, we addressed our letter to the void.

×××

It has taken me a while to realize how insignificant I am to others.

I was propelled, in youth, not by beauty—I was never a beauty, far too intense & strange for that! But my lovers did not find me insignificant. Far from it! Quincey marvelled at my concentrated self which he said was as if a pinpoint contained the night. Both he & I were so small compared with the others in our lives—tiny, really, the two of us weighing no more than one normal-sized man or plump woman, he said.

Night-time was for us the most wonderful invention!

. . . & I think it was because Darkness let us dissolve in it & become inky sources of our new wild thoughts. No need to fit expectations. Night covered our strange strength & those nights were the best I have known even if they are shattered now in our memory so that neither of us can be sure of their having passed.

I do not use the word insignificant—once my brother separated himself from me, once he became the husband of Mary Hutchinson—did I come loose from my own claim to being a person whose words were of worth?

Even before London, when only a few of my teeth were gone—I remember telling Mary Lamb, It's all finished now—meaning entanglement with men, even men small or strange. Yes, the teeth went & then it went—my significance. But I am not truthful here. Long before I became invisible did I not see a hundred women cast aside like lumps of old clothes, disconsolate, going about their unimportant business of kneading & needling & needing & keening & all the other insignificant things a lump of woman will do once men render her unseen? Once brother & lover have discounted her, as did her father before them?

Says Mary Lamb when I visited her in London to reconstitute my teeth: You must become felt to yourself. You will look out the window that I have dressed in a bridal curtain for your pleasure, & you will see the fern shines green against it, & the room reflects a projection of shadows from the street, & you will breathe & not succumb to the idea that you are supposed, once again, to find some way to pretend you are indispensable. For you are not indispensable.

What you are, says Mary Lamb, is something else. That something is what you need to find, & to find her, it is good to lie down & allow being, not working. This is nearly impossible I know, but it is your medicine. What happens in your chest-cave then in your bowels & even in your heretofore pronounced dead womb & its dormant orchid? Feel!

How did you do it? I asked Mary Lamb. How, without a friend like you are to me, did you navigate the sea between fifty & sixty so that you stand here intact & strong?

Oh, says Mary Lamb, you forget I have spent many months in a madhouse where for days & weeks & months on end, stretching, yea, into years, no one asked of me a thing. For I journeyed beyond the boundaries of their own desires. So I did not have to unpot a herring for any man, no herring of any sort did I have to provide . . . & in the place of all herrings with their silver scales & their concentrated smells & all else about them, in their place grew a bushel of silver scales for me alone, made of my own vision, my own tolerance, my own feelings & desires. You do not even know what your own feelings are, do you, my dearest Dorothy?

. . . & I had to admit to Mary Lamb that she was right.

For two weeks I was like a sleeping maiden in her shadowy parlour.

She left me alone.

It is not, as some say, as if she polluted my mind with her insanities.

No.

The only insanities have been mine, made of layer upon layer of Unvoiced things that have piled up in my body since I was first the beloved of men who include my brother. In their gaze I was not myself. In their gaze my own layers, my geology, built up & towered flakes of silver & cream-coloured stone made—as stone is made—of components leaf-shaped & changeable & moist. Permeable to begin with, but in the end—though I do not want it to be my real end—impermeable slices nestled one upon the other like leaves of shale.

I remember—& of my two Marys, Wordsworth & Lamb,
the latter would agree & the former would not—I remember
being one of the men or at least akin to them in my own
mind, for years. Sprawled on the ground, thinking.
Marvelling & thinking all the complicated thoughts a
writer thinks when confronted with the majesty of the
world & the squalor—is life convoluted or harmonious? Will
humans destroy the world or learn how to echo its spherical
movement in the heavens' harmonious exultation? I thought
along those lines as I tore our bread in three & shared it with
Wm & Sam. Grass pricked our legs alike & shadows of the
same willows shielded us from the sun. We heard the same
crows caw & saw the same rainbow. Wm & Sam listened
to me & my words mingled on our pages with their own &
many times my words became their own. We all agreed.
Our minds were more interesting than the holy trinity for
none of us was separated body from spirit but manifested
both. There ran transparent stairs from the cellars in our
bodies to the resplendence of our minds, & our words were
the light. I was lit & I was one of them.

No, says Mary Wordsworth—just because you & I were
deprived of mothers does not mean we should not learn how
to be proper women! Look around you. Remember correctly
instead of in a longing daze. Who made the bread you tore
in three?

When I knew I was no longer one of the men—once Wm
married Mary & she became—everyone called her—I had

to call her—my sister—though Wm promised me—he promised on their wedding night she would be our wife. But the world called her my sister & Wm did not correct the world.

. . . & with my sister I was now suddenly left behind—I have never got over the shock of this.

Again it happened with Quincey. Oh he found me to be a wild boy with startling eyes! A boy small like himself, tattered & dissolved at our edges & fit only for the out-of-doors in a storm, along with the ragged leaves & all the things that were like us windblown—until he found the little farm-girl & married her! Then I became no longer Quincey's boy friend. I suddenly faded into the same woman I had become in the eyes of Wm & Sam . . . & this was the second shock from which I am still reeling, & which causes my bowels to shut down if I do not wrench myself with an effort far greater than anyone knows.

The first shock was realizing I was no longer one of the boys.

The second shock came after Wm & Sam stopped including me, & after Quincey also found a wife—what is it about their finding wives that made me obsolete? The second shock was that, No, I had never been one of them.

Not in our youth & not in our age. What had I been? They loved my thoughts, it is true, but did not hear me utter them. Rather, they imagined that my ideas had flown to them from the same invisible wind that flows to all men, & that my ideas counted among their discoveries.

Once married, they somehow remembered I too was feminine, like their wives.

Whereas before they were wed, I was a magic stick blown from a wild tree & accompanying them in their windblown travels. A pointer, a wand, a branch from the Tree of knowledge.

After their marriages Wm & also Sam & Quincey would listen for an hour to the yammering of the most menial servant—yes even James our poor manservant who grew up in & out of the workhouse, Wm regards as superior to me in matters requiring any decisiveness . . . hired him—a poor, simple soul, thinks Wm, but reliable enough to coax my beloved sister Dorothy out of her troublesome agitation here at home or in the house of Mary Lamb, a woman who has refused to swallow a thing. Mary Lamb, a dangerous influence!

Mary Lamb, with whom I am not one of the boys, have never been one of the boys, am not interested in the boys.

With Mary Lamb I knew this.

Not interested in the boys is the meat I chew on with my
new teeth after our fortnight in London. This is the carnage
I am damned if I will be prevented from swallowing & once
I swallow it, I will work on digesting it for the rest of my
life. My bowels will thrash like seaweed thrashing offshore,
& the household here at Rydal will have to accommodate
my wildness. James Dixon are you still reading this?

Are you with me?

You, who are different in some elemental way that my
brother has failed to notice. You, who are also not one of the
boys. You, who have built our little carriage in which we can
travel wherever we want to go, without them.

×××

Of course, Mary Lamb is right again.

Our brothers do not worry in the least, upon waking,
whether or not they are useful. They, no matter how old they
grow, do not think, There is as if a layer of powder settling
upon me & rendering me less & less useful not only to the
outer world, but to myself.

They do not then ponder, & what is the entity I have just
named Myself & why is it still lying down at noon?

Our brothers can sleep, geniuses as they are, through noon & on until ten o'clock at night with only a changed word in a second verse to show for it & perhaps not even this. Perhaps there is no change at all in their work, only a subtle change in their minds, a change bestowed by sleep, the sleep necessary to men of great thoughts & words. Men whose words are worth something or whose silence is worth even more & is different from the silence of their sisters.

The silence of sisters is reproachable! For should sisters not be talking of tasks, of errand lists & prices, of economies & time? Women face the clock-face unlike the way in which men face it. Men face the clock not to gauge where they have fallen short of time, but to note how long it might be before the next meeting with another man. Which meal is imminent & which visitor must be given sway? Get the sisters to set the table while we veer to the sill & gaze on distances & conclude, If this therefore that.

Whereas for sisters it is, If this, well then, *this* it is . . . & if that, then, simply that. Thus the world for sisters develops into myriad efflorescences; a panoply of surprises! Whereas our brothers must control each minute, & if their minutes prove uncontrollable, well, it is because they are forced to live in a maddening world containing sisters & trees & thunder.

So it is that on waking I am beset by forces, colours, sensations, crowding in on me & making it hard to get up while at the same time making it impossible for me to remain lying down, or to claim reverie, or to—forbid this!—wonder what it might be like to let things be & not work each second of the day towards my life being considered worthwhile.

My brother, says Mary Lamb, is worthwhile simply by placing his silhouette against the window & resembling a dark poet. I could say the same thing of Wm if I dared.

Accomplishment, says Mary Lamb, is a woman's word. A man has no need of this word as he fulfills it by virtue of having been born & having not yet died. Simply by occupying space in his neutral-coloured garments that we have stitched with our thousand thousand tiny hand-stitches & clapped with our irons & bleached & starched & laid on the rocks to brighten in the sun with a bright-ness of angels . . . simply by donning this angel-white shirt & partly-covering it in a cloak so as to hide the brightness until needed in some important conversation . . . simply by being clothed in this bright & dark garb, by standing straight & tall, by gazing abstractedly into an inner poem . . . thus do our brothers outrace us while we labour toward accomplishing all they have set out for us to do by their mere existence. Accomplishment does not exist for them as a word, because for it to do so would imply that there is a time before perfect completion in themselves— a hole, if you will; a gap or a lack preceding the whole & complete man . . . & no such space exists.

But sisters are space embodied without form. We are the void. We are the gap, the hole, the time before. Accomplishment is our word & our reason for lying in agony for some time before rising, if we are able to rise at all. Accomplishment is for us inaccessible. Evasive. Always ahead. A state of being whole by gazing into our inner word that isn't a poem but is some other form of story or meaning—this is a wholeness that cannot exist for us as long as men stand like gnomons & define timelessness for themselves alone.

So says Mary Lamb.

Oh, she cautions, but we love our brothers.

We love them, she says, with a sick & pitiful persistence because we have been made to love them through a demon calling to us in the night whilst we sleep, & in the day we have been made to cry after that love, that nightmare, half-remembered yet wholly compelling—our disease of the soul.

. . . & Mary Lamb will soon go off again to the madhouse but I will not.

I hang on well enough to remain in the land of normal people. Wm, for one, could not bear to have me disappear into the place where Mary Lamb goes. Without my gay shadow at the hem of his days, he might not believe quite so hard in himself, in his genius, in his poetry. He might fall off the edge into a kind of bog with nobody, not even our wife Mary, quite understanding what it is that he needs daily spooned for him to continue with his usual abilities.

One line after another, spoonful by tiny, exquisite spoonful, do I feed Wm the words the world thinks are created by himself alone.

Alone, for Wm, means Himself plus his insubstantial Sister.

Only in bed in the morning, in the ghastly time before I get up, do I dare imagine that my brother Wm & I are two, not one, not himself alone. Once I rise I cease to be Dorothy & recommence my twinship, my kinship, my death.

Oh but that is your voluntary death, insists Mary Lamb. Entirely up to you—& off she goes again to the madhouse to be wrapped in forgetfulness. Not her own forgetfulness. The madwoman does not forget. The world around her is the forgetful substance. She, on the other hand, is mad because she remembers.

Are you not angry? Mary Lamb asks me.

—& this is the question with which she leaves me, steeping in what she has named my unacknowledged rage. This, says Mary Lamb, is the poison causing your paralysis of the limbs, your agony in the bowel.

—& off she flies, light as a fairy, into her sanctuary.

XXX

I love Rydal when the sun slips onto the water at morning—
even if the distant sound of the hammer begins & rings
incessant through the mist—Sun & mist whiten the water.
You cannot really see the mist. It's only sufficient to diffuse
the light so the lake looks as if it is made of . . . crystal . . .
milk . . . Sometimes there's a little bit of ice at the edge, just
a little bit of ice & a few flakes floating white . . .

The sounds that infiltrate are getting worse & worse. The
smells that infiltrate are getting worse & worse, stench &
racket from industry & progress. But our sycamore with its
serious beauty—it's not a nonchalant kind of tree, it's a—hear
that echo, hear that hammer—the sycamore moves in the
very slight breeze, its dry leaves uttering a whisper that—can
it not remain on the—just on the—hopeful side of sombre?

The Terrace saves me. Sounds roar beyond it. Horrible
buildings loom outside it. The new road snakes around it.
Inside the Terrace sighs the influence of the trees, much like
the influence of the stars in that book I hardly read—*Who
can bind the sweet influences of Pleiades?*—Scripture can be
beautiful but I admit I just don't have a taste for it when the
air itself inside the Terrace is pregnant & alive—

& no, I have never been pregnant, but I have been alive,
even now when the branches are nearly bare, winter a thing
nobody loves enough. The architecture. Skeletons. Bones of

the trees, & the air clinging & dancing all around & hanging there grey & white, white & rain-coloured. Those are the colours of the living air in winter. Those are the colours of the Wordsworth siblings. The living air inside the terrace is like a mind. It is my mind teeming, slumbering, dreaming—flying, floating, hanging, moving in wind-riven play—

I must beg James to drag me out onto the Terrace again.

×××

But the wind!

The wind had scattered willow leaves on the moss & the moss caught them in perfect formation where they fell & clung. So that as Dixon dragged me by it in the cart, I saw the image of the willow tree on the moss, created by its cast-down leaves. There was something violent about them, yet each leaf retained its perfect oval beauty with its graceful elongation & points at each end. It was as if somebody had shed . . . their work. Someone had created work beautiful & alive, & had, in a fit, cast it on the ground—

& when I looked up at the naked willow, blackened leaves shivered on a single branch, the rest denuded.

The tree was aghast, its bark down below incised deeply.

At that moment it flung a few last leaves down—

& when a mere handful of leaves—dry & rattling in the
storm—is cast upon your face with that much force, it stings
like a rain of nails—

ACKNOWLEDGEMENTS

I thank my family, friends and colleagues, without whose help and support the research and writing of this book would not have happened. With special thanks to the following: Jean Dandenault and the Dandenault family, Helen Humphreys, Jeff Cowton and The Wordsworth Trust in Grasmere, Dr. Polly Atkin, Dr. Will Smith, Dr. Shelley Snow, Char Davies and the Reverie Foundation, Quebec Writers' Federation, Lynn Verge and the Atwater Library, Syd and Maureen Boulton, Barbara Muir Wight, Elizabeth Dillon, Brenda Keesal, Meredith Fowke, Elise Moser, Mini Carleton Group, Tiny House Farm, Michael Winter, T.L. Winter, Paul Winter, Christine Pountney, Margaret Spooner, Daniel Karrasch, Rebecca Krinke, Enid Stevenson, Arthur Griffin, Art Andrews, Anne Hardy, Ernest de Sélincourt, Susan Levin, James Dixon, Esther Wade and Juliette Dandenault. I thank my agent Shaun Bradley, assistant editor Rick Meier, copy editor Melanie Little, and designer Jennifer Griffiths. Very special thanks to my editor Lynn Henry, and to the land and living entities upon it that have nurtured and inspired Dorothy Wordsworth and all of us, especially trees, rock, water and plants. I thank Sufi my rescue dog, who has rescued me. And thank you, Dear Reader.

KATHLEEN WINTER's novel *Annabel* was shortlisted for the Scotiabank Giller Prize, the Governor General's Literary Award, the Rogers Writers' Trust Fiction Prize, the Amazon.ca First Novel Award, the Orange Prize, and numerous other awards. It was also a *Globe and Mail* "Best Book," a *New York Times* "Notable" book, a *Quill & Quire* "Book of the Year" and #1 bestseller in Canada. It has been published and translated worldwide. Her Arctic memoir *Boundless* (2014) was shortlisted for Canada's Weston and Taylor non-fiction prizes, and her most recent novel *Lost in September* (2017) was longlisted for the International Dublin Literary Award and shortlisted for the Governor General's Literary Award. Born in the UK, Winter now lives in Montreal.